RAVEN
BOOK 1

BIRTH INTO DARKNESS

WJR PARKS

-5th Edition-
Copyright © WJR Parks, author, 2020
Christabel Samuel, editor, 2020
Edd Sowder, editor, 2020
Mayhem Designs, formatting, 2020
Cover Model: Charise Jeanine, 2020
ISBN: 978-1-953795-00-7

This book is dedicated to all my family and friends that helped me through the long journey to completion.

Special acknowledgment:
Without the help of Christabel Samuel, this book would have never seen the light, or better yet, the darkness of the world. Thank you.
Charise Jeanine, thank you … for everything.

The Hidden World Series

BOOKS

Raven: Birth into Darkness Book 1
Raven: Demon of Darkness Book 2
Allegiances: A Raven Walker Novella
West Texas Blood: A Raven Walker Novel
The Corrupted: An Elspet Novella
The Undying: An Andreea Novella

SHORT STORIES

The Lilin: An Elspet Short Story 1
The Pact: An Elspet Short Story 2
Vampire: A Raven Walker Short Story
Churiphim: A Leonette Short Story
The Umbra: An Andrus Kallian Short Story
The Umbra II: A Ciarda Short Story
Ashia Storm Mage: A Short Story

Los Angeles, present day: 2:00 a.m.

I crouched on the edge of the building, watching as Kylie hid in the slanted shadow cast by a grimy dumpster. She pressed herself against the greasy wall of the alley, which reeked of urine mingled with feces. I had found her a month past. Since then, I had shadowed her.

Kylie was around my age, but small in frame, her brown hair loose and flowing down half of her round face.

She'd run away from home not too long ago, and there were areas in the city no decent person would enter, day or night. She had wandered into such a place. *Idiot, girl.*

Her heart thrummed in my ears. The blood sloshing through her veins, her sweet flesh, moist and tender, made my stomach rumble.

Her wide eyes darted from shadow to shadow. She huddled into a ball and kept as silent as possible, but her body trembled, her teeth-chattering amplified in the stillness. The night was not a human's friend.

"Please, please, God," she whispered, as she pinched her eyes shut. God wouldn't help her tonight, for she had been found.

Unlike Kylie, I was not normal. I stood taller than most girls my age, five eight. Though I'd been bitten at thirteen, the curse had enhanced my body and aged it for survival, giving me the look of a sixteen-year-old. It had heightened all of my senses, especially my hearing.

Three men had been chasing her. Their hearts drummed; the thudding chimed in my ears from both entrances to the alley. Malevolence erupted from their pores, its stench permeating the air. The evil sheen I had learned to hone in on. I licked my lips in wait.

Lust burned within the men. They didn't care that she was thirteen, only that their yearning be satiated. They'd cornered her, seen her run into the alley. At two in the morning, there would be no one around, not in this area.

Except, perhaps, the monster lurking in the dark watching them.

"There you are. Keep running but you can't hide."

Kylie jerked her head to the right. A man as large as a truck towered over her; bald, wild-bearded and a toothy grin painted wide.

"Over here," he called to his two friends.

The girl shot to her feet, dashed out from her cover and whimpered when she slammed into another man's arms; his form as lanky and greasy as the bald one.

The third, the leader, lashed out with a thick tattooed arm and slapped her, silencing a scream. They dragged her, dazed, back behind the dumpster into the darkness of the shadows.

The bald one ripped her black T-shirt. A thick, leathery hand pressed over her mouth stifling another scream. The side of her face smacked against the slimy pavement. The lanky man held her feet while the bald one pulled at her shorts.

Their malice, their cruelty, proven, I stepped off the ledge and glided down three stories landing silently behind the rapists. Kylie's eyes flashed wide when she saw me, her dark brown orbs tinged with fear and confusion.

"Foolish girl." My voice spun them around.

"The fuck you come from?" The leader's gaze rolled over me. "This your friend? You want to get some action too, you little whore? This just turned into a party." He chuckled. Moron.

"Fuck yeah. Shit, you can have this one. I want her." The lanky man released Kylie's legs and climbed to his feet, his eyes aflame with lust.

Coming at me, he snapped back to reality when I punctured his skin with my fangs. My venom worked its way through his carotid artery, the white-hot burn paralyzing him. He crumbled, knees knocking on the pavement, followed by his head.

"The hell did you do to him?" The leader jumped to his feet and I was at his side before his muscles twitched to move. The sound of his intestines hitting the pavement with a wet splatter sent the bald man scurrying on all fours, stumbling to stand.

"Fuck, fuck, fuck. Holy shit." He managed to get to his feet and staggered to a stop when I appeared in his line of escape. "Holy mother of Jesus, help me."

I smiled fangs. He turned to run. I pounced and tore a handful of his throat.

He fell to his knees gurgling bubbles of blood. Blood like sweet perfume making my nostrils flare. My body hungered for it. I complied by biting into the shredded flesh and feasting on the honey liquid. Ecstatic waves washed through every parched and hollow vein; shock and pleasure reverberated in my muscles, as they breathed once more to life. I allowed my mind to linger in the moment, the nirvana of fuzziness soaking my brain, muffling the world.

I made sure all life was sapped, and then I turned to the other two and drained them as well. I would have my fill tonight.

Soft whimpers pulled my attention back to Kylie huddled against the wall. Her heart fluttered and her skin paled when I noticed her.

"Please, please, please." She curled tight grabbing a glass bottle next to her. As if it would help her.

I moved to her side and jerked the bottle away before she could even move a muscle to protect herself. She yelped and shielded herself, lifting her arms for cover. Silence lingered for a few beats before she dared to look and find me offering a hand.

"Stupid of you to wander in such places," I said.

She was reticent. I relaxed my arm. "These men are not the only wicked things that walk the night." I leaped back to the roof, making the three-story jump effortlessly. Kylie stood, watching in awe.

"Wait, please." She pulled her torn t-shirt around her. "I don't know this place." Her eyes darted to the streets silent shadows. "My name's Kylie... Kylie Deland."

I lifted my backpack from the roof and slipped it on. "I know who you are."

A bewildered look glazed over her. "You do? Do I know you? What are you?"

I leaped back down. She coiled back as I landed. I headed toward the back exit to the alley shrouded in darkness. "Are you coming?"

"What about them?" She stared at the corpses.

"Would you like to hold conversations with the dead?" Her skin paled, and with reluctance, she followed.

"What you did back there, what was that?" She stopped walking. "It's like the movies. You sucked their blood. You're a vampire." Her eyes grew round. "You're saving me for a snack. You're going to lead me to your den and suck me dry."

"Do you know your way back home?"

"I'm not taking a vampire to my home, no way." She backed up a couple of steps.

I proceeded on my way. I had no time to explain.

"Hey, where are you going?"

"To find a den." If she didn't follow, I would have to find her again, eventually morning would come and I had no intention of seeing the sunrise.

Kylie looked back toward the other exit, past the dead bodies and the waiting darkness. "Shit... okay, wait." She caught up to me. "So, you're not going to suck me? I mean vampires don't save people, right?"

"I made a promise to protect you." I quickened my pace.

"Promise? To who?"

"We must hasten to the bus stop; it takes twenty minutes for the next bus to arrive, and we're about thirty from the nearest stop." Unfortunately, Kylie was an annoyingly slow walker.

Eight streets later, beads of sweat crawled down her face. Kylie perched herself on the mucky bus bench stamped with movie ads. Unless the bus had been early and already left, it had not arrived.

"Are you going to tell me?" Kylie had a nettling persistence.

"I have been protecting the Deland family for over two hundred years. A promise I made to the person who gave me a second chance at life."

"Like whoa, brain-boner. Who was the person, like my great-great-great-great-grandfather or something?"

"The bus is coming."

From the dark, repressed lagoon of memories, flashes of my death floated to consciousness. Fear cornered me in my dreams and travels in those times. I had not then discovered my power's potential and the significance it would have in my first years as an undead.

It had been easier to keep my faith in humanity during those times, but now it was an ever-pressing battle. Technology was the new magic; money was the new faith, and the pursuit for power the new God. Nothing had changed I supposed; the veil showing the true face of humanity had been lifted. The invention of the internet, cell phones and social media unified all the world's people. Through those electronic windows spilled out the judgments, the hate, the condemnations, and the true face of the race. I'd learned to adapt, to look for the few innocents who could possibly survive in this human world. The rest were my cattle.

Two buses and a barrage of questions later, Kylie and I arrived at a three-story rundown building claimed by squatters, and hidden between two larger dilapidated structures.

I had worried she would fear me, be hesitant to accept my explanations and the reality of my being, but her reaction was the complete opposite. Her curiosity burned further and her questions flowed like a river.

She crawled in through a boarded opening in the basement and washed the area bright with a small flashlight. When I did not follow, she turned back.

"You coming?"

"I cannot enter without invitation."

"Oh, wow, that's pretty cool. I mean, not cool like that, but that it's true. Vampires can't enter and stuff."

"I can find elsewhere to sleep."

"My bad. Not sure how this works."

"You have never invited someone into your home?" I furrowed my brow.

"Oh, that easy, huh?" She stood straight and swept her arms into the building. "You are invited into my home."

I slid my backpack into the hole and crawled in. I had no time to find another place to slumber safely. Not when the morning was biting at my heels. This would have to do.

Kylie led me to her room. Other squatters' rhythmic heartbeats resounded in my ears. I was thankful for drinking the three rapists dry. At least twenty bodies slumbered in other rooms and their blood's scent was thick. The stench of feces and urine wafted through the walls. The punch of moist, molded carpet and wood mingled with them like twined wire. My nostrils flared from the reek, which helped assuage my thirst.

"You would rather live here than in your own house?" I asked.

"Anytime. This is way better than living with my parents. Man, I can't wait to tell everyone about you."

I snapped my gaze to her. "No, no one must know about me. No one."

She lifted her hands in surrender. "Okay, okay. Cross my heart."

Kylie watched as I pulled a laptop from my backpack and a large blanket, then reached for a heavy pouch emptying the earth from it over the blanket, and lay down.

Once situated upon the soil on which I slept, Kylie plopped down on her bed; a yellow stained mattress. "Can I at least know your name?"

"Raven," I said.

"Coolness." She proceeded her questioning once again. She wanted to know everything. Too much for my taste. I closed my eyes and slept.

CHAPTER 1

Pittsburgh 1776

Raven crouched behind a large gnarled tree waiting for Phillip to pass. The crunch of twigs signaled he was near, and when he came around the trunk, she leaped out and gave her best monster roar.

Her brother squealed and fell into the dry creek. Raven dashed toward home.

"Not fair." Phillip jumped to his feet.

Raven raced across the field, veins thumping in her head, heart drumming, the wind slapping her face and swirling around her hair, making a swooshing sound in her ears. Behind her, her brother's feet thudded against the ground. He had gotten fast and would soon be within arm's reach. She pushed her legs to work; flaming heat washed through her muscles and her lungs burned as she sucked air and summoned a jolt of speed.

She focused on the door to her home and its matching shutters on either side. Its safety mocked her from a few yards away, but his steps faded behind and Raven allowed herself a confident smile.

That summer, she'd gained inches over other girls her age, and her long legs gave her the advantage when playing anything that required running. She arrived at the porch and leaped onto it, knocking over the butter churn. Ha, made it! She skidded to a stop and let out a breath of relief. Heaving, she dropped onto the stool with a smirk and waited.

When Phillip reached the porch, she stood and shouted. "Olly, Olly, oxen free. "

"You cheated," Phillip said.

"I did not."

"Yes, you did. You pushed me into the creek. That's cheating."

"I did not push you. You fell. You are just jealous. Let's go in before Mother gets angry. We should have been back hours ago."

Phillip crossed his arms over his chest and glared at her.

"Stop pouting."

Raven reached past him, opened the front door, and pushed him in. Stomping through the house, they shoved at each other, fighting to cram through the kitchen door at once. A waft of savory smells filled the warm air. Both their stomachs rumbled.

Their mother stopped stirring cake batter and turned to stare at them. "Still haven't learned to get home on time!"

Raven pushed her silky black tresses over her shoulder and dropped her head to stare at the floor. Her mother walked behind her and lifted the thick mass of hair that flowed evenly to the middle of her back. With a twist, she looped it into a chignon and secured it with a comb pulled from her own dark locks.

Her mother let out a soft gasp. "Raven, did you wear that to the tutor's house?"

"Yes," Raven said, while her brother grinned to himself. Her mother turned her around and eyed her white boy's shirt, brown coat and loose breeches.

"I don't see why you worry about my clothes," Raven frowned at her.

"A lady doesn't dress like a boy," her mother said, shaking her head. "At least you didn't go into town. But I want you dressed appropriately for your lessons."

"It was only Phillip and me. The others went with their parents for a meeting in town."

Her mother smiled. "You're wearing a dress next time."

"Yes, Mother," she lied. Footsteps echoed in the living room and Raven perked up.

"Hey, birthday girl!" Raven's father steered Phillip's twin brother, Matthew, through the doorway. He'd taken Matthew with him into town to help carry things. Phillip had sulked when he found out his older brother was going instead of him. Unlike Raven, Phillip hated going to a tutor. Matthew had to go too, but Father would let him miss a day or two when he needed his help in town.

Matthew walked over to Phillip. "What you moping around for?"

"Nothing."

"Raven beat you again?"

Phillip shrugged and looked away.

His father patted him on the back. "Don't worry, son. One of these days your legs are going to catch up with your feet and things will change. You'll see."

Giving Phillip a sideways glance, Raven giggled under her breath.

Their father looked back and forth between her and Phillip, and grinned. "Go wash up boys," he wrapped his arm around Raven and hugged her tight to his side, "it's time for our girl's celebration."

Both boys shoved at each other and took off racing, another game of who gets there first.

"Matthew, Phillip. Keep running in the house and you're not having cake tonight," their mother said as she raised her brows at their father.

"Boys, listen to your mother." He winked at Raven. "And you, young lady. Come with me."

She followed him into his small study, tingles of anticipation setting in her belly. He set down his large satchel on the mounds of muddled papers on his desk.

Her father's study was the one place he did not have to worry about presentations, and it was her favorite escape when she wanted to leave the world of everyday life. She could always find something fascinating to quench her mind's desire for knowledge, losing herself in the many books that lined the walls of Father's shelves.

"How's the new tutor? You haven't run her off already have you? This is the seventh one. They are hard to find. The good ones at least."

"I know," Raven sighed.

Tutors were hard to find. Ones that taught more than the normal things that young girls learned. Things like music, painting or needlework.

She could never imagine herself confined to such education. No, her mind wouldn't allow it. Her brain always hungered for more. More mathematics, writing, reading ... How could anyone ever understand the world without knowledge of those subjects?

Mother never understood this. She always wanted Raven to be a normal daughter and what everyone expected a girl to be. Father understood though. He'd grown up with the same hunger. He knew she wasn't any normal girl, and while boys could go on to more advanced education, girls were left behind. Her father said that would never happen to Raven. She was too smart.

"She knows more than most. Though, I do find myself having to dumb myself down to her level."

"Raven, you shouldn't demean people," her father scowled.

"But I'm not. She is a nice person. Really, she is. I do not understand why I have to explain my mathematical solutions. I feel like I am the teacher. I can work them out in my head faster than I can write them down."

He turned to face her and sat on his desk. "Okay, I guess you do have a point when it comes to Walker family shrewdness." He rubbed his eyes with his thumb and finger. "I'll have to find a genius for you to torture."

Raven shifted her body, trying to peek at the item he had pulled out of the satchel and conveniently set behind him. He meant to torture her. He was being mean. Simply mean.

"Did you get a new medical book to study?" she asked.

"I did. The illustrations are perfect. I'll learn much from this one." He brandished the small book and flipped through the pages, taking his time scanning each one, and with deliberate slowness, moving on to the next.

She stomped her foot on the floor and crossed her arms. "You know exactly what you are doing. You are being vicious, Father."

"Whatever are you talking about?" he said, painting a perfectly innocent look on his face.

She let out a heavy huff and intensified her glare. Unable to help himself, he broke into laughter. No doubt, she looked pitiful. She turned to stomp away.

"Alright, alright." He brandished another book and she raced over to him, beaming and wide-eyed. She snatched the book and turned it over to see the front. *Philosophiae Naturalis Principia Mathematica.*

"You found Isaac." She lunged at him and embraced him in a tight hug. Father was the best. "Thank you, thank you, thank you."

"Alright, keep it down. I don't want your mother knowing I got you two gifts for your birthday." He ruffled her hair.

"Two? Another book?"

He walked over and sat behind the desk. "That's enough greedy inquisitiveness. You will wait until tonight," he said. Father knew how to spark the flame of curiosity and leave her in suspense.

Raven noticed the letter that had arrived a week earlier. It was sitting on the desk as if it were like the rest of the papers. Her stomach tightened every time she saw it.

Her smile faded and she hugged the book to her chest, wanting to be angry with him. Actually, she did not know what she wanted. Perhaps that was how the adult world worked. The world she was becoming part of and probably why her father never hesitated to pay for tutors and books. He was preparing her. Nevertheless, she *was* angry with him. Angry that he would be leaving.

"Washington has not done well against the British. The Continental army is running," she said.

Father followed her gaze to the letter and he placed a book over it. "That's why they need good doctors."

"Papa, doctors get killed too."

"Come here."

Raven trudged over. He sat her on his lap. "Oh, you've become heavy. What have you been eating?"

She pushed herself away. "I am not heavy."

He held her tight and smiled. "Alright, alright. Get over here."

She relaxed and laid her head down on his shoulder. His skin's husky scent was comforting, nostalgic. It reminded her of the many times he had held her on his lap growing up. Soon, that would be gone. He would be gone.

"You're not my little girl anymore. You're my little lady now. After I come back from the war, you'll be meeting boys and I will have to be chasing them away."

She twirled in her fingers the small cross around his neck. "You promise?"

"To chase boys away? You better believe it."

Raven giggled and nudged him in the chest. "No, you promise to come back?"

He poked her on the forehead. "Stop worrying. Worries are the worms of life eating you away. Now go find a pretty dress to wear for your mother."

"A dress?"

"Your mother has been laboring all day for your celebration. You could show some appreciation by wearing a dress, don't you think?"

"I suppose." Raven stood and kissed her father on the cheek, and scurried out after setting her new book on her own desk for later reading.

She tripped over one of the twins. Both were snooping outside the study.

"You were eavesdropping on us?" Raven glared.

"We weren't dropping anything," Matthew replied.

"You have to wear a dress tonight!" Phillip ran off, followed by Matthew.

Raven raced after them. "I'm going to make you wear a dress."

The twins flew out the front door, Raven following right behind them and catching a glance of her mother shaking her head at them from the kitchen.

Both boys ran into their father's shed and shut the door as Raven reached it. She shoved it open and dashed inside, catching a glimpse of Matthew's feet as he scurried out the other side of the shelter. Raven raced after him. When she reached the door, Phillip flew out from the side and pushed her. Raven tumbled into their father's tools and paints. A loud crash of falling boards and clanking metal tools tore through the shed.

A hammer cracked over her shin. Jolts of raw pain shot through the bone. Tears welled up and exploded from Raven's eyes.

Phillip froze.

Matthew ran in. "What did you do?"

"I didn't mean to push her so hard," Phillip said, as he rushed over to her side. "Raven, please don't cry."

Matthew hurriedly picked up the tools and started to place them back. "Father is going to whoop you!"

Raven pulled up the cuff of her breeches and inspected the bruised bone. "It isn't broken."

Phillip hugged her. "I didn't mean to push you so hard. I wanted to get you back is all."

The twins both helped her up. She grimaced when she shifted her weight to her left leg and another jolt of tingling pain fired up.

The damage around where she fell was nothing much, except for the most important things. Their father had been working on wooden frames for large portrait paintings, and now they were all cracked and broken from Raven's fall.

"You aren't going to tell Father, are you?"

Both twins stared at her with dark round eyes. They looked like mirror images.

"He's going to be angry. All his frames are broken," Raven said, wiping tears from her face. "No hiding that."

Both boys frowned.

"I'll come up with something. I tripped or some such thing," she said.

"What about your birthday?" Matthew asked.

Phillip kicked at the ground, hanging his head down. "He's gonna whoop you and you won't get to celebrate your birthday."

Raven walked slowly, getting used to the pain and trying her best not to limp.

"He isn't going to know until morning." Their father liked working at first light. He would probably take her book away and whoop her good for breaking his frames. She and her brothers knew not to be playing around in the shed. She wasn't worried about the whooping. That hurt for a little while, but the book – he wanted to read it.

"Let's go back, before Mother and Father start wondering where we are." She steadied herself against the jabs of pain.

"I'm sorry Raven. I don't want you to get in trouble," Phillip said.

"Father will not be so coarse with me. Not like he would with you two." Raven replied. At least she hoped he wouldn't.

She had never been in much trouble compared to the twins, and when she did get a whooping, it was usually because she had taken the blame for either Matthew or Phillip. She was definitely making Phillip wear a dress for this.

By nightfall, her family had gathered around the dining room table for Raven's birthday feast.

Father placed a large roast turkey on the table, pervading the house with its savory aroma mingled with the warm waft of buttered bread, sweet yams and delicious spices. The twin's mouths smacked with anticipation and they licked their lips.

Their father lowered his head and joined hands. "Our Father, who art in Heaven, bless our family. Each and every one, and forgive us our sins, for they are many. I ask a special blessing for our daughter, Selah, who turns thirteen today and begins her own journey into adulthood. Lead and guide her, oh Lord, that she may stay on the path of righteousness. All this we ask in your name, for all things are possible through you. Amen."

It was a great feast with stories and smiles. Raven enjoyed every moment. She knew these would be the last for some time. Stuffed with chicken, it was time to receive gifts. Her mother gave her a beautiful quilt with Raven's name embroidered in the center. Her brothers gave her a hand-carved box they had both worked on.

Phillip beamed. "It's to keep your knicky-knackers in."

Raven gave them a warm look and happily thanked them. Her father's gift was her favorite. He handed her a miniature painting that he had done himself. He'd captured the family's happiness within the varying lights and shadows of the colors; the twins' rosy cheeks and he and his wife's passionate love. Tranquil warmth filled Raven, and she gave her father a wide smile.

"So you can remember your roots," her father said. He gave her a tight hug and kissed her on the forehead, then went into the study. He returned soon after with a square piece of board.

Raven grinned when he started setting the pieces. She held the winning streak and was not about to lose it. He winked at her when he noticed her eyeing the chess miniatures in expectation of the game.

Matthew rested his head on his palm and sighed. "You and Raven going to play your board game again?"

"It's not just a game, son. Life is a kind of chess. Learn to play the game well and you will acquire habits for all occasions."

Raven smirked. "You took that from Ol' Ben."

"Who's Ol' Ben?" Phillip asked.

"Benjamin Franklin, of course." Raven shook her head at him.

"Don't tease your brother, Raven. Be nice," her mother said. "And don't forget. We have cake."

"And as soon as we've eaten it, the game shall be ready to play." Her father stood and kissed her mother on the cheek.

A loud knock startled them and the house fell silent. "Awfully late for visitors," their father said, and retrieved his flintlock from over the fireplace mantle.

"Probably one of the Williams' wanting to borrow logs," their mother said.

Their father motioned for them to stay. He cracked the door open and relaxed his pistol. A low murmur of conversation proceeded.

Their mother smiled and cleaned the table. "Why don't you children play a game while I set the table?"

Seeing that their father had recognized the visitor and invited him in, Raven and her brothers settled down to play a game of jackstraws. Phillip released the colored sticks from his hand and started the game.

Matthew frowned and sat back on the floor with a sigh. "We should play another game. This one is boring."

"It is not," Raven said.

"That's because you always win."

"Yes, because she always cheats," Phillip said.

"I do not. You're a sore loser."

"Leave her alone, Phillip. You're already getting her in trouble—"

"Shhh." Raven lifted a finger to her lips.

"Trouble? What trouble?" Their mother asked.

The twins looked at each other, speechless. Raven turned to say something to her mother when the shout from her father pierced the house.

Raven snapped her body around to see what happened. Her father was standing in an uncanny way. What was wrong with him?

His head drooped back. His arms were limp.

His pistol fell from his hand.

It clanked on the floor.

He wasn't standing.

The stranger had his hand buried inside their father's chest, holding him up.

Vertigo crashed into Raven. Her stomach tightened and terror iced her body. Disbelief spiraled with reality, twisting and turning. Her legs went numb.

A wet ripping, cracking sound followed before her father fell to the floor, a pool of blood flowering under him. The stranger stood over him, his hand filled with her father's crushed heart.

Raven didn't comprehend. Didn't want to. She was unable to cope with the image. She screamed.

The stranger leaped and his feet thumped beside Raven. Her mother banged a pan flush against his head.

"Run."

Raven crawled away, scraping her knees and elbows, climbing to her feet. Her brothers raced to her.

Her mother turned to run but the stranger wrapped his pale long fingers around her throat, shutting the airway. Her mouth etched the shape of words, as her hand reached for Raven.

The man buried his mouth into her throat. Her mother's face crinkled, her eyes cried a dreadful pain. Matthew tried to run for her, but Raven held him firm.

Blood oozed in tiny trickles down her mother's neck. Her eyes rolled to the back of her head, and the man let her go, her body clunking to the floor.

The brothers screamed, the sounds humming in dreamy delirium. The man looked at them, the corners of his pointed lips forming a smile, and two canines peeking from the upper lip.

Deep nausea spilled, rancid, through Raven's body, tingling at the tips of her fingers and toes. A swoon engrossed her as things became motionless. Dreaming, dreaming, she was asleep in her bed and the whole day was probably a delusion. Soon she would wake and tell her father and mother about this awful dream. She would scare her brothers with it one day when they deserved to be scared.

The man took a step toward them, and sound and motion dripped back to Raven. Her heart thumped in her ears, tingling sensations wrapping around her head. Her mind peeled away the fuzziness of a hallucination that said horror like this could only be a dream.

The man hissed.

Raven bolted with the twins into the kitchen; they fumbled to unhinge the lock to the back door.

"Hurry!" Phillip squealed.

The door released them and they raced outside, making for their father's shed.

The shed door was open from the day's earlier events. They slammed it closed but it had to be locked from the outside. Raven's heart pounded.

"Out the back," Raven whispered.

They rushed out and the foliage greeted them. Raven led them deep into it and they huddled into a ball taking cover. The sharp twigs bit into their skin like little insect legs creeping up and down her arms, reminding her of the thousands of little spiders crawling on her in that black hole she'd once fallen into.

She felt her brothers' pulses drumming hard against hers and she hugged them tightly.

Clanking sounds screeched from the shed. They tensed. Phillip's teeth made little chattering noises. Raven laid her hand on his chin trying to calm him.

Around them, the trees cracked their joints, pressing in on Raven and her brothers. Shadows danced at every corner and twigs snapped from somewhere behind them.

There was no possibility he could find us, Raven told herself. *No. Not with so many places to look, and at night. He would never find us.*

More twigs snapped closer to them; a hush fell over the woods, and Raven knew. She felt they were not alone. Felt the evil presence near them.

"Run," Raven said. "RUN!"

The twins bolted. Raven turned and found two gleaming yellow eyes piercing into hers. She threw dirt she'd had clumped in her right hand, and the man screeched in annoyance.

She chased after the twins. They sped back to the house. Raven's feet felt as if they were being clutched by the ground and felt the stranger's hands inches away from her neck.

Her brothers jumped through the kitchen door. "Hurry, hurry, Raven," they squealed and pleaded.

Fingers wrapped around her shoulders like vice grips and the twins screamed.

"RUN!" Raven cried. Then fiery pain surged through her veins and she screamed. She imagined white-hot spider webs weaving themselves through her body and scalding her flesh.

The twins shrieked and darted into the kitchen. Raven fell stone still, her eyes wide open and her mouth only twitching when she tried to scream.

The man twisted her black hair around his hand and dragged her by it, scraping her body up the stairs, into the kitchen and back into the living area. Raven's head thunked against the floorboards when he let go.

Her father lay on the floor, his lifeless eyes staring at nothing, his mouth agape in a silent scream.

The man walked toward the twin's room. She needed to move, needed to protect them. She tried to cry but nothing would escape her mouth. Their screams filled her ears. All the candles went out. Darkness flooded the house, suffocating vision. Raven cried.

The murderer, slim and tall, glided over and crouched beside her. With one cold, pale finger, he caressed her cheek. His fangs oozed droplets of blood that landed on her silky-smooth skin and slid into her hair.

Tears spilled down to her ears. *He'd killed them.* Her brothers. *Only children.* Raven strained to move. The burning she felt in her veins had not only paralyzed her, but it had also numbed her body.

The moon gleamed through the window and the devil savored revealing his rancorous grin, his sharp canines protruding at the sides of his mouth. It was part of his game and it was working. Fear gripped her heart with ice-cold fingers.

Exposing his gums, he opened his mouth wide to bite.

The top of the front door shattered and rained into the house. The remaining bottom slammed to the floor with a bang. The hinges ripped from the casing. Six men rushed inside, armed with crossbows, daggers and stakes. "Jonas, you filthy demon. You will burn," one shouted—an older man, thickset from broad bone and muscle.

Jonas. The monster had a name.

Raven rolled her eyes sideways and gazed at Jonas who stood and hissed at the strangers. He unleashed an invisible force that hurled three of them into the wall. The thickset man pulled the trigger on his crossbow. A heavy arrow cut the air and thumped into the monster's chest.

"James," the thickset man shouted.

James shot a second stake into Jonas. The wretch let out a guffaw. His body formed into a thin mist, coiling and slipping like vines around their feet. In a second, he was gone. Nothing made sense to Raven; all she knew was her family was dead.

"Three of you go after him. He cannot remain in that form for long." The thickset man turned back toward Raven, eyeing her motionless body. "The rest of you stay and help me look for any survivors."

Raven made an audible gasp. James turned and stared at her, uncertain as to where the sound came from. Then, as stealthy and strong as any twenty-year-old, James lunged his middle-aged body toward her. Placing an arm under Raven, he sat her up and inspected her.

"Wyman, here," he called to the thick man. "She's alive."

Wyman rushed over. Discovering the wound on the side of Raven's neck, he sat back on his heels and signed a throat-cutting gesture with his hands, "Kill her."

Raven's eyes widened. Trying to speak, only a low moan escaped her. James gritted his teeth and pulled out a stake with a sharp silver end. Seeing it, Raven fought harder, forcing her mouth to obey. Placing the stake above her heart, he raised his mallet.

"Please ... don't ... kill me."

R

James stopped his strike mid-air. No one had ever been able to function once bitten. Amazed that the girl could move and speak, he crossed himself and raised her so that she sat upright, propped against his leg.

"Please ... I don't want ... to die," the girl said, raising her trembling arms toward him. What the hell was he going to do?

James stared into her eyes. If he let the girl live, she would become a Lilin. She would feed on humans and be cursed to Hell. Shaking his head, he placed the stake over her heart.

"Please…"

James closed his eyes. "You're already dead."

A hunter's life can be a damn nightmare. With one thrust, he drove the stake into the girl's chest.

She would live, but only he knew that. He'd never killed a child. Couldn't bare it, and it would haunt him. No, she would live and when she'd turned into the Lilin demon, he would use her and train her. It was possible. He had heard it done before in the old world. They used captured Lilins to work for them.

"James," Wyman called. "Found two survivors."

James walked over to the small room Wyman stood by. Two boys were huddled together, trembling in a corner behind a large shelf.

CHAPTER 2

The stake ripped through her chest. Pain. Sharp and slicing pain. Raven tried to scream but her mouth only quivered. Her eyes became heavy. Her heart stopped and her stomach churned. The last warm breath escaped her lungs as they deflated. Ink blackness ate her vision. It was cold.

Voices swirled around her, howling and shrieking. It was the damned in agony.

The lava hot toxin within her veins seemed endless. Raven screamed continuously in the dark void, but the nothingness swallowed it. She couldn't linger on the gripping despair before the scalding fire ripped her mind back to the agony.

Time was unmoving in this place, this existence. Hell was the one thought burning in her mind, filled with gnashing teeth, weeping, and wailing. On it went—the burning, the eternity of burning flesh, the scalding liquids inside her.

She cried to God, pleaded with him. Nothing. Only the fire and the screaming.

Raven tried to lash out, to move, but felt nothing. Not her hands, nor her feet. An entity of existence. An existence of pain. This was a soul burning in Hell; a presence hovering in blackness without form, burning forever.

Exhaustion joined the agony. Exhaustion from the mental cries, the mental screams, the reflection of her suffering. Raven's mind could only linger on herself and her torture.

A chilling sensation sliced through her skin as if she were being wrapped in a cocoon. The fires of the toxin were being quenched.

"Let go. Let go of your soul," voices repeated. *Who were they? Where were they? Would this ever end?*

Holding strong to her father's teachings and God's words, Raven steeled her mind and refused to give in to such thoughts.

The darkness, the eternity surrounding her, and its cold chill increased. She had always stayed faithful to God. Why did he send her to Hell? *Please, God help me.* After many silent shrieks, the icy hold diminished the raw fire in her veins. The pain subsided and the darkness faded.

Sound and smell seeped back ever so slowly. The smell of dust, mold, and dank wood mingled in her nostrils. An endless chiming oozed into her eardrum. Somewhere, heartbeats drummed. There were two of them, but she could not hear or feel her own.

Raven's body crept back to life, tingling prickles crawling up her limbs, her torso and then to her head. She lay on smooth hardwood. She touched her arm. It was neither warm nor cold. She opened her eyes and though it was dark, her vision cleared followed by sudden terror to comprehend her situation.

Was she in her mother's root cellar? The walls were empty. The jars of vegetables and fruit that her mother had so laboriously made were gone.

Everything had such detail and clarity; it had to be a dream.

Each particle in the air, each crack on the wall was clear and sharp. There came a drumming again, two heartbeats from a distance. The sound of a surge each time the hearts pumped blood from chamber to chamber created a lust that she did not understand. She wanted to drink. Her lips were cracked and numb. Her thirst devoured her thinking.

"Stay the hunger and be true to the teachings of the Father," a man said, his voice smooth and calm.

A rush of shock jolted her. She leaped feet away from where she lay and landed without a sound. She scanned the room and focused on the furthest corner, catching a glimpse of a winged man, before a blinding radiance burst from where he had been standing. She slammed against the wall trying to recoil from the light. A loud hiss issued from somewhere. Clapping her hand over her mouth, she was stunned. The hissing sound had come from her.

What had she just seen? The man was gone.

The beating of the two hearts above drew her attention and she placed her hand over her churning stomach. She felt voracious, as though she'd been starving for days. Moving toward a wooden staircase, cautiously, she made her way up to the landing, halting only when she came face to face with a large statue of an angel. A cross stood at the opposite end of the room. She walked down the aisle past the empty pews. There was a figure of a man sitting in the front row, his heartbeat reverberating in the hollow of her ears. It wasn't a dream. Whatever she had gone through was real. The stranger looking at her was real.

"Who are you?" Raven asked. Her voice sounded different and harmonious, like sweet honey.

"My name is James. If you remember our last conversation, we made an agreement that I expect you to keep."

What conversation? Faint visions of the man swirled in her mind. Each image merged with sharp stings of pain. She remembered a promise. Yes. Something about innocents, dying, and demons. She was dying. Dying in this church, and he made her promise something.

"What happened to me? Why do I speak so strangely?"

James stood and she backed away.

"You don't need to fear me. I'll explain everything, but first, we have to feed you." James walked behind a pew and dragged out a bound and gagged man. The man's heart quickened. Its pace amplified her hunger.

"This man is a rapist and murderer. Take him. Feed on his blood."

Raven's eyes widened. "No."

This man is demented.

"The hunger you feel is the bloodlust of the Lilin. A demon that feeds on the blood of man. Jonas was such a demon, and when he bit you, the curse transferred to you. You are a Lilin. A *vampire*."

Raven shook her head. "Vampires are not real."

"They are. You're one," James said. "And unless you want to lose your soul to the demon curse, you must quench your hunger before your mind turns pure evil, and that I won't allow." James pulled out a crossbow armed with a stake and aimed it at her.

"What are you doing?"

"I didn't kill you. I only disabled you. But before I did that, you made a promise to never feed on the blood of innocents. If you let your hunger control you, that will happen. Now feed, before you lose the last ounce of humanity you have left!" His voice sounded more demanding.

Raven's hunger was mounting. That, she could not deny, but to feed on human blood? To kill? Her mind was growing distraught. The idea of ravaging and tearing into both men played in her head. She clenched her teeth, wrestling to take control of the whirling storm of thoughts.

James had told the truth.

She stared down at the man. The pulsing of blood under his skin sent a fire of hunger pains crashing through her. Raven looked back at James. He stood quietly, studying her with the wicked point of his crossbow, waiting. She looked down and felt the strange sensation of her fangs growing.

Survive. She must survive.

CHAPTER 3

Raven awoke in the church basement. It had all been some horrible nightmare, invading and stealing her memories, but slowly, awareness stabbed at her, oozing reality in.

A man bound by rope flashed in her mind.

She'd drunk blood. The man's blood.

She recalled the sensations that had rushed through her body. Spasms of pleasure that vibrated through her muscles, making every inch of her feel like it was breathing to life for the first time.

James lingered somewhere in that fuzzy image, warning her, telling her to stop, but she couldn't. She kept drinking the sweet honey warm liquid, bringing moisture to every parched crevasse of her body.

A thumping of hearts, a dozen at least, brought her back to the present.

The low simmer of voices seeped through the walls. A door squeaked open somewhere, followed by footsteps resounding on the floor above. Raven lost herself in the clarity of her hearing.

A fog of fleshy scents swarmed into the room and made her stomach growl.

She wanted to kill and to rip into that delicious tissue.

No, she didn't.

It wasn't her.

It was the voices.

The voices thieving her mind, devouring her from the inside. She pinched her eyes shut and curled against a corner. *Stop it. Leave me alone.*

Her mind raced, conjuring explanations. There were always explanations; that's what she was good at. Finding answers. But her brain wouldn't work, as if it was soaked in muffled confusion. Her emotions were clouding her logic.

The room spun, a sharp pressure tearing through her skull.

Her father's eyes. Lifeless and empty.

Phillip and Matthew, they were screaming. They were dead.

Her mother was dead.

No, it's not true.

The images flashed, one after the other, drowning her thoughts. Lightheadedness followed. A snarling sound issued from somewhere.

An animal?

Her throat vibrated.

It was her.

She was the animal.

The door to the basement creaked open.

Without thought or reason, Raven jumped into a defensive crouch. A group of men stepped down the stairs holding a candle lantern toward her. The light washed over their faces, outlining every wrinkle, and darkening every shadow of their features.

Raven remembered the graying hair and thick build of the man called Wyman. She pressed against the wall like a cornered animal. They were watching, their eyes focused as if they expected her to harm them. *Afraid of her. A little girl. Why?*

Wyman nodded at the man next to him who pulled out a crucifix and brandished it toward her. She stared at it, confused, and the group shifted uneasily, looking at each other.

"It has no effect," one of them said.

"How can it be?" another asked.

"She didn't become the full Lilin," one answered from the back of the group. It was a voice Raven was familiar with. James pushed through the hunters and came to stand next to Wyman.

"We can use her; train her to hunt their kind. She can even the odds for us. Give us an edge." James pulled out a vial of water and walked to Raven. "I'm not going to harm you."

Don't trust him. Kill him. Rip him apart. Raven studied the vial.

"What is it?"

"Holy water." James poured the liquid into his palm. "Hold out your hand."

No. She hated him. He'd made her kill that man. But James hadn't killed her. He was trying to help, wasn't he? Why wasn't her mind working correctly? Why couldn't she think? She held her hand out and James poured the water over it. It rolled cold over her skin, and trickles splattered on the ground. The hunters watched curiously.

"She isn't harmed. Her will is her own." James gripped Raven's wrist and, with a harsh tug, presented her hand to Wyman. James's veins pulsed against her skin. The scent of his flesh warped into a suffocating cloud of honey-sweet fragrance, maddening her thirst. Her brain soaked in the effective intoxication of it. *Rip into him.*

Raven fell back and clutched her head, wrestling the thoughts away.

"It's too dangerous. If she should ever completely turn, who knows which of us she will kill," Wyman said.

"Lilin attacks are becoming more common and we haven't the resources to hunt them, especially with the war. It's our duty to protect all humanity from the demons, and we are not doing that job."

"Look at her. She battles with her mind. How will she help us?" Wyman pointed at Raven, who fought to regain her composure.

"She's not trained. I will take her and instruct her."

"Instruct a vampire?"

"I have tracked and killed more than anyone here. I know their strengths and weaknesses. Who better to train one?"

What were they talking about? Run, run now. Raven peered at the stairs following them to the door to freedom.

"I want to go home," Raven bellowed.

Wyman looked down on her, distaste in his eyes. "I won't endanger our men. Finish the job you should have done. Kill her."

Tendrils of fear crept through Raven. "No, I do not understand what I'm doing here."

Two hunters aimed crossbows with silver tipped stakes at her. She slid against the wall.

Myth. Silver stakes for killing vampires.

Vampires don't exist. I am not one, am I?

James stepped between her and the hunters.

"I'll take her, and I'll take the damn risk. If she turns, I will kill her myself, but I need to do this. Each day more people are being killed, families slaughtered. The Lilin plague grows stronger." James held his stare firm on Wyman.

After a few moments, Wyman shook his head and let out a heavy breath. "Fine, this is your responsibility. If anyone is hurt, I am looking for you."

"She won't be hurting anyone except her own."

"For your sake, I'd make certain. Find a place to train the thing and be quick about it. I don't want the filth desecrating the house of God. I will inform Archer, but if he says no, I can't save the demon." Wyman glared at

Raven then ushered his men out. James followed them up the stairs.

Raven ran behind him. "I want to go home."

He reached the door and turned to face her. "You have no home. Your family is dead. You're dead." James shut the door and locked it.

Raven's mind swirled. Vertigo stole her strength. She had to get out of there. She yanked on the handle, but the door, thick and stout with metal trimmings would not yield.

"Let me out. Please. You cannot keep me here. Please let me out." Outside, horses raced away, their hooves knocking on the ground and fading. The beating hearts of the men fell to a whisper. She dropped to her knees, sobbing.

Hours passed. She hadn't moved from where she sat, streaks of crusted blood tears lined her cheeks. There was a heartbeat.

Footsteps echoed outside. Raven leaped to her feet and hammered on the door.

"Help me. Let me out."

The lock unhinged and the door opened. James greeted her with a cold stare. Raven cautiously stepped back. "Will you let me go?"

James tossed metal shackles that pooled with a heavy clank by her feet. Raven stared at them and turned her gaze on James with a questioning look.

"Lock those around your ankles." James pointed at the heavy chains.

Raven's lips quivered. "No."

"Do it or I will, and you'll not like it." James pointed a crossbow at her.

Raven fell back on her rump. "I have done nothing. Please... let me go."

"Shackles. NOW." James waved the crossbow at the chains.

Frightened sobs stole Raven's breath, a long silent inhale burst out in broken heaves. She turned on hands and knees, ever so slowly crawling toward the chains. Raven picked them up and rocked back and forth, puddles of crimson tears forming on the dusty floor, eyes turning to James, pleading.

"Put the damn things on." James punched the doorframe.

Raven slowly locked the shackles around her ankles.

When she was done, James walked over with a second set. "Hold out your arms."

Raven gave him one more abject stare. James avoided her eyes and locked the manacles around her wrists. Though they should have been heavy to her, they were light, weighing nothing at all.

James pulled at the long chain attached to her hands and led her out of the church.

It was night and the stars were bright across the barren sky. She could see the dim light of morning coming. She felt its warmth.

He led her to a horse-led carriage. James opened the door and stepped in, pulling Raven with him. The cabin was solid, no openings, and made of thick wood and metal bindings. The smallness of it was overwhelming. She imagined herself trembling though her body wasn't. James latched the chain to a metal hinge and locked it firmly.

"This is your home for the next few days and there is where you will sleep." He pointed to a pile of soil. "Lie on that earth to rest. It's part of you now."

When James stepped out Raven realized that this was a prison. Dark, empty and confined.

"Wait, I cannot stay here."

James slammed and locked the door.

"No." Raven ran at it, jerked back by the chain. She burst into tears. She wrestled with the manacles and screamed. Nothing. James disregarded her pleas. What had she done? He'd let her live, why was he doing this? She was suffocating; her body quivered.

Calm, calm, her body didn't need to breathe anymore. *Too dark, too small, it's too small.* She wouldn't die, she was dead. James said she was dead already. *Calm down.*

She fell to her knees. "Papa..."

It was long after the carriage had started moving that Raven calmed and curled on top of the earth as James had instructed. She was too exhausted to think anymore, her body drained of all strength. The burning sensation and thirst was overbearing, enough to make her forget the confined cage.

The carriage moved along and she concentrated on the rattle of the wagon wheels. The heavy clack of horse hooves became a hypnotic rhythm and she succumbed to the world of dreams.

R

Raven was running with Phillip toward home. Their father was smiling, waiting for them on the porch with Matthew. Their mother came out and gave their father a kiss. The sunlight washed over the grassy field and various flowers were aflame with colors. Normal, safe, happy. She ran faster—something was wrong, the house was blurring. The faster she ran, the further away it moved. She stumbled and fell.

Suddenly it was dark. She was trapped in a suffocating prison of earth. Her arms pinned by her body, hundreds of little spiders crawling on her. Phillip stared down the crevasse at her, his eyes wide.

"Phillip—help me, Phillip."

He shook his head, trembling. "I... I can't."

Raven shrieked. The baby spiders were crawling into her ears and over her eyes.

Phillip disappeared.

"Phillip. Please," she cried. They were swarming into her mouth; hundreds of little spider legs clinging to her tongue. Frantically, she tried to spit them out, their little bodies popping against her teeth when she rubbed her tongue to spit.

Raven snapped her eyes open and sat up, shaking the evil nightmare away. It had been some time since she'd had that particular nightmare violate her dreams. It was a memory that she couldn't wipe away. She scooted against the corner of the cabin, once again surrounded in darkness, this time without hope that anyone would come for her. Her family was dead; she was a prisoner, constantly burning with hunger. She imagined her father's smile. She would never see that smile again; never go hunting with him again. She wanted to hear her mother's voice, play with her brothers, wanted to go home, wanted to make sense of everything. The darkness of her cage stole any hope of that.

The door opened and Raven scurried to her feet. It was night. A whole day had passed while she'd slept. The smell of human flesh made her wince. Hunger burned hot coals in the flesh of her throat.

James stood by the door. Two strangers came around, dragging a third unconscious man, whose feet were bound by thick rope. They lifted and shoved him into the carriage. Soon after, the two strangers left, leaving Raven and James alone with the unconscious meal.

"You know what to do. This time restrain yourself. Do not drink so fast, lest you are overwhelmed. Your body hasn't fully adjusted to your demonic alterations. Now, feed," James ordered.

"You want me to kill him? I will not."

"Drink or die. Those are your only options."

"I will not."

"Are we going through this again?"

"I want to go home. I have done nothing, and yet I have been locked in chains with none of my questions answered."

"Forget your home. Your old life doesn't exist anymore. Now drink!" James' voice grew stern.

Raven stepped toward the back of the carriage, away from the bound man. "I will not let you do this to me."

James hopped into the cabin and over to Raven and wrenched her by the hair. He dragged and forced her down by the man who was gaining consciousness. Her body was becoming weak, the chains were heavy; the world spun and stole her power.

"You will drink. Do so before he wakes." James shoved her face into the man's neck. Tears smeared her skin.

"I will not."

The blood pulsing so near to her was enthralling. The warm heat and smell made every particle of her body scream. It wasn't until she felt the warm liquid dripping from her chin, that she realized she was drinking.

Raven leaped back. The man was pale; on the edge of death. James was standing outside the carriage. Raven had lost track of time, lost her mind within the invigorating sensation, the orgasmic taste of blood.

James dragged the dying man out of the carriage and dropped him on the ground with a loud thud. He pulled out a stake and rammed it into the man's heart, driving it in through to the other side.

James peered at Raven. "That will keep you to the end of our travel."

She curled against a corner, fresh crimson tears washing over her clothes. James closed the door and locked it. Moments later, the carriage creaked on its way. Raven fell to her side and rolled into a ball, losing herself in past memories of her old life. Crinkling her eyes shut, she tried pushing away the despair that ate her from inside.

What had she done that was so evil that God would do this to her?

"Please, God, help me. I am sorry if I made you angry. Forgive me. Please get me out of here. I will do everything you ask of me. I will read the Bible as Papa said. Just make things right again. Please, please, please."

Only the dark silence answered her.

Raven lay unmoving for the entirety of the journey. A sense of time lingered indefinitely with sorrow and despair; her trance broken when the door opened. James set down a candle lantern by the entrance and stepped in.

"We've arrived," he said.

Raven sat up and shifted to gain a better view outside. With her inhuman sight, she could see that a thick wall of trees caged them. James unlocked the hinge to her chain and tugged her up.

"Are you right of mind?" James aimed his crossbow at her.

Raven stared at the loaded silver tip of the stake.

"Are you right in the mind?" He asked again.

Raven nodded. Both of them stepped out of the cabin. A two-story house stood within a jungle of weeds, encased by gnarled trees that clawed at the windows. The house looked as though it had been unlived in for some time. It would have probably been a grand sight to see in its time. James led her to the steps. Dabs of orange candlelight broke through the blanket of dust on the windows. A couple of people moved inside.

"You'll train here." James walked inside the house and Raven followed, tugged along by the shackles. "The first lesson, you will learn well."

James closed the door behind her. A burning sensation spread through her body, intensifying by the second, and she screamed. Her skin fumed and burned black.

"What is happening? Help me."

"Never enter a home without being invited," James said.

Raven fell, rolling on the floor and screeching.

"Ask to come in," James ordered.

"I am burning," she shouted.

"Ask permission to come in."

His words were mumbles; the pain drowned her senses in lava. James dragged her by the chain. Outside the house, the burning stopped and Raven curled into a ball. Her skin was black, but in moments it healed and soon it had its pale tint again. When she looked up, two other men glowered down at her.

"All the arrangements have been made. The house is yours," one of them said to James. Both men stomped down the porch steps. "Deliveries every three days," he finished, before both of them left on horseback.

James pulled Raven to her feet. She was drained, and her skin shriveled and dry.

"Your second lesson shall be to hunt."

CHAPTER 4

Twelve British soldiers trudged through a thicket of tangled woods. Thin frames of trees and silhouetted canopies of leaves were wrought by the dim moonlight that broke through the black forest, leaning in on them. An eerie silence lingered, and each soldier felt the back of their necks prickle from the sensation of something watching them.

Their steps sank into the moist carpet of plant life, which was fine, as they did not want to make noise for fear Continentals would discover them. They feared arousing the evil presence that oozed from the dark.

The captain's horse shifted restlessly. The men scoured the trees as if expecting something to jump from the inky mass of shadows that enclosed them.

Captain Benton remained resolved, hiding his unease, but he couldn't dismiss the sense that a presence lingered. As though on cue, the air became cold, sending chills up his arms. The horse reared and flung him off and galloped away.

"Godforsaken beast," he shouted.

His men shuffled around him and helped him back to his feet. The sound of movement in the bushes caught their attention and they all rushed to form a line, aiming their muskets at the blackness.

Silence.

A scream from one of the men sent their hearts racing. He was gone. Only his musket remained where he once stood. The men looked around wildly.

"Where did he go?" Shouted one.

"Calm thyselves," Benton ordered.

From the bushes, the decapitated head of the missing soldier flew at the Captain who caught it by sheer instinct. Benton immediately flung it down. The men fired frantically into the woods.

"Hold your fire, damn you. You'll have every Continental on us," Benton said.

"Something is in the woods!" A man yelled.

"Some beast," another said.

A pack of large snarling wolves crept from the edges of the woods to surround them, eyes gleaming and teeth bared. Hands trembling, the squad feverishly reloaded their muskets. The wolves swarmed in, ripping into them before they'd finished.

Benton pulled out his pistol, took one of the animals down, and unsheathed his saber.

Screams ripped through the dark woods. Benton stared at a losing battle. He had to move, find an advantage, if there was one. "Too many of them. Run." He ran with a couple of the other soldiers following behind him.

The screams faded behind them as the three men found themselves further into the thick forest, barely able to see a few feet in front of them.

"We're trapped. This is the Devil's work," the younger of the three said.

Benton silenced his fear trying to remain calm. "Get a hold of yourself, soldier."

"What should we do?" The second man asked.

"Keep moving, and quickly. We must get out of the woods," Benton said.

A woman's laughter echoed around them.

"What was that?" The young soldier swung his musket aiming at the shadows.

A pair of eyes gleamed from the darkness. The clouds unveiled the full moon. Its light broke through a small clearing of branches to reveal a beautiful young woman. She had perfectly smooth skin, pale white. She was enchanting.

"Don't leave me here. I'm lost and alone." The girl sauntered to the young soldier and caressed his cheek.

"How did you get way out here?" Benton asked.

The young soldier dropped his musket, submitting to the girl's caresses.

"I was with my husband." She gently kissed the young man.

"Where is your husband?" Benton stepped closer to her.

The girl gave Benton a sly look.

"Behind you," she said, as fangs jutted from her mouth. In less than a second, the girl bit into the young soldier's neck, near his throat... A grumbled yelp escaped him, but only for a moment.

Benton turned to look for the other soldier. He was dead at the feet of a stranger. The man was tall, at least six foot five, with a firm jaw and a thin nose. He was at least in his late teens to early twenties. Strands of long flaxen hair fell over his shoulders and his skin was porcelain smooth like the girl's, but his eyes were yellow, rimmed with silver.

"What the devil are you?" Benton asked, as he turned his attention back to the girl. She did not look up from feeding on the blood of the young soldier.

"I am Dumitru. And that is my mate, Andreea."

Dumitru moved toward Benton, who swung his saber at the large man. "Stay back."

Andreea giggled. "I want to keep him. He is a strong one."

"Demons, I do not fear you. God is my shepherd." Benton rushed at Dumitru and swiped his saber. He hit nothing. Dumitru moved behind him in that instance, gripped him by the neck and hurled him into a tree.

Andreea leaped on Benton, "Shhh, quiet. Be still. I will keep you," she whispered. "Darling, he is so adorable."

Benton could not help but succumb to this girl's deep melodic voice. Her face was serene, her touch gentle; chills of ecstasy covered his skin. She had a sweet scent, pleasing; it sent his blood racing. She pressed her body against his, her breasts soft against his chest and her lips plumb against his skin. She tenderly kissed him.

"He is strong, a perfect addition." Dumitru studied Benton then turned back to the woods leaving the pair alone.

"What do you want with me?" Benton asked.

Andreea smiled.

R

Raven awoke from the clutches of another nightmare, or more like haunting memories—scenes of her family that she had forgotten. She forced herself not to dwell in that happy past. It was too draining to think about.

A lone candle desperately fought off the darkness that tried to swallow the underground room she slept in. It was there not for her, but for James when he came to check on her. He didn't trust her and kept her shackles hinged to the floor. She accepted what she was or had become: a vampire. The very same monster that had killed her family.

A month had passed and James had forced her into training, teaching her how to hunt, which was an arduous task more so for James than for her. She refused to kill, but her bloodlust would win over her will, clouding her judgment.

James stayed nearby, watching when she fed. He would kill her if she fully lost her mind to the evil. He'd made that clear.

Men from the Order of the Sons of Light would bring murderers and the vilest of criminals for Raven to feed on. Only the blood of humans could quench the hunger of a vampire, James had explained. The longest Raven could go was three days at the most. After that, her mind would sway to the demon curse.

Raven had asked James how they found these criminals, but he always sidestepped her questions.

Loneliness suffocated her in the long hours that passed when James would leave her locked in the prison, and her mind would busy itself with the wraiths of her happy past. Raven longed to talk to someone. *Anyone.*

Thinking came clearly and emotions would flood in, always disrupting her logic, but she was gaining more control. Images in her mind were detailed, her brain working like some device, envisioning possibilities and searching for understanding. There was no doubt that she would think of a way to escape. The isolation was unbearable. The need to return home to find closure became the one goal she could not put aside in her thoughts.

That night, when James brought her out, Raven surprised him by following all his instructions. No doubt, he was probably wondering what the ruse was. Though it weighed on her, Raven was precise in her kill. A large man who James explained had slaughtered a family with young children. Raven couldn't help but feel a small sense of satisfaction killing this one. However, there was an ulterior motive to her actions.

When the night was done, James brought her down to her lonely prison.

"I did everything you asked of me," she said.

"You did."

"I want something in return."

"No." James locked the shackles.

"I will follow your instructions, I promise. I just want one thing."

James turned to leave and Raven clutched his arm.

"Unhand my arm, or I will end your demonic existence. What do you think you are doing?" he demanded.

"Will you sit and talk? Talk like normal people."

"Let go of my arm." He jerked his arm away.

Raven released her grip and James climbed the stairs out.

"Please, it is so lonesome down here."

R

He ignored her, shut the door, locked it, and stood for a moment in silence. She wasn't a child.

James hadn't expected this. Hadn't thought through all the aspects of training Raven. Those damned feelings. It was too damned difficult to keep himself detached emotionally from the vampire.

She is dead, no longer a human. No, she's a little girl fighting to keep whatever humanity she has left. Stop it. There can be no attachment. She will turn into a full Lilin and will kill without sympathy.

His hands balled into fists. *Did I make a mistake keeping her alive? Probably. And what about her brothers?*

A knock at the front door disrupted his thoughts. James went to open it. *Perfect.*

Wyman and his group of hunters stood outside. James let out a sigh. He felt his blood simmer. Wyman was head of the northern hunters. He was good at keeping people in line, but that was about it. Wyman had once chosen to use people as bait in a trap for vampires. It failed and innocent people were slaughtered. The Core Order didn't see it that way, but James did. Now, both men had to work together, each one tolerating the other.

"You're early."

"Are you going to let us in?"

James stepped aside for them to pass.

"Can the creature track her kind yet?" Wyman asked.

"It's only been a month and she is a fledgling, what do you think?"

"There's been a massive spree of butchery in the past week. British and Continental troops have been slaughtered in groups."

"A couple of vampires couldn't achieve that level of killing," James said.

"We believe it is a gathering of vampires," Wyman walked over to the door that locked Raven in. "We need your vampire dog to track them."

"Vampires roam in pairs."

"They are amassing a coven and it must be stopped."

"Raven isn't ready. I need more than one month. I need three at the least."

"By instinct, she'll find others of her kind." Wyman loaded a stake into his crossbow. "Open the door."

"Fine, if she's the only thing that can help track them, then all hangs on her ability to do so. If she's not ready and doesn't do as you ask, then what? You'll kill her?" James shook his head. "Do that and your journey here was nothing but a waste of time. You lack patience."

Wyman shot James a cold stare. "The one who gathers the vampires is Dumitru."

The name shook James' world, forcing him to collect himself.

"What say ye now, James? You believe we should wait months and let Dumitru gather an army or escape? You would let your son's murderer flee?"

James' nostrils flared. "Two weeks."

"What?"

"Two weeks more and she'll be ready. I won't lose an opportunity to find Dumitru." James walked over to Wyman, moving close enough to whisper into his ear. *"Don't ever use my son's death for leverage again."* He landed a hard right to Wyman's chin that sent the man slamming to the floor. The other hunters rushed in and Wyman held up a hand to hold them back.

James had climbed the stairs by the time Wyman got to his feet with wobbly legs.

"You have two weeks and not a day more," Wyman said, trying to regain some pride. "Let's go." He stomped out with his men at his heels.

James stood by a window watching the hunters ride off as the sun peeked over the horizon. A rush of emotions swirled inside him. Dumitru was close and he was gathering an army.

It had been twelve years since his son had died. James had made it a personal vendetta to find the one who'd killed him. When he did, it wasn't what he expected. It was when he'd found Dumitru and tried to avenge his son's death that he discovered vampires existed. A group of vampire hunters were also tracking Dumitru. They'd saved James from being one of the Lilin's next victims. Since then, he'd become a member of the secret society that hunts the demons, the Order of the Sons of Light, backed by the world's religious institutions.

Dumitru was one of the few remaining elder vampires who possessed great powers. He was very skilled at evading the hunters. He was a vampire similar to Jonas, the one that had bitten Raven. Jonas was the first to be turned by Dracula, and considered the most powerful of all the elders. As vampires created other vampires, the powers would diminish, and fledglings would have no special abilities. Raven was Jonas' first sire.

James suspected that Raven would soon realize her powers. The girl was an accident that Jonas had never planned to let live. A mistake that James planned to use to find Dumitru.

R

When James opened Raven's door the next night, she was standing, waiting for him. James came down and unlocked her shackles. She knew that hatred in his eyes. They shared it. One of the monsters had killed his son, in the same way her own family had been slaughtered. Unfortunately, he thought of her as one of the demons. The difference was that she would never kill a family. Never.

"I heard everything last night. I understand what you are doing," she said.

He pulled her by the chain and walked her out. Raven was relieved to see the open night sky again; an escape from the enclosed walls of her prison. James loaded a silver-tipped stake into his crossbow and coated it with Wolfsbane, a poisonous toxin to her kind, he had warned.

If she should ever try to escape, he would use it on her. She couldn't get far, even if she managed to elude him. The house was the only shelter for miles around that would protect her from the sun. He had let her try to walk out in the daylight once. She'd neared the door and felt the intense heat of the sun's radiance. The white heat blinded her.

He explained that she would burn should she ever be caught in the direct light of the sun; this always ensured she would return to the house after a hunt. She had contemplated running, but feared death more than her prison.

She was mastering her ability to think without emotional disturbance and soon, perhaps, would visualize a way to escape.

Raven looked around for her next victim, but after scouring the area, she neither saw nor heard anyone else. It was only herself and James.

"You are not making me hunt tonight?"

"Yes."

"I see no one."

"If you're to hunt your kind, first you must learn to track someone who is skilled at stealth." James released Raven. "I'm your prey tonight."

He walked toward the thick trees, then stopped. "If you decide not to participate, I revoke my invitation to the house. You have until morning to find me or burn by the light of the sun."

Raven's mouth opened in shock. "What if I cannot find you?"

James proceeded into the woods. "When you hear the sound of my pistol, that's your signal."

Raven paced and stared out past the tops of the trees. She could see the dim light of the evening sun that only her eyes discerned. The fear of imminent death flooded in.

Raven's attention was jarred by the blast of James's pistol and she sprinted to the trees, moving swiftly toward the direction of the sound, the blurred mixture of black and green land rushing past. Raven listened carefully for James's heartbeat and sniffed the air to catch his scent.

She was relieved when a strong breeze carried the smell of flesh and forest with it. She would not die. James wasn't as good as he believed himself to be. Raven followed the trail, running toward the source of the scent and arrived where it was most profuse only to find a piece of his shredded tunic.

"No."

A flood of emotions washed in. She was lightheaded and churned with anxiety, her ability to think faded into the storm of emotions.

She caught another whiff of James's scent and sprinted off. He was near. Another piece of his clothing flapped on a branch. James was throwing her off, tricking her sense of smell.

The game went on into the late hours of the night. Raven tried to push away the river of emotions swelling in her, and tried to think rationally. What use was it being precocious when you couldn't even think? She thought she'd heard the sound of James' heartbeat a few times, only to discover it was that of some forest creature. She was, however, starting to discern the variation between the rhythms of the beats.

Worry gnawed at her. The late hours of the night were ending. She didn't want to die, especially by being burnt alive. If only she could find shade from the sunlight. Raven recalled how intense the heat was from the open door where the sun spilled through.

She raced forward desperately sniffing the air for his scent, hoping it wouldn't be another decoy. Then there was the drumming of a heart. It was the right pace to be human; she made sure this time. And there was a second, stronger heartbeat. A horse. That's how he was matching her speed.

"I have you."

Raven raced toward the thudding. She sensed something off when she neared. The scent was wrong. It had to be another trick. Not falling for it, she turned past a few thick patches of bushes and trees and came behind James mounted on the horse. He was moving at a relaxed pace. Raven lurched down and leaped many feet off the ground landing on top and pulling him down. He landed with a thud. The horse reared and snorted.

"I win," Raven said, proudly.

She was greeted with a cross held to her face. It was then, with the inhuman vision, she saw it wasn't James at all.

"Away from me, demon!" the stranger shouted.

Raven stepped back, "I'm sorry. I thought you were someone else."

The young boy stood and flung water on her. Raven was surprised and so was the stranger staring at her as if something should have been happening. He quickly brandished his handgun crossbow and aimed it at her. He was a hunter.

"No, wait. I am not going hurt you."

"You're right about that."

He pulled the trigger. Raven was quick enough to twirl and avoid the thick stake striking her heart. It drove through the side of her chest instead with a jarring crunch. Her bellow sent sleeping birds flying.

R

James darted across the thick web of woods. The fragments of moonlight that broke through the branches provided enough luminance for him to make out his path. He rubbed his clothing on a tree every few feet to leave his scent. There was no single point of reference for Raven to pick out his scent. It was everywhere.

He was tracking her as well. One of the first skills a vampire hunter was taught was to control his heartbeat. Through meditative training and breathing, James could lower his heart rate dramatically enough that only a very few vampires could sense his location. This provided a great advantage for the hunters when they needed to ambush the demons.

James sat down to rest. He didn't expect for Raven to find him the first night, and of course, he had lied to her about revoking his invitation. Once a vampire had been invited into a home, it would be free to come and go from that point on. He did expect to use more drastic measures in the next few weeks to get her ready for the hunt. *To catch my son's killer, if it would mean being cruel to Raven, then so be it. She was a demon.*

He'd left his wife and two younger daughters for the pursuit of Dumitru. He had only seen them a couple of times in the years that he'd joined the Order. He'd lost his son, but his lust for vengeance meant he'd sacrificed the rest of his family. Was he wrong?

A piercing scream snapped him back to a heightened awareness. He jumped to his feet and darted in its direction.

R

Raven felt the hot sting of the stake penetrate deep into her chest, and a burn pour into her body. She could feel it like boiling water coursing through her veins. The stake was coated with Wolfsbane, and while she had blood in her system from the last time she'd fed, her heartbeat sent the poison flowing through her. Her shrieks echoed through the woods. She willed herself to pull the stake out. The hunter ran toward her with a Machaira, the hunters' blessed weapon.

"Stop," she cried.

He leapt at her and swung at her throat. Raven held her hand out to shield herself. To her surprise, the hunter was hurled a few yards away. Raven stood in quandary, the heat swirling from her wound stole her focus and she staggered to her knees. She let out another scream when her flesh singed from the movement. The veins near her outer skin were black and burnt through.

"James," she screamed.

Another stake slammed into her stomach and sent her on her back with a thud. The hunter had come back. The burning numbed her. She could only cry out, as the hunter stood above her and swung his Machaira down.

CHAPTER 5

James leaped over a bundle of bushes.

"No!"

He tackled the young hunter who swung his weapon down on Raven; its sharp edge sliced the side of her neck.

James pinned down the boy.

"You don't know what you're doing," the young hunter shouted.

"I'm with the Order and she is under my watch." James pointed at Raven.

"What? Get off me."

James stood and let the hunter stand, only after he had relaxed.

"Why are you watching over a vampire?"

James rushed over to a groaning Raven.

"James, it burns." He examined her neck. A small cut on the side. It was already zipping together, though slow due to the Wolfsbane.

"I am sorry. I blundered," she curled into a ball and let out another cry.

He lifted her into his arms and hurried to the boy's mount. "I need your horse."

"What?"

"Keep walking north. You'll find one of the Orders' holding houses, and your horse." James placed Raven on top of the horse and mounted right after.

"Walk? That's my horse."

James nudged it onto a gallop before the young hunter could protest further.

James arrived at the house and quickly dismounted, hauling Raven in. The sun was peeking over the horizon when he slammed the door shut.

"Make it stop. Please." Raven's grip crunched down on his arm. He winced but held her firm.

James took her to the basement and laid her on her soil.

Raven heaved out long breaths. "I am burning."

"It must run its course; I can do nothing. The soil will help." James tried to stand, but Raven's fingers clenched tight to him.

"Don't leave." Raven's face streamed red tears and she trembled. *She was a vampire but her mind was that of a child.* He'd tried only to see the monster that was in her. He had been cruel enough, hadn't he? She was a father's child. Could he have been so callous if she was one of his own daughters? He could not find it in him to leave her, and knew he would come to regret the emotions swirling in him. But not today.

Raven writhed for the next couple of hours before the Wolfsbane ate the last of the blood in her system and she became exceptionally cold to the touch. James moved her to a more comfortable position on the bed of soil. She slept soundly, as an innocent child at rest. Her heart wouldn't beat until next she fed, and her skin was becoming tight over her muscle and bones. The Lilin curse would eat her away without fresh blood.

Wolfsbane was an effective weapon against vampires. It indeed was like a poison that destroyed a vampire's tissue from the inside and weakened them. The vampire's system would use existing blood to keep constantly healing. It was blood that gave them powers and inhuman strength. Raven's last feed was meant to last another two days when a prisoner would be brought to her.

She would be fiendish when she awoke, which would be extremely dangerous. The thirst could make her succumb to the full control of the curse. James left her to rest. There was a knock on the front door.

R

The boy hunter had found the house. He'd been looking for his horse, which James had given back when he'd joined him outside. The boy had introduced himself as Nathaniel Hughes. He was seventeen and freshly out of hunter training.

"You never answered my question. Why are you protecting one of them?" Nathaniel demanded.

"She is to be used... to help us. I'm training her to track her kind."

"That's a foolish thing to do. What does the Order think it's doing? It's the same as bargaining with the Devil," Nathanial said.

"It's the lesser of two evils. What are you doing this far in the middle of nowhere?"

"Tracking two vampires. They killed my partner, and I aim to pay them back in kind." Nathanial looked toward the north. The flare of youthful determination gleamed in his eyes.

"Two to one odds are not favorable on your account."

"I don't fear death. God guides my way and protects me."

"As he protected your partner?"

Nathanial turned a cold stare to James. "Watch what you say, old man."

"Old enough to understand that blind faith is foolish. If you wish to go on your path, then die a fool's death. God wouldn't have given us a brain if he didn't want us to think." James walked past the young hunter and up the steps to the house. "If you don't want an imprudent demise, wait for tonight. I and the vampire will help you go after the demons."

"They will be miles away. They move by horse carriage."

"And only one path to take."

"The more reason for me to go on. They travel slowest during the day."

"Indeed, but I have a vampire to feed."

"I'm not hunting with one of the Devil's minions."

"Then you have a rough journey ahead of you. If those vampires travel a long distance, they will no doubt have guards to keep them."

Nathanial contemplated James's words. He was smart enough, but if he wanted to find an early death, James wasn't stopping him. His mind lingered on other problems and he didn't need to mount more to the mix.

That evening, Raven woke to pain like coals burning her from the inside. Her throat felt rubbed raw. Black veins crawled like spider webs to wrap every part of her skin. It made a sick feeling wrench itself in her stomach.

"James!" she screamed.

Footsteps scrambled outside. James unlocked the door and rushed down. Raven stood to examine herself, "What is happening to me?"

"The Wolfsbane ate what blood you had left. Now, the Lilin curse is eating your flesh," James said. The young hunter walked in.

Upon seeing the young black-haired boy, Raven stepped back. He pulled out his crucifix and hid behind it.

"Put that away. It has no effect on her," James ordered.

The young hunter kept it out.

James shook his head.

"Why is he here?" Raven stared daggers at the boy.

"We're hunting vampires tonight. You need to feed before you become crazed with hunger."

When James explained the situation, Raven wasn't pleased having to work with someone who had tried to kill her. Nathaniel feared her; it was evident in his eyes, and fear could make him dangerous. Nonetheless, all three set off in search of the vampires that night. Nathaniel made sure to stay clear of Raven, and both kept cautious glares on each other.

The hunters rode on horses while Raven swiftly followed by foot, hard-pressed without blood, and the hunger was increasing every hour.

Kill them. Feed on them. The annoying voices rang like wailing bells, injecting her mind with images of ripping into warm, delicious blood. She shoved them back into the silent dungeon of her psyche.

By late night, Raven's worries gnawed at her. Morning was a few hours away. They had been following a small path and no sign of a carriage. She voiced her concern to James, but he was confident that they would soon be upon their mark. Raven was more troubled for getting home. There would be no way to return in time before the sunrise. She was relieved when her eyes caught a hint of dancing lantern light and smelled flesh streaming down the path. The exhilarating scent punched her senses and stopped her mid-stride. She fell to her knees clutching her stomach. A deep growl issued from her throat.

James and Nathaniel stopped.

Raven looked forward with clenched teeth, "Ahead, I smell them."

"Control, don't lose control. Do you hear me?" James asked and gripped his crossbow. Nathaniel readied himself with his.

Raven clenched shut her eyes and nodded. "I am fine." Her words were deep and graveled. Nathaniel's heart quickened. "Don't let him shoot me."

James looked over at Nathaniel who relaxed his trigger finger.

"What?" Nathaniel shrugged.

Soon all three came close enough to see the warm glow of candle lanterns lighting the path for the three human guards that protected the vampires. One rode on the carriage while the other two rode horses to the left and right of it.

"Raven, I need you to take out those guards. Feed from them."

Raven shot James a curious gaze.

"Only the sinful would protect a vampire. They find victims for their masters in hope to be turned themselves," James said.

Nathaniel smirked. "Ironic that you protect and feed one yourself."

James ignored the jab.

"We'll wait for you to take them before we attack." James dismounted and made for the woods. Nathaniel followed on his heels.

James looked back. Raven slipped into the forest, swallowed by the blackness.

"You trust her to kill her own kind?" Nathaniel asked.

"No."

"You're testing her?"

"Quiet. Calm your heart, lest you let the demons know we're here."

They tied the horses and made their way through the thick brush and gnarled trunks, keeping enough distance from the carriage that the guards wouldn't hear them. Each twig they stepped on cracked and rung loud in the night.

"What if they're out hunting?" Nathaniel asked.

"They have to return," James said.

An ear-piercing scream from one of the guards broke the calm of the forest and more than a few creatures scurried or flew away. Nathaniel nearly dropped his crossbow.

Raven had leaped on the rider on the left and ripped a chunk of throat, leaving him gurgling for air from his spewing blood.

He fell like a sack of sand. The other two pulled out pistols.

The second rider darted around the carriage. Raven was already gone within the forest's shroud of darkness.

"They're not coming out," Nathaniel said.

Raven came again. With blurred speed, she hurdled on the carriage driver pinning him down. The second rider fired his pistol landing a hit.

Raven fell off the side. She let out a scream holding a hand over her wound. She crawled under the carriage. The rider came around.

The driver jumped down after her. He was pulled under by his feet. Raven in desperation clawed and ripped into him.

James scoured the area for the vampires.

A shadow descended on them and Nathaniel was lifted into the air. A woman flew above James holding on to Nathaniel by his tunic. She threw him against a tree and he landed face down in a thick mass of bushes.

She went for James next. He ducked low under her swipe.

"Flyer. She's a flyer." Nathaniel shouted.

"You're good at pointing out the obvious," James said. "She is a damned elder. Why didn't you say so?"

The women vanished into the darkness.

"I didn't know," Nathaniel said, regaining his bearings, and ducked under a swing from the woman when she shot out of the woods.

"I remember you," came a man's voice.

Both James and Nathaniel pulled out their crucifixes and scanned the shadows. A large wolf leaped out of the foliage and bit into Nathaniel's hand, dragging him out of the woods onto the trail. The creature ripped into his wrist. He screamed and dropped the cross.

James shot his crossbow at the wolf and landed a hit into its mid-section. It let Nathaniel loose with a loud howl.

The male vampire rushed to James, tackled him, and hurled him into a tree. His shoulder impacted and hung loose, his face twisted like someone having a heart attack. The vampire came in for the kill, but James brandished his crucifix, making it hiss in retreat back into the woods. "Come out, you son of a bitch."

R

Raven finished off the driver and turned to face the second rider. He shot under the carriage with a second pistol. He missed and she lunged out, startling the horse. It reared and the man tumbled off. She jumped on him and pierced deeply with her fangs into the backside of his neck. The hunger took over. The taste of the crimson liquid was ecstasy and her body shivered with pure euphoria. She closed her eyes losing herself in the fiendish curse. She could feel the hollows of her veins soaking in the fluid with a voracious hunger. Every particle of her body breathed back to life as waves of ecstasy sent spasms through her muscles.

Let go, embrace bliss. Kill them all and live forever. Forever young. The voices filled her mind.

R

James ran toward Nathaniel and was tackled by another large wolf. He dropped his crucifix in order to hold back the beast, its teeth inches from ripping into the side of his face. He could smell the hot breath of the creature.

"Raven!" he shouted.

Nathaniel was vulnerable without his cross, and the female vampire came at him, grabbing him from behind and pinning his arms. The male vampire walked out from the woods, a wicked smile shaped on his lips.

"Well, this is exactly as I remember your partner. How curious. It's like déjà vu." The vampire bore his fangs.

"Raven, damn it, snap out of it." James could see Raven lost in the bloodlust. If she had turned, it would mean the end of him and Nathaniel. His plan may have backfired.

The male vampire clutched Nathaniel's throat.

"Go on then, have at it. At least I won't be the one to burn in Hell," Nathaniel said, through half breaths.

"Do you think I am killing you? No, I am giving you eternal life," the vampire smiled.

"No." Nathaniel tried to break the woman's hold but his strength was useless against hers.

"Raven, remember your promise," James yelled. He kneed the wolf then reached for a dagger hidden in his boot cuff. Holding the wolf away by its neck, he stabbed the dagger deep into its side. The wolf howled and jumped away, tripping and yelping.

A voice like a distant dream weaved into Raven's mind. A promise, James's face, images of her family flashed in the dark void of her mind. She opened her eyes. James and Nathaniel. They needed her. She fought the voices, pushing them to the back of her mind, locking them there.

The male vampire went in for Nathaniel's throat and was then flung by a force into another incoming wolf. The vampire and the beast slid over each other like a tangled ball, rolling on the ground, and slammed against a thick tree trunk. The female vampire was taken by surprise for that instant. She stared at Raven, bewildered.

Raven rushed to the woman who released Nathaniel and leapt into the air.

James jumped back to his feet and sprinted over to both. "What the hell was that?" he asked.

"I don't know," Raven said.

The female flew out of the dark and grabbed Raven, both of them crashing into the woods, hissing and clawing. Raven attacked and defended herself on pure instinct. Her strength was superior to the vampires, who looked confused.

R

James locked and loaded his handgun crossbow while Nathaniel clutched his wounded wrist.

"Don't pass out on me," James said.

"It's nothing. Get him." Nathaniel grabbed his crossbow.

The male vampire was on his feet glaring at the two men. A pack of wolves joined him. Each stared at the hunters with hungry eyes.

"Who in God's name, was your teacher?" James asked.

"Adam Blake."

James snorted, "Figures. He was never any good at fighting elders."

Raven flew past both of them, landing on her feet. Her clothes were shredded and blood oozed out of large cuts that were healing. The female vampire looked no better when she stepped out of the brush.

"Here," James tossed Raven a crucifix. "Use that."

"Great. A vampire that is immune to crosses," Nathaniel smirked.

"A vampire that saved you," Raven growled.

"Children, mind our predicament," James said.

The female joined her mate who was surrounded by at least a couple dozen large black wolves.

"Well, I doubt the crucifix will help against wolves," Nathaniel pointed out.

R

Raven found herself gazing into the eyes of one of the wolves. *If vampires could control animals, then why wouldn't she be able to?*

"Take him out first," James said.

As he finished speaking, one of the wolves dived on the vampire, tackling him and clenching down on an arm. The rest of the pack became disoriented, looking around confused. The female vampire was taken aback. She ran to help her mate, but was pulled by a force and fell. Clawing at the ground, she was dragged toward Raven.

James and Nathaniel stared at Raven, puzzled.

"Are you doing that?" James asked.

"I cannot hold her long," Raven said.

James quickly aimed and shot a stake into the female's heart, paralyzing her. The male vampire knocked the wolf away and saw his mate in danger. The rest of the pack ran back into the forest after his control was lost on them.

"I will rip you all apart!" He shouted, and lunged for James. Raven shot an invisible force that slammed him down. Nathaniel fired his crossbow but missed.

The power Raven used was wearing on her strength; her legs went limp and her knees thunked on the hard ground.

The vampire twirled to his feet and James threw holy water on him. The water sizzled on his skin, sending him into a wailing frenzy, while Nathaniel tried to load another stake into his crossbow, proving quite a task with only one stable hand.

James pulled out his Machaira and lunged in for the kill. With one strong swing, he decapitated the vampire.

The female watched and let out a shriek. James walked over with his sword. She snapped her teeth at him, hissing and glaring with deep red eyes. "I'm going to…"

James swung down and her head rolled from her body.

"Did Adam Walker teach you how to shoot as well?" James asked, walking past Nathaniel over to Raven. She was hunched on hands and knees. She steadied herself, letting her strength return.

"You discovered new abilities?" James helped her to her feet.

Raven nodded.

"It came by itself … when I was protecting myself … from him." She looked at Nathaniel, who was wrapping a piece of his tunic over his hand.

The heat of the coming sun alarmed her. With her enhanced sight, she could see the horizon brightening. "The sun is rising," she said. "We are far from home."

"What a shame," Nathaniel remarked as he walked to his horse.

"You'll be fine," James said, directing Raven's gaze to the carriage. "That will protect you well enough to get you home."

Of course, the vampire's carriage was built to protect them from the sun. Raven smiled wide with relief.

Inside the carriage, Raven sat looking out the front through a slit of drapes. James held on to the reins outside from where she watched the trail. The vampires had fashioned the inside of the cabin to be comfortable, and spacious enough for two. It was elegant—a plush and glossy seat and bed fitted perfectly together. James noted her peeking through the slit.

"You will burn your eyes and you will be no use to me. Close the drapes," James said.

Raven frowned and sat back. He was right. The glare of the sun did warm her eyes, but her curiosity and longing to the see bright world needed to be satisfied. *They would heal again, wouldn't they?* Outside the carriage, she could hear Nathaniel riding alongside, groaning.

Once they'd arrived at home, James took time to gather a few thick hangings around the house to wrap and cover Raven and lead her inside. James closed the door and guided Raven to her cell. As they walked down, Raven pulled off the drapes and turned to James.

"Are you going to lock me in? I did as you asked. Even saved your own." Raven looked pleadingly at James. Nathaniel groaned in the other room. "I can help him. If he does not treat the bite, he may become ill. He could die."

"I can hear you. You're not making me feel any better," Nathaniel said.

Raven kept her gaze glued on James.

"What do you know of medical treatment?" James asked, skeptically, at which Raven beamed.

"I have read all the guides. From housewife companions to the theories of Hermann Boerhaave. I will need you to find a few things, herbs and such, but I will have him feeling better," Raven said.

Soon enough, after James had covered all the windows to keep sunlight from washing in, Raven was mixing herbs in a boiling pot. James and Nathaniel watched curiously as the spicy and bitter mingling of smells took over the house. A aura of joy had enfolded her. She had on a new set of clothing James had found for her. They fit large on her, but a bit of sewing fixed it fine. She was consumed by her work, and for her age, knowing advanced theories of medical treatments was no small matter.

"Are you sure you know what you're doing?" Nathaniel asked. Raven was certain he was more than a little worried to have a minion of the Devil performing any aid on him.

Raven came over to inspect his wound, at which point he tensed.

"Calm down, if I wanted to kill you, I would have let those vampires do it. Now let me see." She held his hand while gently removing the wrappings around the lesion. The bites were deep and had pierced the skin to the bone. The sudden smell and warm touch of skin raised an inner hunger. Raven coiled away which made Nathaniel flinch.

"What's the matter?" James asked.

"Nothing, I need you to open the wound. We have to drain the blood, at least ten ounces."

"Why, what for?" Nathanial covered his arm to protect it from her.

"To clear some of the infection and I need garlic, four heads. It has to be rubbed on the wound and mixed with the herbs so you can drink in doses."

James carried out the instructions as directed and found four heads of garlic for Raven. She grabbed for them, their odor and touch sent a burning sensation familiar to the Wolfsbane. She dropped them immediately.

"It burned me."

"I didn't think it would have affected you, but I suppose it is the same as Wolfsbane. They are used for keeping evil away." James walked over and gathered the garlic.

"But ... I am not evil."

"Perhaps not, but the curse that runs through you is."

She frowned. "Well, then, you will have to cut and ground the garlic. Rub it on the wound."

R

Two days after Raven had completed the whole procedure of treating the wolf bite, Nathaniel was beginning to feel better.

"Medical theories, eh? I'm impressed."

"My father said I was gifted, that I learned things easily." Raven frowned, remembering her father's words. "He taught me most of the skills I know. He studied medicine for years. He did many things. He was good at games too. I loved playing with him, our favorite was chess."

"Chess? You know the game?" James perked at the mention.

"It is not merely idle amusement, according to Benjamin Franklin." Raven's words were interrupted by a bored sigh from Nathaniel.

"I'm going to feed the horses. If anyone needs me, I'll be outside." He stood and made for the door when James stopped him.

"Back door, please."

"Oh yes, we don't want the demon child to burst into flames." Raven gave Nathaniel a narrow-eyed stare.

"Let us see how good you are." James stood and beckoned Raven to follow him to his study. There on his desk sat a board with chess pieces.

"You play?" Raven asked, excitedly.

"I do, but worthy opponents are hard to find in the frontier. Are you up for a challenge?"

"I have never lost a game." Raven sat down and moved a pawn.

James smiled and sat down, accepting her dare.

It was a pleasant morning. James had acknowledged Raven and there they were, playing a game of chess. It had been some time since she'd felt so content.

R

Nathaniel perched himself on the top beam of the porch railing. He shook his head looking out at the undergrowth and arbor that shrouded the house. There was a whisper of a track that led out through the thicket. He looked at his injured hand, appraising the bandages. Raven was an exceptional healer. He lingered back to the night he had almost severed her head.

His feelings ground like rocks in his head. *Damn vampire.*

That's what it was, her vampire charms trying to get to me.

By all that's good and Holy, her dark amicable eyes were hard to ignore when she spoke to him. She had the kind of sweet face that invited friendly conversation, the kind that made her approachable. It was small and pretty with half of it draped by glossy black hair that flowed to the middle of her back. He had taken notice of this because he had caught himself unknowingly admiring her callipygous figure on a few occasions. This he attributed to vampire witchery. *Of course, it was some demonic charm that made me look.*

Raven had turned thirteen on the night she was cursed. Her height and appearance, willowy and well built, had given him the impression she was closer to the age of fifteen.

What in God's name am I doing? This is all irrational. He spun around on the beam and jumped down. Trekking over behind the house, he loaded his crossbow so he could practice his aim on a wooden dummy. Her image remained lingering in his head.

CHAPTER 6

James let out an exasperated sigh and laid down his King. For the last two weeks of Raven's training, it had become routine to come home and play the game of chess, which James was determined to win.

Raven made him feel like an oaf, however hard he tried. Raven, in fact, was good at adapting, and had accepted the situation that had befallen her. She was able to control her emotional responses. She was thinking rationally in training and had improved on the techniques James had taught her. She'd tracked him down every night.

Nathaniel had stayed with the two of them until Raven was sure his wounds wouldn't become infected. He'd participated in the training, mainly as a practice dummy for James while he taught Raven how to fight and defend herself using hunter weapons.

James and Raven were deep in concentration after starting a new match of chess, each one intently envisioning their moves. Nathaniel watched them from where he sat in a corner of the study. He had become more like an annoying older brother to her. He had almost affectionately nicknamed her the demon child.

"Face it, demon child is using her powers to win," Nathaniel said, a sure sign he was bored.

"Stop calling me that," Raven bared her fangs, all in fun. When Nathaniel's hand had shown considerable healing, he had grown to trust her.

Five games later, James let out a grunt as Raven trapped his King once more for a checkmate. "Damn it all to Hell."

Raven beamed. "Another?"

"No, you should be off to bed. Wyman will be here tonight and wanting us ready." He stood and grabbed the keys that would lock Raven in her cell.

Nathaniel was snoring already, sure to have a neck crick when he awoke, from the way his head was draped over the back of the chair.

Raven stopped at the door before going down the steps.

"Why do you lock me in? I have never tried to do harm to you. I always listen, but you do not trust me?" She asked.

"It is not a question of trust."

"You believe I will lose."

James looked at her curiously, not understanding.

"You believe the curse will win and I will no longer be myself."

"It's my hope that it doesn't, but it's my fear that it will."

"I will never let it. I will not become the monster that killed my family." Anger flared her eyes, anger that James understood all too well. The hunters had not been able to capture Jonas the night he attacked Raven's family. "Wherever he is, I am going to find him, and kill him." She stared at James. "The demon took everything from me. I am alone. I will not become a monster."

Such was the determination in her eyes that James' faith in the girl raised. He wanted to believe in that conviction. He had failed to keep detached. His bond with Raven was growing, and that worried him. He was becoming lenient with her each day, and felt that one day, he would come to regret it.

R

That night, in a small Pennsylvania town, a thick fog rolled in, bringing with it an unnatural quiet. A little girl woke up and watched the white mist roll against the small window of her room, like some living thing feeling the edges for a way in. It oozed over the ground, rolling against the other houses that huddled close to each other.

A piercing scream woke her mother in the next room who rushed to the little girl to find her curled and crying against the back of the bed, shrinking back from the window.

"What's the matter? You're safe, I'm here." The mother cradled her.

"There was a man by the window." The little girl pointed toward the window, but only the white mist crept against it.

"It was a nightmare, that's all." After a few minutes of the mother soothing the little one, she was back to sleep. She draped a warm blanket over her daughter and walked into the main room. A loud knock at the door made her jump. She grabbed her husband's pistol she kept in a drawer.

"Who is it?" She asked.

"Captain Benton of His Majesty's army. My men and I need quarter for the night."

A cold finger of worry played at the bottom of her heart. She opened the door. Eight redcoats stood with the white mists coiling around them. "It is only a modest home; I do not have much room."

"It will do, may we come in?" Benton asked.

The mother looked back toward her daughter's room.

"Are you denying His Majesty's men quarter?" Benton pressed.

"No, come in." She stepped aside and let them pass.

Her mother's scream woke her. The little girl sprang to a sitting position, wide-eyed. She jumped down and crawled under the bed. The door creaked open, but she didn't see anyone walk in. Her heart felt like it would drum out of her chest, and she tried to calm her breathing. It was quiet for a long while, not a sound in the house.

She crawled her way toward the edge of the bed. The silence pressed the air in on her. Slowly, slowly she neared and saw nothing. She knew that her mother was dead, deep down she knew. Her mother's scream, then its sudden silence, meant she was dead. Still, she clung to hope.

Closer to the edge, a board creaked in protest to her weight. Her heart fluttered in response and she froze, holding her breath. Her tiny hands clenched white. No one entered the room. No movement outside.

The shadows of the room danced, summoning monsters from her nightmares. Her stomach felt glued to the floor. In the heavy silence, there was the ruffling of her bed sheets. A groan escaped her. She stayed paralyzed.

Perhaps whatever was out there hadn't heard her. It didn't know she was hiding under the bed. She would be safe; she would run to her aunt's in the morning and tell her, tell her about the yellow-eyed man. Tell her about mother's scream.

A hollowed face popped down.

A scream shattered the air of silence. Like roaches, the vampires crawled down the walls. They swarmed and clawed and sank their teeth into the little girl, shredding her apart.

More screams followed. The new fledgling vampires led by Captain Benton roamed the small settlement. Mothers hid with their children and the fathers took their muskets to fight, thinking it was an Indian or British attack.

Deep in the woods, Dumitru stood, unmoving, listening to the screams. Andreea walked up beside him.

"Our captain proves to be ferocious," she said.

"As are all fledglings."

Behind her, a dozen more vampires appeared from the darkness of the woods.

"May we go and join them, master?" one of them asked.

"Indeed. Feed to your heart's content," Dumitru said in a deep, crisp voice. The vampires swarmed into the town.

"Our small army is growing, perhaps too quickly," said Andreea. "We will draw attention to ourselves. How long do you plan on doing this?"

"Until every town that houses a hunter's family is destroyed."

"The Order will call more, perhaps from the old lands. As our numbers grow, so does our need to feed."

"There is safety in numbers."

"There is safety in unity. These are fledglings. They won't play well together forever." Andreea finished and Dumitru turned a cold stare to her, a warning she was overstepping her bounds.

"They took something precious from me and I plan to return my pain upon them tenfold," he hissed, bile in every word.

"Will you always love her more than you love me?"

"She was my wife." Dumitru's answer stung Andreea deep. His emotionless response amplified the pain.

"If she had never died, I would have been some night's food for you? Why did you turn me, to satisfy your desires and not mine?" Andreea was cut short when Dumitru clinched his hand around her throat and held her off the ground.

"Yes, I made you for my own pleasures, as surely as I can make another. Do watch that mouth before I decide to find a new mate that knows when to shut up." Dumitru released her and left to join his vampire army.

Andreea fell, sobbing, against a gnarled tree. Though she was angry, she couldn't come to hate him. She hated the wife he once had—the ghost of her that lingered in his mind. It was a foolish idea, competing for his love with a woman that didn't exist anymore.

R

Dumitru arrived in the town. Musket fire sounded around him. Men's entrails and dismembered limbs painted the ground crimson.

"Set the houses on fire, and be careful not to set yourselves aflame," Dumitru commanded. "I want every man and woman dead."

The swarm of vampires went about lighting the houses on fire, and soon the sky was bright with the luminance of the flames. Dumitru scoured the area for survivors. The rapid pace of three hearts grabbed his attention. He followed the sounds into the woods. He smelled the scent of fear nearby, and by the cover of bushes, he found a young girl about ten years of age. She was clutching her younger brother and sister.

She stared at him and clasped her siblings tighter, her face and eyes wide with anticipation of the unknown. All three burst into sobs.

"Master, riders approach," Benton called out at him.

He stared into the eyes of the girl. "Run, far from here. Run." The children jumped to their feet and ran into the forest. Dumitru turned back to the town and joined his small army.

More than two dozen horsemen arrived armed with crossbows and stakes. Vampire hunters. They pulled out crucifixes, brandishing them at the fledglings that retreated from the holy symbol, their arms wailing as if to deflect the image.

The hunters dismounted quickly and slew a group of vampires in short order. Dumitru's army was disoriented; their first time facing soldiers from the Order of the Sons of Light.

Dumitru, unfazed, walked into the fray, his hair blazing in the glow of the fires. A young hunter ran up and shot a stake into his heart. When Dumitru didn't fall, paralyzed, the young hunter took a step back. His eyes grew round. Dumitru appeared behind him driving a fist through his back ripping out the man's heart through flesh and splintered bone.

"He's an elder," a hunter yelled.

Two more hunters rushed at the demon, brandishing crosses. Dumitru waved his hands and set the holy items aflame.

"You shall need to have more faith in *your* God," he said and sent the two hunters flying with a powerful thrust of telekinesis.

Two more stakes punctured into his chest. This time he let out a low groan. They were coated with Wolfsbane and the older hunters were producing vials of holy water. Others held torches and used them to set fire to his fledglings.

"I will not yield here," he said. "Benton, distance yourself and your men," he shouted at the Captain.

Use muskets and cover of smoke. Lure them to you, do not go to them. Dumitru made his voice heard in Benton's mind as he did the other vampires, telepathically giving them orders.

He vanished into the woods with blurred speed. Only the hunters scuttled in the open luminance of the burning town.

"They're running," one shouted, right before a musket ball went through his head, splattering brain matter on a couple of hunters behind him.

"Take cover," the older hunter ordered.

The hunters ran for the nearest refuge, dividing their unit. One by one, a vampire jumped from the shadows to slay them.

"Stay together. Watch your backs," the leader shouted, and screams of dying men issued from every direction. Muskets took down the other hunters who tried to run into the light for safety. Confused shouts and screams echoed in the air.

The cries of men trickled to silence and soon only the leader was left standing. The vampires slithered from the shadows to surround him. The hunter tried to shoot his crossbow only to have Dumitru rush in and knock him down.

"Devils, you cannot escape the judgment of God," he brandished his crucifix driving away the younger vampires. Dumitru cackled.

"You will make a fine addition to my army."

"I'll join no demon army of yours."

"That is not a choice you have. Let us see how your God places judgment when you become one of us." Dumitru lifted the hunter by his throat and dug his canines into soft flesh.

The man tried to fight. He felt his muscles burn and numb. He felt the scorching toxin from Dumitru's fangs course through his blood, paralyzing him. His vision blurred until only darkness remained and he faded into unconsciousness. Only the fiery sting in his heart let him know he was still alive, that he would become one of the demons he vowed to destroy, and his soul would be damned to Hell because of it.

Andreea joined Dumitru and scanned the inferno that had once been a town. "We should leave, before more arrive." This was the largest slaughtering she had witnessed. She was certain Dumitru's actions that night would prove to have terrible consequences.

CHAPTER 7

Raven awoke when James opened the door to her underground room. Behind him, Wyman and a few other hunters lurched at the steps.

"You don't have her shackled?" Wyman quickly observed. The hunters all grabbed for their crossbows and crosses.

"Stay your weapons. She is free to roam as she pleases in here. Raven, it's time," James said.

Raven sauntered up the stairs, and the hunters, four including Wyman, stepped back giving enough room between her and them. She was rather amused by the whole spectacle.

"For being vampire hunters, you seem to be pretty afraid." Raven's comment gained her a couple of scowls.

James simply smirked and led her outside to where Nathaniel waited on his horse.

"You are coming with us?" Raven asked.

"Of course, you think I'm letting a demon child run around loose? I am coming along to help keep an eye on you."

"Splendid," Raven said.

"Get her into the carriage," Wyman ordered, directing her to a small wooden cart. It was large enough for Raven but wouldn't allow much of anything else. Her memories of being stuck in an underground hole flashed in her mind. She turned to James.

"I cannot go in there. It is too small."

"You'll do as we say," Wyman said.

"James, please. I want to go in the other carriage." James looked into Raven's eyes. She had told the story of her ordeal, of being trapped. He understood why she feared to be confined to such a small area, unable to move.

"I have her carriage prepared already. We shall take that one." James pointed to the carriage they had procured from the two vampires they slew.

Wyman's face flushed red. "She will go in ours."

"Her home soil is already placed in the carriage. She'll need rest, unless you don't want her abilities at their fullest." James gave Wyman a stone-cold stare.

Wyman tightened his lips around clenched teeth. "*So be it*." He stomped down the steps and mounted his horse. "Be quick."

Later that night, Raven peeked out of the front drapes of the carriage watching the trail lit by the candle lanterns. James sat holding the reins beside the hangings.

"How far do we travel?" She asked.

"We go south to Virginia. The settlements have been attacked by British troops."

"You believe it is vampires?"

"Yes." James's face became serious. Raven could see his mind lingered on something. *Dumitru most likely.*

"You know we're heading straight into the war," Nathaniel said, riding up to the side of the carriage by James. "The British have been arriving at the coast down in Carolina. The Continental Army has been looking for volunteers."

"A lost cause. The Continental army will fall to Britain's might. The Sons of Light are loyalists," Wyman said.

"Speak for yourself. If I didn't serve the Order, I would be fighting with the Continentals," Nathaniel remarked, to which Wyman turned, his eyes flaring. He was about to speak but was cut off.

"It's not our concern, but the boy does bring up a good point. We may run into the British army," James said.

"We have nothing to fear. Our charge is to do God's work, not intervene in mortal affairs as you so clearly put," Wyman explained.

"Do they know that?"

Wyman held out a rolled paper to James. "We have documents from the Church of England with King George's seal. They grant us the protection we'll need."

"So, what if we run into colonials?" Nathaniel added.

"Unless you joined with them, I wouldn't worry about it." Wyman rode forward when Raven's head poked out of the drapes.

"Make yourself scarcer. It was hard enough to convince Wyman not to place you in shackles the whole journey," James said.

"I have done nothing that would make them fear me." Raven squinted her eyes.

"You drink blood, you have control over animals, you can throw things around with a thought and you're the walking dead," Nathaniel remarked.

Raven crossed her arms. "You would be missing a hand now or close to death if I had not treated you."

"Probably sold half my soul to the Devil for it too."

"Enough. Nathaniel, ride on ahead and help Wyman scout and you..." James turned to Raven. "Get back inside."

"I am inside," she remarked.

James shoved Raven's head back; she frowned and sat back on her bed. A book flew through the drapes and landed beside her. "Read it; it will give you something to do."

Raven picked up the Bible.

The small group made camp in the late hours of the night. Raven's wagon was held at a distance from the site and two guards kept watch over it. Raven busied herself inside reading the Bible, while James and Nathaniel sat by a small campfire with Wyman.

"Your bond with the creature grows too deep. She is not a child," Wyman said, coating stakes with Wolfsbane.

"I know what she is." James looked at the carriage.

"I'm telling you for your own good. Be cautious, or one day she will be the death of you like a rabid dog does its master."

James pondered Wyman's words.

By mid-morning, the group was well on their way. Raven lay in her bed of soil and felt the heat of the sun seeping in. The group traveled into the early hours of the night. Hunger burned in her core. The scent of the men only increased her thirst. Her sense of smell always amplified when the hunger came. Because of this, she picked up on other odors.

Raven poked her head out of the drapes and James turned to look at her. "I smell others. A large group of people—" Before she'd finished, the blasts of musket fire reverberated through the woods. The screams of men and shouts of commands came from further ahead.

"Take cover in the trees!" Wyman ordered.

Raven leaped out of the carriage, her feet padding the ground. James jumped off and made for the cover of woods. The musket fire came closer until Raven could make out colonial troops retreating from the British army. They were mowed down as they ran. As some of the Colonials surrendered, they were shot.

"They're killing them." Raven took a step forward.

"Silence the creature," Wyman told James, which produced a glare from Raven.

"It is the way of war," James whispered to her.

"It's not right."

"That's the might of British rule for you," Nathaniel said.

The fight was short and when the alabaster mist of gunfire cleared, only the dead bodies of colonials littered the ground. The redcoats shot anyone that was alive. None had seen the carriage hidden on the small trail within the woods. The troops moved ahead pursuing the Colonial Army. After a long wait, Wyman gave the signal to come out.

They had to drag a few bodies off the trail so that the wagon could pass.

A low moan issued from a wounded colonial. James walked over and inspected the young man. His skull was cracked and blood oozed out the large open wound. A flap of his scalp clung on with shattered bone.

"Raven, come here," James called and Raven stepped by his side, looking down on the dying man. He groaned again. "End his suffering."

Raven glared at James. "You want me to kill him?"

"Nothing can help him except for a quick death to ease his pain."

Raven studied the man. James was right. She closed her eyes and bent down caressing his forehead. His eyes moved to look at Raven's face. He smiled, perhaps imagining an angel. "I'm sorry." She whispered. *I'm no angel.* She gave him a kiss on the side before giving him a quick death.

The rest of the men watched in silent revulsion. "If you don't like it, don't watch," James said walking past them.

The rest of the journey was hushed until the later hours of the night when they made camp. Raven stood in silence watching the moon.

James came to stand next to her and studied her for a while. The physical changes of the Lilin curse were becoming pronounced. Raven's skin was completely unblemished and her hair had gained a silky luster to it, a beautiful dark angel.

"You're quiet tonight," James said.

"I am human, not some creature to be treated like a dog." She faced him, "I know what it is that happened to me. I understand why you did what you thought was needed. My father once said that no man is truly against another, he is only for himself. I do not know if other vampires have feelings, or could care less for killing. But I am human, and I have to live with the memory of those faces I kill." She stood and turned toward the carriage. "I will help you get your revenge, but I want you to acknowledge my humanity. You have forgotten yours." Raven trekked off.

James felt the sting of guilt as he watched her crawl into the carriage cabin. True, while they had been talking more the past couple of weeks, the relationship between Raven and himself was nothing more than part of his plan. He thought of her as a weapon, a creature to be used.

His fists clamped, his nails digging into his flesh. *But, she wasn't a creature, was she? Who was more human?*

It would take a full week's travel to reach the encampment where they would meet with a larger group of hunters. Nathaniel kept Raven company through the night hours when they camped. She had grown to feel safe around him, comfortable. He was more talkative than James at least. Yet, Raven couldn't read Nathaniel's intentions. He was warm at times, yet never cared to share anything more than casual conversation with her.

Mid-week, they met a small group of hunters who had an Indian with them. There had been a raid and many colonists had been killed including woman and children. The Indian had led the attack. They brought him to Raven bound and blindfolded. It had been longer than three days; she had been restraining the red-hot sting of hunger. The voices and thoughts of ripping into the hunters had grown stronger during the fourth day. She accepted the meal without argument and hated herself for it.

Another day of travel and they arrived at the camp after sunset. The air was tense and tinged with fear. Raven could smell it, feel it around her like a lingering perfume. There had been death here.

This was not a camp; it was a burned down village. The smell of soot and charred wood seeped through the carriage drapes. There was an underlying scent too. That of flesh, burned until barely any remained. It stung in Raven's nostrils with a pungency she did not care for.

There had been a large vampire attack and hunters had been killed, a great many of them. Samuel, the crinkled-faced leader of the second group, explained the situation.

Wyman and James listened while a lone survivor, Henry, explained the battle.

"It was not two; it was a group of vampires. We would have eradicated them if it were not for an elder. He commanded them, used our weaknesses against us. The vampire knew strategy and used the cover of smoke and darkness to divide us." A few whispers broke through the group of hunters.

"A vampire gathering a coven and able to command it?" One asked.

"We can barely keep the plague controlled as it is. How are we to fight an army of undead? We've never had to fight them in groups," said another.

"By slaying their master. Kill the one who leads them and they shall fall like all others," Wyman explained.

"Yes, the one who we've not been able to capture. His power is strong and he eludes us easily," an older hunter countered.

"We have the ability to track him." Wyman pointed toward the carriage where James stood with Raven.

The assembly quieted and glanced over, at first not knowing what it was they looked at, soon enough, they realized they stared at a vampire.

"What is this?" Samuel demanded.

"You bring a demon with you," another shouted.

"Aye, she can track her own kind. We will use her to our advantage. James has trained this creature to hunt on our side," Wyman explained.

"We do not use the Devil's abominations. It's sacrilege," a hunter protested. The rest joined in shouting words of disapproval.

"The Core Order has used vampires they've captured to aid them," James shouted. "They have done so for generations. Why should we not do the same?"

"They do not let them run free as we see this one. They are caged and chained on sacred ground," Samuel said, acid dripping from each word. "That is where this creature ought to be, not running loose. You place us all in danger by bringing her here."

"The Core has sanctioned this," Wyman shouted.

Raven eyed the large group of hunters glaring at her, each armed with crossbows. She didn't want to feel that smoldering sting of Wolfsbane again, especially being struck by multiple points of stakes. The immediate threat of death sent tendrils of fear tugging at her. Her vampiric instincts told her to run, to seek safety but she couldn't. With so many hunters, there was no way to make it without one of those vicious stakes piercing her.

James could see the worry in Raven's eyes when she turned to look at him. "And we allow more innocent lives to die by not using her."

"Don't speak to me of innocent lives. The demons took my wife from me. Take her to The Pits and burn the sin out of her." Samuel glared at Raven with inner hate that intensified her fear.

"And I've lost a son. Make no mistake; I hate the demons as much as you." James pointed toward Raven. Her heart dropped. "I would see each one suffers and screams in the fires of The Pit." He stabbed his finger toward her with fervent heat. "But if I can use their own against them, by God I will. I'll use every opportunity presented to me until they are all sent to Hell, suffering for what they took, suffering in their damned eternity."

Those words cut Raven to the core. She could feel the hatred in each word. Betrayal and anger sliced through her.

He would see all vampires burn in Hell? His words confirmed that she was a tool to him, nothing more. For the present time, she needed to stay alert and her mind focused on the current threat.

"The plague is growing each day and our numbers are strained. If you have a better idea then please present it. Until then, we use one of their own to hunt them. For the longer we wait to find this vampire, the stronger his army grows, and more innocent people are slaughtered. Are you willing to risk the death of innocent people for the fear of ours? One demon, that we can use, we can build a link to track their own, to give us a chance at fighting back and saving lives, and you are willing to lose it." The hunters' shouts became groans and whispers.

After some time of arguing and protests, Wyman and James calmed the men. Raven, not wanting any part of it, walked through the town followed by Nathaniel. Wyman ordered him to keep an eye on her. James had to threaten the hunters to keep them from binding her in shackles. *What did it mean? If he hated her, why would he protect her?*

"You picking up on any trail with those demon powers of yours?" he asked.

"Your job does not involve talking." Raven's tone was sharp, which caught Nathaniel by surprise. He had become accustomed to teasing her, with her doing likewise. But she had been quiet since the hunter's meeting. She hadn't meant to be so cold. He stayed silent. "I am sorry," she stated honestly.

"Was damn tense back there. I'd be wetting my breeches If I were a vampire and had all those hunters itching to stake me."

"Vampires don't wet themselves," Raven said, matter-of-factly.

They stared at one another then burst into laughter.

Raven looked about. "I don't know how I am supposed to do this. How am I to find clues to track vampires if I do not know what to look for?" Her sense of smell increased each week and her sense of hearing was becoming even more acute as well as her touch, neither of which were of any help.

Nathaniel rubbed his chin. "What about the vampires we killed? How'd you track them?"

"By luck. I had caught the scent of the humans, not the vampires." She should have studied them.

"I guess they don't smell like a rotten corpse—at least I don't think they do. You don't reek of dead," He shrugged.

"I do not know how to respond to that." Raven furrowed her brows, sniffing herself.

"Vampires' hearts beat, though they beat less as blood is used up."

Raven looked at him. "How is that of any help?"

"Aren't you supposed to be a genius?"

"My emotions are not helping the matter. I could use more help and less of being teased." She crossed her arms.

He smirked. "How's your hearing?"

"Annoying. I think some nights I can hear the flutter of moths; it does not help when one is trying to sleep in the early hours of the morning."

"And there is your answer." Nathaniel snapped his fingers.

"Moths? I am supposed to use moths to track vampires?"

"Don't be silly. Heartbeats. If you can hear a moth flying around, you can hear a vampire's heartbeat. Isn't that how you found James—and confused me for James when you were hunting? You need to either listen to faint heartbeats or strong, depending on when vampires have fed. Either way, vampires' hearts are discernibly different to humans, or so I'm told." Nathaniel rubbed his chin again, pondering. "You learned to pick out humans from animals, now take it a step further and pick out vampires."

Nathaniel was a genius. Well, maybe not, but he did have his good moments.

Raven stood motionless and closed her eyes, losing herself in the sounds of the woods, feeling the ground and the micro-vibrations of movement and heartbeats. She imagined the beats like waves of light as they traveled the hard surface of the earth.

Her ears picked up on the air rushing through Nathaniel's nostrils and into his lungs. Then the movement and various beating hearts of animals in the woods. Their scents became strong. She focused on a group of animals; they traveled in a pack. Raven figured them to be wolves and imagined them.

It was strange when a clear image of the woods flashed in her mind. Though it could be her own imagination, it was too lucid, too defined. The grain of the underbrush, the sweet smell of crisp air, the soft padding of feet was real.

The view shifted and she could see the pack of black wolves and understood. She was looking through the eyes of one of them. Another power discovered.

When the wolf looked into a thick covering of brush, a jolt of alarm flooded through her as it focused on its prey.

"No!" shouted Raven and bolted into the woods.

Nathaniel was startled, then astounded by the blur of movement. James and Wyman heard Raven's cry and saw her disappear into the woods.

Wyman mounted his horse and chased after.

"The demon is trying to escape!" he yelled.

James and the large group of hunters mounted and followed in quick succession.

CHAPTER 8

Was she plotting something, Dumitru asked himself? Andreea was being far too sweet after his last outburst of anger. She showed no hint that she had been scorned by his actions, and had been loving towards him. In truth, he did feel a stab of guilt for being so brash. He hated hurting her, but he felt a strong conviction to avenge his wife's death. Though it had been well over two hundred years since her slaughter at the hands of hunters, being a vampire, emotions held strong a long time.

The pair had found a large plantation home to hide their coven. At the moment, the fledglings were hunting for the night, which left Dumitru and Andreea much needed private time.

"What are you scheming in that head of yours?" Dumitru fell over a cushioned sofa and Andreea mounted on top of him.

"Scheming? That is your expertise. Not mine," she said outlining his chest with her fingers. Each one felt like a brand against his skin. She possessed such power over him when she was ready to share her passion. A look of innocence and curiosity lingered in her eyes and his desire was raised. They had finished feeding and their blood raced to warm and intensify each sensual touch from her lips. She repeated the process each time, withdrawing long enough to drive him mad. Andreea let out a squeak of surprise when he pulled her tight into his grasp. He gave her a fierce kiss proclaiming his hunger.

R

Later that night, Dumitru slept with his arms wrapped around Andreea, cradling her to his body. If only times could always be as serene as this. Through the years, she would try to get Dumitru to forget his old life and love. She would make him want her passion; make him miss her touch the nights they were separated. However, for all the time together, he had never professed his love. It tugged at her core, for she didn't know if it was only passion that held him to her. She loved him dearly. *Did he feel the same toward her?* Though her body no longer needed air, she took in a long breath and sighed heavily, slid out of the bed and dressed.

She found herself in the great room of the house where sat a curly red headed girl by the name of Elspet. She was a slender thing with catlike eyes and a sweet face that would make any man bend to her will. Andreea sat down on one of the seats lost in deep thought.

"Ye look the perfect paintin' of pitiful. What has ye in such sour mood?" Elspet asked.

"Dumitru." Andreea frowned, and slumped deeper into the seat.

"Oh aye, A mon can do that verra weel. Such a troublesome sort they are."

"I don't understand him. His actions would show that indeed he cares for me, but he clings to his old life. I feel the fool being jealous of a dead woman."

"Mon are strange. He does care for ye, cannae doubt that."

"But I do. He has never mentioned a word that would let me know his feelings of me, or if his passion was truly the seed of love. You would think that seed would have blossomed by now."

"Tis there and he kens it, though he willnae admit it to himself. The mon is afraid."

"Afraid? Dumitru and 'Afraid'; never thought I would hear those two words used in the same sentence." Andreea raised an eyebrow.

"Oh aye, he is afraid, dinnae doubt that. The mon has ken the loss of a loved one and has shielded his heart for fear of feelin' that pain again."

"He doesn't show a hint of jealousy, I toyed with our newest fledgling and he simply cared not. I throw myself at other men and he cares not?" Andreea pouted and crossed her arms over her chest making the most pitiful look. It drew a giggle from Elspet.

"Wee lass, ye are inflamed. Dinnae fret. In his mind, if showing such anger, it would be signs of weakness, and truth of the lad's love for ye. Nay, he will deny it to himself and tis ye part to break those barriers. Dumitru lost his love near close the time he was turned to the undead life. The mon holds the memories deep. Dinnae forget, it takes a verra long time for us to disregard such things and feelings hold strong for our kind."

"I hope I can break those barriers down before we are faced with the whole army of vampire hunters upon us."

Elspet tossed an iron poker at Andreea who caught it with quick reflexes. "What is this for?"

"Some mon need a beating over the head." Elspet tossed another poker at Andreea.

"And what is this one for?"

"The mon has a verra thick head." The women laughed.

Dumitru was awake by the time Benton returned with the rest of the vampire coven. The vampires gathered in the great room.

"I trust all fed well; we have a long journey ahead of us." Dumitru stood looking out one of the windows. Everyone fell silent when he spoke; his voice coupled with his tall frame was intimidating. Most of the fledglings had traveled with him long enough to know to never anger the Master. Dumitru used fear to rule his small group and delivered a slow, agonizing death to those that fell short of his expectations.

"Yes, we shall be ready for our excursion tomorrow night," Benton answered.

"Our ranks need to grow. I'll expect everyone to have a mate by the week's end. There will be consequences for those who fail to strengthen our coven."

"Yes, Master." Benton turned and ushered the rest of the fledglings out. Andreea walked over to stand by Dumitru, wrapping her arms around his waist.

"What is ye plan, tis quite a bit of preparing for the journey?" Elspet asked.

"The Assembly of Saints."

Elspet widened her eyes. "Ye gone mad, ye isnae thinking weel."

Dumitru turned a sharp glare at her.

"Dinnae be given me ye wee little looks. I isnae intimidated like the rest of ye mindless zombies."

"What are you two babbling about? What is the Assembly of Saints?" Andreea interrupted.

"Aye lass, ye mon has gone mad. Tis the main church of the Sons of Light this side of the world, only their headquarters in New York is more fortified. Ye love plans on marching us to their gates."

Looking at Dumitru's determined gaze, Andreea's face changed from confused to worried. Elspet stood and walked over to stop only a few feet from the large vampire.

She was a tiny thing next to Dumitru; one could mistake her for a child, though she was in her eighteenth year when she was turned.

"Have ye lost all ye senses? I'll use much strength to take them." Elspet stood firm against Dumitru's hard stare, she was the only one who dared. Considering they were of the same generation, though no vampire had ever seen what powers she possessed, Dumitru would not cross certain boundaries with her as he did all others.

"Don't think me a fool. I know well what we face there." He broke the uncomfortable silence.

"Do ye now? Dinnae think I ken ye brilliant mind. Ye have ways with strategy, but tis a dangerous road ye take. Ye cannae think ye will defeat that place without repercussions, then what will ye do when the ire of the whole army of hunters is stirred?"

"That is precisely what I intend to do."

"Then ye have lost ye mind!" Elspet snapped.

Andreea had never seen her so animated and infuriated before. This was serious.

Dumitru simply grinned, amused by her reaction.

"Do you think I haven't planned this for some time? Why do you think I beckoned you here? You possess some of the more potent gifts of the curse. Especially a certain one that will help in defeating any large army that would come against us. And with our addition of the new Captain, we have another strategist in the way of field battle." Dumitru looked over to Benton who stood quietly listening to the conversation.

"Aye, ye do that, but ye need a larger army."

"You need not worry on that." Dumitru walked away leaving the three vampires by themselves. Andreea and Benton stared at an obviously irritated Elspet.

"Ye mon has lost his mind." She said to Andreea, and stomped off.

R

Raven rushed through the woods, the sound of sprinting horses behind her. She concentrated on the one wolf, commanding it to hold back from attacking. Near the vision she had seen through the wolves' eyes, she leaped as the creatures rushed in after their prey.

Raven slammed into one of the beasts and knocked it down with a yelp. With deep growls, the rest of the pack turned their attention to her. Raven let out a hiss. The group of hunters raced in, momentarily surprised by the wolves.

In a knot of gnarled underbrush, three children clenched to each other. Raven stood firm in front of them ready to fend off the large black animals. The wolves ran off upon seeing the large assembly of hunters arrive.

Wyman and James quickly dismounted and headed straight for Raven, who in turn headed for the three children.

"What the hell were you thinking?" James shouted.

"Keeping them from becoming dinner." Raven pointed into the area of brush where the youngsters hid. The rest of the hunters encircled Raven, crossbows pointed.

"Hold your weapons." James walked over and looked at the oldest girl who held a younger boy and girl in a tight hug. He shook his head at Raven and looked back at the frightened children she had saved. "It's alright, you're safe now."

Wyman marched in for a closer look. "Are they bit? Are they vampire?"

James gave him a sharp glare while he helped the children out the brush. Wyman tugged them over roughly checking them for bites, making the little girl wince.

"You could be gentler," Raven scowled.

"And if she is bit, she will be dead same as any demon," Wyman replied.

The little girl's eyes grew wide.

"Be less barbaric, they are children," James agreed.

"And can kill the same as an adult vampire. I have not the pose to be relaxed with the responsibility of lives," Wyman said.

James snickered. "Really? Was that same reasoning you had when you let a village get slaughtered?"

Wyman burned his glare on James then turned to Raven. "If you force us to chase you again, I'll have your feet hacked off."

"If I had not been quick, they would have been a meal for wolves," Raven said.

Wyman mounted his horse, ignoring her.

R

The three children had survived in the woods for days. It was some miracle considering a pack of wolves roamed the territory. Lydia was the name of the eldest girl, which Raven tended to. A few cuts and insect bites, but nothing serious. Peter, the youngest at five years and Tabitha, seven years of age, were sitting quietly by the campfire the hunters had provided.

"You are one of them," Lydia said, as she sat on a large log. A few guards stood by keeping a close watch on Raven.

Raven wrinkled her brows and looked at her. "Them?"

"You have teeth and hissed as they did. They killed father and mother." Lydia frowned and stared down; she was on the rim of crying.

"They killed my father and mother too." Raven sat next to her and wrapped an arm around her. "No, I am not like them. I was bit by one and it made me sick, but I am here to find them and stop them from hurting people."

"I want Mama." Little Tabitha cried which set Peter to sobbing. Lydia went to them and clutched them both. "Mama and Papa are not with us anymore."

Raven kneeled by them and pointed to the stars. "You see all those stars." The two children looked up at the many twinkling lights. "They are pretty, are they not?"

The two nodded.

"It is God's Kingdom up there. Heaven. And it is where the people we love go when they die, so they can look down on us and protect us." Raven smiled at the little girl who hugged her sister close.

"They live with God now?" Tabitha asked.

"Yes, they will always be with us, waiting until the time comes for us to join them, with God."

Nathaniel and James leaned against the carriage and watched. "That is something I won't be getting used to anytime soon," Nathaniel said.

"What?" James asked.

"A demon speaking of God."

Raven looked to have heard him and gave him a sharp glare.

Nathaniel returned a smirk. "So, what are we going to do with the children?"

"We'll take them to the Assembly of Saints. They will find them a home."

"Somewhat off our trail."

"Wyman intends to gather more men. If Dumitru commands a coven of vampires with such tactics to defeat two dozen of our men, we'll need to make certain we're prepared."

"Vampires that believe in God and now gather armies too. The new ways of the world." Nathaniel shook his head.

"A new age. We move into the modern world and the demons have adapted to our ways. They've met us with strategy and found our weaknesses." James studied Raven soothing the children.

"Having doubts?" Nathaniel followed his gaze.

"Always," James walked off.

Nathaniel stared at Raven a while longer and sighed. The glow of the fire fell soft on her face. She could pass as a normal human girl sitting with the three children.

R

Raven finished putting the children to bed and studied them for some time. A guard kept staring at her, a look of worry etched on his crinkly face. She retired to the carriage. He was probably thinking she was brooding to feast on their blood.

She opened the thick Bible splayed on her bed of soil and immersed herself in reading it. Her memories of her father sneaked in, reminding her of happier times when he would tell stories from the book. It helped her to sleep and eased her fears, so that peaceful dreams would fill her night. How funny it was to fear monsters in her nightmares and now she was one. A hard lump clung in her throat.

Images of feasting on the children would eventually invade her mind. It had been a day since last she fed and the dry heat of hunger clawed at her from deep within. Images of ripping and tearing into people haunted her.

Unable to settle her mind, Raven stepped out for a walk. Two guards eyed her and made sure to keep their crossbows loaded while they followed her around the camp. James convinced Wyman to let her walk free despite angry protesting from the group. Though he'd fought for her, she could not shake his words.

He would watch every vampire burn in The Pit? The words burned into her memory. She could not help but wonder, if there were no more vampires in the world, would he kill her the same as he would any other vampire?

R

Nathaniel was sitting by the fire.

"Nathaniel." A low voice tinged with sadness pulled Nathaniel from his musings. He turned to see Raven standing behind him, along with two guards a few feet further.

"Demon child." Obviously, her sense of humor had not returned when she grimaced at her nickname.

"May I sit with you?"

"You can do as you please, just don't set yourself aflame so close to the fire."

"I am not a bumbling idiot," Raven scowled as she sat right next to him. He didn't expect her to sit so near.

Nathaniel glanced at her and knew she felt his discomfort from the look of her eyes. He noticed the hint of a frown.

Raven scooted away giving him space. "You do not trust me, do you?" She bowed her head and stared at the dying campfire. Trying to cheer up a vampire. He was not used to this.

Nathaniel tried to find the right words to say and joined her in looking into the crackling flames. "You know, when I was younger, I was deathly afraid of dogs."

Raven wrinkled her brows. The story was probably a bad idea.

"I did not trust them. I had been bitten, twice. Because of that, I thought all dogs were evil creatures. When I was fourteen, my uncle had a dog that always tried to catch my attention. Of course, I was scared of the thing and always avoided it." He smiled, recalling the memories. "That year I would've died had it not been for that dog. A pack of wolves caught me out in the woods alone. I'd been lost and it had followed me. He fended off the wolves until my uncle and his friend found me. They had heard the growls and barks. From that point on I become attached to the dog and trusted it."

"Lovely story," Raven drawled.

"Well, the point was that it was hard for me to trust dogs because of what I had come to learn and believe of them. With the experiences of them biting me, I thought all of them were the same, and it wasn't the case."

Raven gave him a discerning look. "So, you are comparing me to a dog?"

"What I was trying to say is that I've been taught to fear and kill your kind. You can't expect me to change those teachings and feelings in a short time. It's not that I don't want to, it's that I have to convince my mind."

"I suppose it is my life now."

"Quit being so gloom and doom." He gave her a friendly nudge on the shoulder and smiled.

She broke a smile and nudged him back scrunching her knees to her chest and wrapping her arms around them. "What is The Pit that James mentioned?" Raven asked.

He stared back at the flames. "Not sure you want to know."

"Oh please, do not act as if you are worried about my feelings now."

"Pff, I just don't want to be blamed for scaring you off."

Raven rolled her eyes and waved her hand at him.

"It's a hidden fort deep in the woods away from any settlements. The Order takes vampire prisoners there to punish the sin from them. They'll make them give names of other vampires and where they may hide." Nathaniel stopped and his face tensed. "I only went there once; my mentor took me. I hunt the vampires, but I couldn't shake the images I had seen that night."

Nathaniel contemplated if he indeed wanted to go on, Raven's eyes took on a shade of worry, but she had asked.

"Vampires were bond to all manner of torturing devices. Red-hot steel pierced through hands and feet and eyes. Their screams haunted my dreams for some time after." He shivered and went silent for a second. "It is my duty to kill the things, but what they do there, I couldn't wish upon anyone or anything. It's Hell on earth."

"You were right; I should have not asked." Raven stood up.

"I did warn you," Nathaniel said.

CHAPTER 9

The sunlight washed over Dumitru, warming his porcelain skin. He closed his eyes and his mind traveled to faint recollections, a ghost of a past that was happier. His wife's face, it was becoming clouded. He could no longer see the perceptive fires of her eyes, the smile that filled him with joy. *What did her voice sound like?* She had such warmth when she spoke, but he only heard the screams. The fierce whipping of flames with the stench of burnt flesh that suffocated his memories with hate. There was no compassion in the eyes of his wife's murderers.

Sensing a presence, Dumitru pushed the images back and opened his eyes. Elspet stood by him staring at the feathery clouds floating lazily to cover the sun. The trees danced to life when a soft breeze rolled across the plantation. The ground was carpeted by lush grass and patches of flowers soaking in the sunlight that poured down. Though their skin felt its warm embrace more so than humans, through the years the two elder vampire's tolerance for it had increased.

"It seems nothing but a dream now. I cannot remember the shape of her face, the warmth of her touch." Dumitru's voice was heavy with the years of sorrow.

"Ye memories dissolve and so do ye feelings as the sands of time run away."

"Time is nothing to us."

"Nay, time is ever our thieving enemy as it is for humans. It can charm us to its depth of regret for things never done and things that should have been. Ye mind is lost when time enslaves it in the past as it has done with ye."

"You take Andreea's side. You believe I shouldn't attack the church." It was more of an assertion than a question.

"The lass loves ye, fool that ye are. I dinnae take a side, I do wish to rid ourselves of this plague, these hunters that drive us to extinction. But to incur war when we have not the numbers for it, make ye a fool."

Dumitru jerked his head stabbing a glare at Elspet.

"Ye ask me questions, dinnae expect me to lie, I tell ye the truth. I will follow ye, I simply warn ye to play the game weel. Ye seek to avenge a lost love, yet yer blind to the love that fights to earn yer heart now."

"Andreea knows the boundaries of our relationship." Dumitru clenched his fist and stared into the sky. "I cannot stop my journey. What are we to do, run for the rest of our eternal lives? Hide in the shadows for fear of death? God curses us then forsakes us as he did Tepes."

"Ye plan to be a Lilin hero?"

"I plan for us to spread our plague, to curse God's creation as he cursed us. I plan to make humanity live in fear."

"Oh aye, Tepes did that verra weel already."

"Then, I shall carry on his legacy. We move on to The Assembly of Saints tonight."

"The place has an army of hunters. Even should the fledglings have found mates by the end of the journey, we stand at thirty." Elspet looked at Dumitru; she was trying to read him. He simply smiled.

"Don't worry your little head. You have yet to see Andreea's full power. When I turned her, she gained another of Dracula's gifts, one that will turn the tide of the battle in our favor." Dumitru walked over, cupped Elspet's chin in his hand, gave her a kiss on the cheek then entered the plantation home.

In the silent home, the polished oak floors gleamed with the reflections of sunlight breaking through the windows. It was a brighter world compared to the first decades of his undead life, the time when his master, Dracula, had kept him in that dark place, the castle that had a life of its own. Dracula, the one who had cursed him, also cursed his wife. They had been freed from that dungeon, free to roam the world and feed on the humans that had become like cattle. They couldn't remember their lives when they were human, when they only knew of the word of God and actually had faith. They only knew they had to survive, to feed and live by the cloak of night. They were demons, the monsters of nightmares.

It was a dim time. Dracula had made his own personal war against God, and the Devil had granted him all the powers of Hell. Waves of hunters came to slay him, only to be slayed themselves and joined into Dracula's army of mindless undead. He had heard it through whispers, as peasants talked in hushed voices, telling stories of vampires and the dead rising from their graves. It was during this great vampire scare that his wife was caught alone one night when they'd separated to hunt. Her shrieks ripped through the quiet village. When Dumitru found her, it was too late. Her murderers had set her aflame. With great rage, Dumitru carpeted the village with the entrails and blood of her slayers and vowed vengeance upon any of those remaining in The Order of the Sons of Light.

But what was it that lingered in his core? What was it that weighted down his mind? Andreea's face flashed through his mind, her lustrous eyes peering into his inner being. The form of her body shaped in the essence of all loveliness. He had to push toward his plans, he could not falter, would not. Andreea knew he could never truly love her... he knew he could never love her.

R

Samuel shifted in restless sleep, his face wet with sweat as if he were lumbering some heavy stone. He dreamt of that horrible creature that walked freely among them. That dark-haired demon. He stood over her as she slept. Her features, though beautiful, were those of a corpse. He could see the decaying grimace of her teeth, the sunken pits of her eyes. He woke, his clothes gummed by sweat to his skin.

That day, visions of the black-haired girl lingered in his mind. He focused on the carriage while they rode, imagining burning it. They were bewitched by her charms. Wyman and James both dared to let that creature walk free. Dared to let her near children. They were bewitched. *She will kill us all.* But she'd rescued those children. That loathsome demon had rescued the children from wolves. Yes, he needed to kill her.

The group stopped to rest and rotate the carriage horses. The sun was high, washing white the blue sky.

Nathaniel kept watch over the three children who ran around exploring and playing, while James and Wyman waved and pointed in different directions arguing over the course to The Assembly of Saints.

Samuel maneuvered himself by the carriage, making sure that no others were nearby or watching him. It had only a single latch to lock the door. He could easily open it and let the light of the sun flood that dark coffin. Let the radiance turn the creature that slumbered inside into ash.

A sudden gust of wind howled through the trees and swept through the little patch of open land. Each man held to their tricornes before the wind could wrench them away.

Samuel cursed to himself when James and Wyman walked over to the carriage with two men leading horses. After exchanging the horses with the new ones, they were back on the move.

A storm gathered in the distance. Every few seconds, lightning painted the bulbous dark clouds with a tint of blue. The sun was devoured by the storm, and night followed soon after. Surely it was the demon summoning the storm. This infuriated Samuel. This hideous witch was taunting them, showing her powers.

R

Raven woke to the rumbling of thunder. She peered out through the drapes of her cabin. The trees rustled and leaves whipped from the blast of wind. She crawled out to join James at the seat of the carriage. Lightning streaked across the sky as if trying to rip it apart. Horses reared and hunters tried to calm them. A sudden realization hit Raven and she turned to look at the riders.

"Where are Lydia and her siblings?" she asked.

"Nathaniel has them." James gestured to his side and Raven climbed on to the roof of the cabin. She felt the fresh kiss of a drop of rain.

"We must get them inside the cabin, it will rain soon."

James shook his head.

"They will get sick out here."

"The men are already concerned with your presence around the children..."

"I will stay out here until the storm passes."

Raven made it clear to James that she would not yield. Drops of cold rain already formed beads on his face. He agreed with an annoyed nod.

Raven helped the children climb into the cabin. Samuel nudged his horse over.

"What is she doing?"

"It will rain soon, the children need shelter," James said.

"With a demon?" Samuel glared at Raven.

"The demon is staying out here," Wyman interjected. "No harm will come to them except that of the rain if we leave them out here."

"The thing has bewitched you both. She has called the storm."

"You forget yourself, Samuel," Wyman said, with a stern glare. Samuel sneered and nudged his horse back to the line of riders.

Wyman turned to James. "If those children are harmed..."

"Yes, you will come looking for me," James finished. Wyman pressed his lips together and rode forward.

"I can imagine the wonderful welcome we'll receive at the church when they discover we have Raven with us," Nathaniel said.

"Perhaps it would be best that I wait outside the walls," Raven offered.

Nathaniel locked his eyes on her. "I can stay and keep a watch on her, in case she tries anything."

"I am not going to do anything except wait, not that you would be able to stop me if I did try anything." Raven rolled her eyes.

"Who is the one that had you crying on the ground? Oh yes, that was me." Nathaniel held his index finger up.

"Only because I let you have a shot."

"Enough, you sound like a bickering old couple," James scowled.

"Pfft, who would wish to be with an oaf," she protested.

"And who would want to be with a demon child."

"I said enough!" James slapped the side of the carriage to quiet them.

Raven made a face and stuck her tongue out behind James. Nathaniel couldn't help but laugh, which also made Raven giggle. James shook his head with a sigh.

The rain lasted into the late hours of the night. The hunters looked like they had taken a swim fully clothed by the time the storm passed. A deathly silence followed after, and not even the wind dared to stir. The men's gaze darted to every shadow that lingered in the deepest parts of the woods.

"It is the demon's doing I tell you," Samuel said.

Raven sneered at him.

"It is simply the silence after the storm," said James.

"I thought the silence came before the storm." Nathaniel rubbed his chin.

"Quiet," Wyman ordered, holding up his hand for everyone to stop. "Do you hear that?"

The group came to a full halt and only the ringing of silence in their ears remained.

"What is it?" Nathaniel whispered.

"A scream." Wyman crinkled his eyes concentrating.

"Raven, can you hear anything?" James peered at her.

Raven listened intently, thinking Wyman was simply unnerved by the eerie atmosphere. But there was the drumming of many hearts. "Wolves. Numerous."

"Are they going to try and eat us?" Lydia asked, peeking through the cabin drapes with her siblings.

"No, they won't attack when we have such a large number," James assured them with a smile.

A chorus of howling broke the silence. It sounded like a hundred screeches of demons singing to the night. It pressed in from all directions, reverberating from the black cover of the woods. The hunters pulled pistols and aimed at the shadows.

"It sounds like an army of them," Wyman said.

"They are not alone." Raven turned to look behind them. "There is something else in the woods behind us."

"Well, what is it?" Wyman's voice went up a notch; strain lined his face.

"It sounds like people, but I hear no heartbeats."

"Vampires." Nathaniel pulled out his Machaira.

The hunters switched to their crossbows and aimed them to the back of the line.

"No." Raven's face contorted into repulsion as she caught the waft of something rotten.

Silence once more descended upon them like a thick blanket suffocating the howls.

The horses snorted their discomfort. Something was gathering behind them, some evil energy in that black pit of the forest.

Raven closed her eyes searching and soon she was looking through eyes of a wolf. Through its ears, she could hear the strange slither of feet over the earth. She commanded the wolf to turn toward the sound and when it did Raven lost the link with it. The sheer shock would have sent chills down her spine if her body allowed it. She had let out a gasp and everyone saw the sudden change in her face.

"What is it, Raven?" James studied her with concern. She looked at him, then at Lydia staring back with large fear-filled eyes.

"We have to go. Now!" Raven's tone set everyone on edge.

Wyman readied his crossbow. "What the hell is it?"

The reek of dead coiled around them, stealing their breaths. A few hunters spewed out their lunch.

The scraping of feet against ground turned all eyes down the small trail. A human figure came out the darkness of the forest. The hunters gripped their crossbows.

"Your name, sir," one of them ordered.

Silence.

The figure neared with its sluggish movement and stopped. A low moan issued from its mouth. It sniffed the air.

The hunters stared at each other, confused.

The thing burst full speed to the nearest hunter who shot a stake into its chest. It only forced the figure to turn with the impact but didn't slow it.

It leapt onto the hunter and everyone could see its rotten flesh. The stench of decay filled their nostrils. The young hunter screamed when the undead creature bit down and ripped into his throat snapping a chunk of skin off.

Crossbows let loose arrows and pistols fired. The creature fell on its side, then sat, and then stood with a moan.

"What in God's name?" Wyman croaked.

"This is no work of God," James remarked.

"We have to go, there are hundreds more coming," Raven pleaded. Lydia began to cry.

A hunter screamed when another of the undead creatures leapt from the woods and tackled him. More emerged. Eyes sunken and flesh shriveled over exposed bone. The men flung holy water and shot stakes into them, but nothing held back the creatures.

"Ghouls!" Wyman shouted. "Run. We cannot win here."

James whipped the horses sending them into a hard gallop. Lydia fell back into the cabin. The ghouls swarmed out of the woods like a pack of rabid beasts. They clawed into the horses bringing them down along with their riders. Raven rushed to their aid.

One of the hunters screamed trying frantically to push away the creature pressing him down. It snapped its mouth trying to rip into his throat with exposed teeth. The dead thing was hurled away and Raven stood over the hunter.

"Th... Thank you."

The hunter scurried to his feet and another of his comrades helped him on to his horse. More hunters remained down the road, the ghouls pulling out the screaming men's entrails. Raven rushed to the aid of the ones she could save, wrenching off and hurling the things away. She used her powers to send many of them flying, but she was overwhelmed. For each one that she peeled off a fallen hunter, three more took its place.

"Raven, we have to go," Nathaniel shouted.

Raven looked at him then focused on a cry from a hunter whose horse was dragged down.

"Help me, help me."

Raven rushed to his aid; she pulled one of the creatures off. Two more leaped on her, their strength was remarkable. They bit into her, ripping and pulling off her skin with their sharp teeth. She screamed, baring her teeth and biting back in return. A reek and rancid taste oozed over her tongue.

She flung them and tore one of the creature's heads off. She turned back to the hunter; three of the things pulled him into the woods. He screamed and clawed at the ground with frantic determination. "Help me. Don't leave me, please."

Raven willed herself, summoning her strength and poured every ounce into a fierce blast of her unseen power. The ghouls were sent hurling into the air, but more came. She rushed at the hunter and lifted him. She threw the man into the air to Nathaniel. He fell feet first into a roll by Nathaniel's horse. A pack of ghouls swarmed on top of Raven.

R

"Raven!" Nathaniel shouted.

He went to help her but was held back by the hunter. "You can't, there are hundreds. We must leave."

"No!" He moved to Raven, again held back.

"Please," The hunter begged. "We have no time."

Nathaniel bit his teeth. "Raven."

The hunter climbed on top of the horse. "Go."

A dozen of the ghouls circled them, one tried clutching his arm and he had to kick it away. They clawed at the horse's legs trying to bring it down, ripping skin.

Nathaniel kicked the horse into a full gallop.

Raven's screams faded as they gained distance.

CHAPTER 10

James whipped the horses and they snorted in protest, their hooves beating against the ground. The carriage bounced and creaked with defiance forcing Lydia and her younger siblings to hold tight to whatever they could.

The greenish, yellow eyes of wolves gleamed in the black underbrush, and soon they were biting at the hooves of the horses. The men took down many with pistols and crossbows. More swarmed out and brought horses and hunters down.

"Do not stop until we are at the walls of the church," shouted Wyman.

The group broke through the woods and arrived at a large open area of land. The moon beamed down its blue light on grassy terrain and the faint light from torches shimmered in the distance.

"The Assembly of Saints!" shouted Samuel.

The wolves stopped their pursuit by the edge of the forest, howling in protest. Half the number of hunters was present when they slowed their horses.

"They're not following," Nathaniel said.

"Where is Raven?" James noticed she was gone.

Samuel scoffed shaking his head. "Joined with the Devil's army."

Nathaniel sneered at him. "She stayed behind to help."

"Aye, if not for her, I would have been dead," said the hunter who'd been saved by her.

"Then, where is the creature?" Wyman asked.

Nathaniel let out a heavy breath and tightened his grip on his reins. "She was overwhelmed. The things swarmed on her; I only heard her cries as we fled." He turned to James who was deadpanned. "I couldn't help her."

"We should be happy it's dead. One less of the demon filth to worry about." Samuel nudged his horse toward the shimmering lights ahead.

Lydia poked her head out, her eyes moist with fear. "Are they gone?"

James nodded. "We're safe."

"Pray for our fallen comrades and let's be on our way. Whatever drives that horde, it's marching them toward the fort." Wyman nudged his horse into a gallop with the others following behind.

James lingered a moment longer scanning the forest. He was lost in the storm of emotions that stung him. The anger of wasted time training Raven, or was it?

"Let's go, we have to get the children to safety." Nathaniel's eyes were resigned, his fists white on the reins.

"Aye." James kicked the horses into a gallop and followed after the group.

Raven screamed.

Razor sharp teeth dug into her skin. Four of the undead beasts held her down pulling her limbs, trying to wrench them from their sockets. Her blood diminished, her wounds healing slower and slower, her skin becoming pale and shriveled.

She summoned the last of her strength and whipped herself free from their hold. She leapt into the trees landing hard against the rough bark. Her legs wobbly, she dashed into the thickest parts of the woods. The ghouls groaned at her heels.

She turned through a thick mass of bushes and slammed into another group of the skeletal things. She stared into the sunken sockets of the ghoul she had crashed into, its shriveled white eyes focused on her.

A clawed hand shoved into her chest. The pain stole her voice; her mouth formed the essence of a scream that never escaped.

She didn't want to die, *God help me*. She closed her eyes and the ground met her. The growls and moans of the beasts spilled over her body. Claws shredded her skin; teeth crunched and gnawed her bones. Darkness.

R

The doors opened, letting Wyman's group through the thick wooden walls of the fort. A few buildings peppered the area, and in the middle stood a two-story structure adorned with decorations and arched windows. The roof was steep and tiled, a large steeple projecting from its centre, brandishing a cross at its point. Men patrolled the fort's walkway with muskets and crossbows held tight, their eyes alert, faces tensed.

A figure covered by a cloak of the darkest crimson quietly waited for them. James helped the children down from the carriage and joined Wyman and Samuel who made their way to greet the silent stranger. Upon seeing Lydia and her siblings, the figure pulled down the cloak revealing a dark-haired young woman. Her deep black eyes roved over the hunters. She nodded and a couple of nuns who waited on top of the stairs came down to greet the children.

"They shall take care of them and show your men to the resting quarters," she said, eyeing the children and the rest of the haggard hunters who were led away.

"I am Leonette. Father Alrick is waiting. Please follow me." Her words were monotone, revealing no hint of emotion. She gracefully turned to enter the building.

Wyman walked up next to her. "We were chased in the woods, an army of the Devil. It is heading here."

"Preparations have already begun."

"You knew?" James asked.

"We have seen what is to come."

James looked at Leonette suspiciously; he noticed a necklace with Celtic carvings. "What do you mean you have seen?"

"Father Alrick will explain. He has been expecting you."

They followed her through an arched hallway lined with bas-reliefs and large gilded paintings. They arrived at Father Alrick's chamber. His walls were also covered with paintings and shelves filled with thick books. The finest furniture colored the room in reds and polished brown wood. Alrick was at least in his late sixties with gray hair puffing out like a small cloud. He greeted them with a warm smile from where he sat behind a polished oak desk.

"Welcome brothers. I'm sorry you arrived in such dire circumstances," he said, with a thick voice unexpected of a man his age.

"How is it that you knew of our arrival?" James asked.

Father Alrick stood and gestured to Leonette. "With the increase of the Lilins, the Core Order sent us their churiphim."

Wyman's lips tightened and he eyed Leonette. "A Pagan."

"A warrior of God," Alrick said, "Though, many do have bloodlines of Pagan and Shanto ancestors. But they are followers of God."

"The Shanto! *Witchcraft*," Samuel said.

Leonette didn't seem disturbed by the remark and moved to stand next to Father Alrick.

"You are not accustomed to the old country. Our alliance with the Shanto is centuries old, but that is not our concern right now." Alrick turned to look out a large window that presented a view of the forest beyond the fort wall. "Leonette saw your arrival in a vision, and the coming attack."

"Then you know who is behind it. Dumitru?" James's face flushed red.

"I cannot delve deep into my visions," Leonette said. "I can only see fragments of things that may come to pass. I saw your group attacked, followed by a larger assault on the fort. But, when the assault begins, I do not know."

"I haven't heard of such use of power since the time of Tepes. No one Lilin could command the undead and summon a storm," Wyman said.

Alrick sighed and turned to face them. "There will be many lives lost."

"You do not know the numbers that come against us?" James asked.

Leonette's eyes were emotionless. "No."

Samuel snorted. "So much for a churiphim's help."

"At least we don't have to hunt them. The Devil brings the fight to us," Wyman said. "It will be our chance to put an end to Dumitru's killing spree. Perhaps it is God's plan."

"If it's Dumitru that brings the fight," Nathaniel added.

"And if we have the numbers to fight them." James clenched and unclenched his fists.

"The fort houses two hundred men and stands on Holy ground." Father Alrick steepled his hands.

"And if they have greater numbers?" Samuel asked.

James frowned. "Pray they don't."

"Nonetheless, the assault shall happen. Keep strong your faith and God will give us victory." Father Alrick turned to James. "I thought you would be bringing one of the Lilins with you." His eyes were soft, his voice warm.

"The demon is either dead or has joined the Devil's army and is now conspiring against us," Samuel huffed, his hands becoming animated.

Wyman made a few throat clearing noises and Samuel calmed.

"I see, I'm sorry to hear," Alrick whispered. "We could have probably used her to aid us."

"That was the intent," James said hollowly.

"I see that it pains you having lost the Lilin." Alrick's eyes were genuinely empathetic.

James breathed in hard. "She was... different."

"I understand."

And it did seem that Father Alrick understood. The way he looked at James, the way his face gave off an expression of warmth.

"You are the one whose son was murdered by this Lilin we go against, this Dumitru supposedly. I have no doubt that it is he who brings this dark army against us." Alrick moved back and sat behind his desk.

"I've been hunting him for some time," James nodded.

"At great efforts. I've read the reports of your feats to capture him. Dumitru, however, is not your average Lilin."

"So I have come to find out."

"His mind and strategic skill are great, beyond any other vampire including Tepes. To hunt him is to engage his mind in a battle of wits. I haven't met one to outplay him. If it is he who moves against us, he is already ten steps ahead, planning his next move."

"You talk as if he is untouchable," Wyman said.

"I simply state the facts. It is my duty to study the most powerful elders, though he is not a true Lilin."

Samuel scoffed. "One in the same. All of them."

"That's where you are wrong. Should you encounter an elder Lilin, a true Lilin, you would do best to run." Alrick held his hand up when Samuel was about to say something. "The matter at hand, gentlemen, is the inevitable attack. Though we do have the manpower to fight them and we stand on Holy ground, I have no doubt the fort will be penetrated. Dumitru would not attack without purpose."

"And his purpose is to wipe us all out," Nathaniel added.

"Indeed." Alrick smiled at him. "But we are the Sons of Light. We'll stand our ground with God."

"And *witches*," Samuel added with scorn.

Wyman shook his head. "I don't see how they could step on Holy ground; I've never seen it."

"As I said, Dumitru is a strategist. He'll find a way," Alrick replied.

"You know much about him," James stated.

"He is the Order's highest target next to Jonas. I've been hunting since before you were born, I've gathered quite a bit of history on him and his methods. Be prepared to fight as if your life depended on it, for it will."

Leonette walked each of the men to their quarters. Samuel opted to have one of the nuns show him.

James stood for a moment in silence before setting his things down on a hutch table in the middle of the room. He couldn't shake Raven's image from his mind.

Raven was a vampire, how long would the Order let her live after they had destroyed Dumitru? She would have died either way. He pulled the folding bed from the wall and slumped down on it. He slammed his fist into the thin mattress. *Get a hold of yourself.*

Unable to close his eyes without Raven's face hunting him, he went for a walk. Apparently, he wasn't the only one who couldn't sleep. Nathaniel leaned against one of the porch columns and stared at the night sky.

His mind lingered back to when he himself was so young and full of goals, ready to fight for a cause. That cause was found in the French and Indian war, though he had been a couple of years older than Nathaniel was now. The isolated pioneers suffered great loses. Indians slaughtered their families while others would take their children. Houses were raided for everything the Indians could walk away with. James had become known as a fierce fighter during the campaign. His experience helped him become a member of The Order.

He leaned against the opposite column.

"Couldn't sleep either?" Nathaniel asked.

"Wasn't tired."

"I was thinking about Raven too."

James simply stared at the sky. The kid was perceptive.

"What is a churiphim? And why have I never heard of one before tonight?" Nathaniel turned to lean his back against the column and face James.

"The elite hunters of The Core Order. Not many are used here, but in the old country they are sent on special missions that require their particular powers."

"Witchcraft."

"Many believe it is since they manipulate the energy that surrounds us."

"Is that why Wyman and Samuel show such loathing toward Leonette? They don't believe we should use witches."

James snorted. "They have blind faith. Puritan beliefs and closed minds. There is a difference between using magic to do the Devil's work and using it to do God's work."

"If they use magic, it is against what the Bible says. Besides, I have never seen magic, it's superstition."

"Because you cannot see, does not mean that it does not exist," Leonette said, startling both men who turned to face her.

"Warn someone before you sneak up on them," Nathaniel snapped.

Leonette's face was like a sculpture, no hint of emotion.

"I suppose that is one of your special powers, sneaking around at night?" Nathaniel said.

"A skill." She moved by the edge of the steps and pointed to a lit torch at the far end of the fort wall. She twirled her hand and waved it up and the torch exploded into a bright orange ball of coiling flames. The men that patrolled on the walkway flinched into a ready position. Nathaniel opened his mouth wide, momentarily lost in the display.

Leonette fanned her fingers into a fist as if calling the fire to her and a long snake-like stream of flames shot her direction. Nathaniel fell on his rump when the flames blasted and coiled around Leonette's hand, washing the porch in its heat and light. A second later it was over. The torch fire was normal again.

She looked back at Nathaniel and walked away.

"Did you see that?"

"Now you know what a churiphim is," James replied.

The walls were slimy and moist. A moldy smell lingered in the air, mixed with earth and root. Andreea stood motionless, only her brows made the slightest movements, twitching every so often. The sound of the small stream within the cave was soothing. It helped her focus. Controlling such a large number of undead was not easy. One or two perhaps, but a hundred felt like her mind would rip, explode from the pressure of many thoughts boiling in her brain.

Dumitru and Elspet had found an underground cave near The Assembly of Saints. Dumitru wanted the undead army gathered around the perimeter of the fort. He was not going to let a single one of the hunters live.

"Tis done lass, ye can set the creatures to sleep," Elspet whispered. It was a great release; she had been waiting for that word. Andreea let loose her hold on the undead beasts and fell. Elspet caught her before she hit the rocky ground. Dumitru rushed to her and grasped her into his arms.

"Ye push the lass hard. She hasnae used the power much, it drains her quick." Elspet shook her head.

Dumitru lifted Andreea, cradling her in his arms and carried her to the back of the cave, feeling Elspet's gaze bore into him from behind. Alone in the dark chamber, he laid her down on a bed of soil and brushed stray strands of hair from her youthful face.

Andreea opened her eyes slowly and peered into Dumitru's. "Did all go well?" Her voice was a faint whisper.

He kissed her forehead. "You did wonderfully."

The sting of guilt and worry bit deep. The strain of Andreea's power was more than he had believed it would be. He had pushed her hard, but it had to be done. These people that hunted them, there can be no mistakes.

Andreea closed her eyes and fell into slumber. She would be less strained tomorrow night, wouldn't need to march the undead army through many miles of forest. Andreea had done well, this beautiful creature that tried so hard to win his love. Why? He never showed or hinted that they were lovers, simply companions in passion.

Was it not only passion that brought them together, after all? Those many decades past, when he'd spotted her on the streets of London, it was her twentieth birthday and she'd wanted to visit the new theater with her father, a well-known nobleman, by which he was introduced to her. She immediately felt an attraction toward him. The increase of her heart's pacing drummed in Dumitru's ears, the enlarged pupils of her eyes, which were the color of deep brown earth, constantly roved over him. The soft features of her face, her large round eyes that reminded him of an innocent child, entranced him. His desire for her burned deep and he knew he would violate the innocent creature. A vile monster would take her virtue.

Three days later, Andreea disappeared from London, her family never to see her again. She had become a fiend, one of the undead. Dumitru was in pure ecstasy the many nights after. Andreea's passion amplified with her change. She could not get enough of the new sensations her body felt. It was like a new world for her and she expressed her need to explore it all. That innocent girl was gone forever. She was a different creature now. A demon like himself.

Maybe that was why he couldn't come to feel that love she felt for him. She was a mirror of himself; a vile beast cursed by God. Cursed for no reason. Or maybe he simply didn't want to betray his dead wife.

Fool, she is dead. Gone. Her soul doesn't exist, only her memory to haunt.

Looking at Andreea, she possessed that innocent child-like face. She filled an empty void in him, and he couldn't imagine going through this undead life without her. So, was it love, or only lust for the passion he would miss if she were gone? He didn't want love; he didn't want to feel that loss again. No, he would not fall into that trap.

Benton walked into the chamber dragging a young dark-haired girl behind him. He pushed her down and she fell to her knees sobbing. "Your lunch, Master."

Benton stepped out leaving the sobbing girl in the black chamber. Dumitru could see her shivering, terrified, and straining her eyes to adjust to the darkness. However, there was no light for them to soak in. He carried candles with him, useful for fledgling vampires whose eyes had not yet adjusted to the dark world. He summoned a small flame to life and the candle bathed the chamber in its soft orange glow. The girl gasped and recoiled from Dumitru who stood a couple of feet from her. She twisted and turned her wrists, trying to wrench her hands free from the rope that bound them behind her.

Dumitru crouched down and wrapped his arms around her. She tensed and closed her eyes, opening them only when she felt him pull the rope, tearing it and releasing her hands.

"Are you letting me go?" she asked.

"I cannot do that; your blood is needed."

She shivered; her teeth were chattering in spasms. Dumitru placed both hands on each of her cheeks and gazed into her eyes. "Calm, be calm."

"You're going to kill me," she said.

"Everyone must eventually die."

"I want to live."

He smiled at her. "Then, you need not worry. I do not intend on killing you."

He wiped her tears with his thumbs and sat next to her. The heat from her body was a pleasant feeling he both enjoyed and missed.

"What do you want with me?" A different look of terror flashed across her face.

"And I do not intend to rob you of your virtue." He pulled her close to his body. She was a small delicate girl and she trembled uncontrollably. "You see Andreea lying there on the ground. She is important to me and needs your blood to regain her strength." The girl tensed, fresh tears streaming.

He pulled out a small blade and grabbed her arm, turning her wrist up, exposing the veins. The girl became hysterical. Dumitru stood, walked over to a satchel, and pulled out a small silver chalice. He set it next to the trembling girl and kneeled in front of her, gently clasping her chin and facing her to him.

"I have always been a man of my word. When I make a promise, I do not break it. It is why Andreea stays with me. It is why I hold such a position of leadership and why my fellow comrades follow me. Because I keep my word. It is something I hold dear. You could say a small piece of humanity. Do you understand?" The girl nodded; he gave her a warm smile.

He lifted her wrist over the chalice. "I promise, you will not die a young girl, but I require your blood." He placed the blade above the small veins and the girl tensed, clenching her teeth and shutting her eyes.

Dumitru grabbed her head and kissed her. At first the girl was surprised and stiff, then relaxed, allowing herself to succumb to his power, her breathing becoming heavy and hot, the pace of her heart increasing, no longer trembling. When he let her go, she looked dazed, confused, staring at him, her eyes asking for more.

"You will feel no pain, relax," he whispered. She was staring at him when the first drops of blood splattered into the chalice. As it filled with the crimson liquid, she regained her awareness. At first, she didn't seem to understand, but gradually she realized it was her blood that made that pouring sound and she fainted.

Dumitru caught her before her head hit the hard rock and gently laid her down.

R

Nathaniel woke late in the morning; grey clouds hid the sky, blanketing the fort in a bleak mood. No wind, no sounds of birds, only the stillness of the air. He spotted Leonette standing watch on the walkway. She was wearing new clothes, a tight crimson tunic and loose breeches, which was strange. He was accustomed to seeing women in either gowns or laced aprons at the most. A large black cloak draped over her and many strange symbols outlined her clothing. Perhaps they were related to the witchcraft she used. He found himself both intrigued and intimidated by her. He was soon making his way toward her on the walkway.

"Hello, I wanted to apologize about last night. I was on edge and—"

"I do not require your apology." Her voice was unvaried, cold. But no, it wasn't that. She didn't express anything in either words or her manner. Her face remained in the same stone expression, looking out toward the forest as if she knew something no one else did. She probably did, considering what she was. A churiphim. A witch. She couldn't be more than a year or two older than himself, nineteen at the most. A large silver medallion hung from her neck bearing more strange markings and roman numerals.

"What are all those markings, anyway? Part of your witchcraft?"

She turned her head slightly to glare at him. "Did Father Alrick send you?"

"No, I want to know who I will be fighting along with. I mean, I don't want you to harbor any bad blood between us in a fight."

"I hold no ill content." She turned her attention back to the forest.

"Are all churiphims like you?"

"Yes."

"Must be because of the witchcraft." Nathaniel leaned over the wall and made himself comfortable looking out into the horizon.

"We do not practice witchcraft. Churiphims are touched by Angels, gifted to protect. We may use the same foundations as witches, but we are granted the ability to do so."

As he watched her speak, though her expression was unchanging, there was something hidden in those words. No. It was her eyes. They were distant, she was no longer scanning the forest; her gaze was elsewhere. There was hidden loneliness and sadness in those dark orbs.

It reminded him of Raven. *The eyes were the doorways to the soul. But, did vampires have souls? Did Raven have a soul? Her spirit was gone, but was her soul? When vampires die they are sent to Hell, or they stop existing all together. Two different theories.* A lump formed in his throat. He should have done more to help her.

"I remember Father Alrick saying something about the Shanto. Are they like the churiphim?"

"You ask many questions." A whisper of a frown etched Leonette's mouth.

"I am a hunter. I'm going to learn these things. Or is it information given to a select few? Besides, who is to say I won't be dead after this battle, then you wouldn't have anything to worry about."

"If only to silence you, I will answer this last question and you will leave me to my duty. Agreed?" She looked at him and he nodded.

"The Shanto are not the same as the churiphim. They are a clandestine order who claim to use their powers to protect the innocent. While churiphim and witches may use the energy around us, the elements of creation, the Shanto use a spiritual power, an inner power. The Order and the Shanto keep watch over each other, balancing the powers and making sure one or the other does not overstep their boundaries."

"Vampires, witches, Shanto, what other things don't I know about?" Nathaniel shook his head.

"Live past the battle and find out." Leonette stared back out to the forest, roving with her eyes. She walked off.

"Great speaking with you, we should do it again." He smiled sarcastically at her.

Nathaniel spent the rest of the day walking in his own world thinking about the conversation with the churiphim. Thinking about all the things he would come to learn as a hunter and a man.

Lightning streamed and flashed across the sky followed by booming thunder that snapped him out of his musings. Darkness snuck up on him. The wind rushed in as if some giant was blowing on the fort trying to tear it down. Men were shouting and giving commands. He couldn't make them out through the loud blast of wind.

Then, as suddenly as it came, the wind died down, the lightning ceased, and all was deathly still and silent. The men around the fort looked at the sky, confused. James and Wyman stood under the Church porch also looking bewildered. Leonette stood in the same place he'd found her this morning, like a statue looking out into the dark mass of forest wall.

"Arm yourselves!" she shouted. "The swarm is coming. The battle begins."

Another roar of thunder shook the ground, followed by rain. Slow at first, then the drops pounded down like millions of tiny feet running across the rooftops of the buildings.

Lightning blasted down into a group of men nearby, and Nathaniel fell. He let out a scream that was silenced by another rumble of thunder. Dazed, his feet tingled, and his strength was sucked away. Men were running and shouting. Others were screaming. He felt someone lift him. It was James. His mouth was moving, saying something. Only a high-pitched hum stung Nathaniel's ear.

A flash of orange light and heat exploded above them. The smell of burnt flesh and hair flooded his nostrils. James was dragging him to the church. Nathaniel looked behind him. Leonette was blasting men with fire. No, not the men, it was the undead monsters. They were on the walkway.

R

Too fast, where did they come from? James thought quickly, dragging Nathaniel up into the porch. Wyman fired his pistol at the coming undead hoard inside the fort walls.

"Aim for their heads," he shouted.

James pulled Nathaniel past the church doors; Father Alrick was there with a few priests who helped lug him inside. James unsheathed his Machaira and leapt down the porch stairs.

He ducked under a wild swing from a ghoul and with a hard, swift whip of his sword, the thing's head flew into the air and its body dropped like a heavy sandbag. He looked toward the gate. That was how they were getting in. The blast of lightning knocked down the left door. Beyond the gate he spotted a red-haired girl, her eyes gleaming in the dark, looking toward the sky. She disappeared, vanishing in a blur of movement.

She appeared behind Leonette. But how? This was Holy ground.

"Behind you!" he shouted.

Leonette spun around. The red-haired vampire rushed her. A wall of fire appeared between the two and Leonette jumped down, landing gracefully, and sprinted away. Lightning cracked and exploded into another group of men, melting away their flesh and killing them before screams escaped them.

"She controls the lightning. Seek shelter; we cannot win in the open. Everyone inside the church," Leonette ordered.

The hunters scrambled to get inside, firing muskets and pistols, hacking the ghouls with their Machairas. The foul creatures flooded through the exposed opening like a swarm of angry hornets. The fort was filled with the screams of men whose innards were being ripped out from them, limbs torn, flesh eaten.

The crimson-haired vampire leaped down on a group of hunters. She punched her fists through two before they realized she was there. Three fired stakes into her, but she simply pulled them out and flung them back with precise accuracy, killing a couple more.

This was impossible, even for an elder. How was she standing on Holy ground? James fired his crossbow and the stake hit on target; the red-haired bitch screamed. The rod was coated with Wolfsbane and garlic. She snarled at him and was gone. From behind, he felt a strong hand lift him. Claws pierced into his neck, and then she threw him through the air. James landed in a roll and stopped in a crouch. He brandished his crucifix.

The vampire hissed. "Ye faith is strong, but isnae going to save you."

Three ghouls lunged at him. A burst of fire set them aflame, the heat singed his hair and the foul smell seeped into his nose.

"Run!" Leonette stood a few yards away.

The vampire curled a brow. "Churiphim? I hasnae seen ye kind in the new world."

James ran for the church behind Leonette. He rushed through the door and turned to see if Leonette followed. Alrick joined him at the door.

"That is no child of Tepes," he said.

"What do you mean? What is she?" James asked.

"That is a child of Lilith. She is a true Lilin before the age of Dracula. Her name is Elspet. She has eluded the Order time and again, for centuries."

Nathaniel regained his bearings and leaned on the door to look. "A true Lilin?"

Wyman made his way toward the church with Samuel and a few men. Another blast of lightning shot down behind them, killing the men. Wyman and Samuel were hurled forward, knocked out.

"Help me." James ran out to grab them, Nathaniel followed with a few other men behind him. A swarm of ghouls rushed for them.

"Get them inside!" James ordered. He pulled out dual pistols and fired, taking down two of the creatures. Then he pulled his Machaira and dagger, hacking down three more. Nathaniel and the others dragged Wyman and Samuel to the church.

A wall of fire swirled up around them, slowing the ghouls.

James looked over at Leonette, one hand held toward them, the other at the red-haired vampire. *The churiphim had the power to summon flames out of the air?*

James ran for the church; it wasn't the time to ponder on such things.

"Leonette, we're all inside, come on!" Nathaniel yelled.

Elspet leaped at Leonette and landed a couple of feet away as if stopped by some unseen force. "Ye smart witch," she said. "A circle of protection."

On the earth, a hint of light glimmered around Leonette in a full circle.

She turned toward a lone torch and summoned a streak of flames that engulfed Elspet. The demon hissed in protest and Leonette ran for the church.

"Shut the door."

James slammed the gate and Leonette pulled a small pouch from one of her pockets. She recited in Latin while tracing symbols on the floor near the door with the white powder.

"That will not hold her long." She stood and stepped back, there was a loud bang on the door followed by clawing. "However, the ghouls it will not hold at all."

"You set her on fire. She is dead, right?" Nathaniel asked.

Leonette faced him. "No, she is a Lilin, the eldest of vampires, she can further resist the powers that would kill normal vampires or keep them from entering a home. What are our casualties?"

"Twenty, and a few injured," James replied. "We'll have to hold them off in here, everyone load every musket and pistol. After each one has fired, move to your Machairas."

"We shall not live past the night," Leonette said. "The force amassed against us, we cannot defeat. Father Alrick, we must use your escape tunnel."

"No, we are safe here, we can dwindle them down." Wyman had regained consciousness holding the side of his head with a bloody hand. "If you take us out there, the vampires that Dumitru undoubtedly has waiting, will rip us apart. Without the Holy ground of the fort to hold them back, we have no power to protect us."

"That would have been true, had they not been able to break through the walls, but they have and there is a Lilin among their ranks." Leonette looked back at Wyman. "We are trapped. We shall go, there is no hope here."

"And who in God's name put you in charge of deciding?"

"The Order."

"It's lunacy," James cut in. "Wyman is right. If Dumitru is out there, he waits with vampires and wolves. We'll have no chance in the forest. You take us out there, we die."

"Father Alrick, have the nuns gather the children and meet at the tunnel entrance." Leonette turned to James. "We are leaving."

CHAPTER 11

Cool waves of air rolled over her skin making her hair flail and swirl. Strong arms cradled her tightly. Raven opened her eyes and saw a face, smooth and beautiful. A dream.

Raven glanced down, trees flew by, or rather she was flying by them, carried by this person. Her vision blurred, large white wings, Angel wings, spread majestically from the back of the stranger. A sheen of white radiance stung her eyes. Yes, she had to be dreaming and her eyes slipped shut again.

When she woke, the lingering wraiths of another dream faded as her awareness crept back. In the dream, she had been back home with her family playing with her brothers as their father and mother watched from the porch.

It was the warm glaze over her legs that brought her out of her serene reverie and back to the here and now. It was humid and the smell of fungus and moisture was thick. A small fire crackled a few feet from her. She scanned the area; it was a cavern and she was not alone. She recoiled immediately with an instinctual hiss.

"That is no way to greet someone who saved you," the man said. He was dressed in pure black; a long cloak covered his face in shadows.

Raven clasped her hands to her mouth and took a second to calm herself.

"Who are you? How did I get here?"

"My name is Gabriel and I brought you here. You were in some dire need of help." His voice was tranquil, filling her with a strange sense of calm.

"But, the undead creatures—"

"Yes." He pulled back his cloak. His features were soft, lacking the chiseled bone structure of a man, appearing feminine and when he stood, was tall. He held out a small brass cup to her. "You must be hungry."

"I am, but—"

"Then drink. You will be quite satisfied."

Raven looked at the cup and the dark red liquid inside. Blood.

"You are a vampire?"

"Certainly not."

"Where did you get it? Did you kill someone for it?"

"It is my own."

"I do not understand."

"I am associated with the Order of the Sons of Light. Do not trouble yourself with worries. I'm here to help." His smile was warm, and his eyes revealed such compassion that she was overcome with a sense of peace. *Who was this man?* All fears, the sadness she felt losing her family, it was gone.

"Drink, you need to replenish your strength."

She trusted this man. She felt safe with him and knew he spoke the truth.

Raven drank the liquid. Its flavor was unusual, the most delicious blood she had tasted and her body was greedy for it, forcing her to drink faster. Her heart exploded to life, beating with such vigor, pushing the blood through her veins. A warm sensation spread through her body; it filled her with a slight panic. Yet it wasn't like what she had felt from the Wolfsbane. More like a warm blanket falling over her during a wintry night.

Images formed in her mind, James and Nathaniel, they were in a fort and there was an old grey-haired priest with them. Then the scene changed, she was seeing the forest through many eyes, she could see the tops of trees glistening by the light of the morning sun. At first, she didn't comprehend, but her mind went to work making sense of it, putting together answers to her questions. These visions came through the eyes of the many creatures that lived in the forest. She knew she could command and see through the eyes of the animals, but to be able to control so many at one time?

From drinking the small amount of blood, her hunger was satiated, and the wounds from the fight were healed.

"I feel... stronger," she said. *Not ordinary blood.*

"Our blood can do that to your... kind, or rather, to Lilins. It gives them strength, enhances their powers. Many of them seek us out for that one purpose, if they know of it and know of us. Lilins need human blood to live, but ours... well that is another matter."

"What do you mean, 'ours'?"

He looked at her with those soft eyes again. The angel wings flashed in her mind. His fingers were elongated, no cuticles, eyes rounder than average, an unnatural presence. Only one explanation, a fanciful one, but he was certainly not human.

"The blood should keep you nourished for a few days."

"Then I will have to kill."

"You do not always need to."

"James said I needed to feed on human blood. He made me kill." Had James lied to her? *Of course.*

"Those men would have died for their crimes, it is true. You did not need to kill them, though. Mortals are not fond of letting things feed on their blood. It is out of convenience as well as evil that vampires kill."

"Convenience? How can you say that?"

"Shall you ask them for blood? And if a mortal should say yes, they would be left on the brink of death and perhaps die in order to fully quench the bloodlust of a Lilin. It is easier to simply dig your fangs in and feed."

"I cannot accept that, I will not."

"Then you will die."

Raven stared at Gabriel; his voice remained soft, gentle and soothing to her ears.

"I do not want to die, but I do not want to murder to live."

"If you stop feeding, you commit murder."

Raven looked at him confused.

"You commit self-murder; you do not trust in God. You will burn in Hell if you lose such faith."

"I do not know about God anymore. This is... wrong. The Order is wrong. They bring people to me to kill when they are supposed to be helping, protecting humanity?"

"The veil of humanity does pervert the Order's original laws."

Raven pulled her knees to her chest. "I hate this, I hate all of this. Why did God let this happen? I do not want to kill. I do not want to be a monster. I want my family." She snarled and tears burst free. The sense of calm shattered.

Gabriel sat by Raven and wrapped his arms around her in a strong hug. Raven had missed such tender compassion in the past few weeks and pressed her head into his chest. There was a sense of familiarity as if she had known this man.

"Know child, that God will never forsake you, so long as you keep your faith in Him. Know that you are important, that you have a purpose, and many shall be watching you. I shall be watching you, as I have always been."

Guardian? Her mind blurred, spinning with mingled emotions. The darkness set in again. She wanted to ask more questions, but she was drifting deeper into that persuasive dream world. She needed to know more, wanted to stay with him, wanted to stay in the safe, caring embrace. But the darkness was instant, dragging her into slumber. Her eyes succumbed to the sweet lure.

You have my blood, use it well, Gabriel's voice whispered in the black of her sleep.

R

A roar of thunder rumbled the ground and Raven snapped open her eyes. The wind howled and the trees around her swayed back and forth. She was back in the forest and Gabriel was gone.

Who was he? A hunter?

But he was different than the other hunters.

An explosion lit the sky somewhere off in the distance, followed by men's screams. By sheer instinct, she raced in its direction.

She arrived at a large opening of flat land. A flash of lightning streaked across the sky and revealed a large silhouette of a fort. Hundreds of the undead things were swarming toward the walls.

A groan came from behind her and she spun around to a dozen ghouls glaring at her with sunken eyes. They leaped at her and she moved to dodge, confused to find herself yards away. Their movements slowed.

One of the creatures grabbed her from behind, digging its claws into her shoulder. She let out a hiss and twirled around and hurled the thing many yards away. She was holding its gnarled arm.

Gabriel's blood.

It must be; it had increased her powers.

Five more ghouls rushed her, Raven focused on them unleashing her unseen force, thinking only to toss them away, instead, their bodies were shredded as they flew from her. She stood surprised.

Thunder exploded, sharpening her focus. She ran toward the remaining ghouls, again they moved slowly, or rather she was moving so fast it gave the illusion they were moving slow. With claws, Raven ripped and slashed into them as if they were thin paper. Effortlessly, she twirled and moved around their swipes. Their movements reminded her of bugs squirming in molasses. When it was done, she stood to scan the butchery, in awe of herself.

Screams from the fort grabbed her attention and brought her back to awareness. James and the children—these things would kill them.

R

Elspet joined Dumitru outside the fort walls, her clothing burnt with dabs of bright orange flakes devouring the last tatters she had left. Tendrils of smoke coiled around her hair and skin. Dumitru wrinkled his nose to the stench of scorched hair and flesh.

"Unexpected obstacles?" he asked, lifting one of his thin eyebrows.

"They have a churiphim." Her lip curled into a sneer. Her skin was already healing, and strands of new red hair grew out like slithering snakes.

Dumitru's face lost expression. "A churiphim? *Here?*"

"Fortunately, she isnae a strong one, though her flames leave a sting I willnae be forgetting soon."

"And left you quite bare." Dumitru pulled off his cloak and handed it over to her. Her skin was healed by the time he did this and Dumitru studied her small curvy frame.

Elspet looked delicate, which was an illusion, of course, for she was a vicious killer. Her breasts were small, not his usual taste, but they were high and round with firm shape. Her stomach was smooth and flat and her hips formed the right arcs into lean and silky legs. She would have made any man happy in her time. Dumitru turned away when he noticed Elspet staring at him with an amused smile.

"Aye, 'Twas my favorite outfit too." She took the cloak and tied it around herself.

"Strange ability you have, to walk on Holy ground."

"Tis that I do have secrets of me awn that ye dinnae ken of," She winked. "Dinnae worry, the fort is ours. They wasnae expecting such power to fall down upon them. They will either stay and die in the church or they shall try to escape, leaving the protection of the fort."

Dumitru grinned. His plan had worked perfectly. "Set fire to it. Set fire to all the buildings."

"This will send waves and the Core Order will ken of it, I hope ye understand what ye do. If one churiphim is here, no doubt their concerns will hae them sending more."

"Waves have been made, our path is set, we have no choice in that matter. After we destroy the fort, we head north to find Washington."

"Ye believe ye possess the power to control such a large army, only Dracula—"

"Dracula failed where I shall succeed. Do not worry about my abilities; fulfill your task. I respect your concern, but I ask that you trust me."

"Verra weel, I'll go flush the mice from their holes." Elspet sprinted away in a blur.

He expected the Order to send more. He'd invited it. Washington, the general of the Continental Army, was his key to defeating any army the Order would send. Mortal minds were easy to manipulate, and Washington controlled a large army, one that Dumitru would use.

James stared at Leonette, who nodded at Father Alrick to direct everyone to the underground tunnel leading out of the fort walls.

"To Hell with the Order's command. You lead us to the wolves if you take us into the forest," James said.

Leonette paid no mind and ushered the nuns and the fort's men down to the lower parts of the church. James twirled her around by her shoulder to face him.

"You're not old enough to know the pains of war. What makes you believe you can lead us to safety, simply because of a title?"

"Stay if you wish."

Before James could respond, a loud crash and shattering glass turned everyone's attention to a ghoul who'd leaped through the window. More crawled in, shattering other windows. The men fired pistols and muskets; a white haze of smoke filled the chamber with its burnt paper and chalk-like smell.

Alrick and a couple of nuns stomped down the stairs with Lydia and her siblings. Two of the ghouls blocked them at the bottom. The children shrieked when they saw the decayed skin and sunken eyes.

James and Nathaniel were busy fending off a group of ghouls from ripping them apart.

"To the lower chamber," Leonette commanded. She moved over to the two ghouls blocking Alrick and the children. She chanted and a blue aura glowed around her hand with which she touched to the two creatures. They slumped over and fell like rocks, banging on the floor.

"Quickly, Father Alrick," she ushered.

Alrick led the nuns and children down past the fray and to the lower chamber. The church door exploded into splintered shards of wood as another swarm of ghouls leaped through it.

Wyman swung his Machaira furiously, trying to keep them away from Samuel who was regaining consciousness.

"Get your bearings Samuel, or become a meal," Wyman shouted.

Leonette chanted and the windows and door exploded into flames, setting fire to the ghouls who were trying to crawl in.

"What are you doing? You'll burn the church down around us," shouted James.

She waved her hands and a stream of fire engulfed the heads of the remaining ghouls, scorching their flesh and dropping them. Nathaniel fell away from the intense heat near one of the creatures.

He flipped onto his stomach and glared at Leonette.

"That's the second time you've done that to me."

Another form of chanting came from the doorway. Elspet was standing outside.

"She is breaking my seal." Leonette turned and headed for the lower chamber.

Nathaniel said, "We need to kill her."

"My strength is exhausted."

"Oh, my strength is exhausted." Nathaniel jumped back to his feet. "You're not the only one here."

"She is too powerful to defeat without my help." Leonette disappeared into the lower chamber.

"Godforsaken witches," Wyman muttered, as he hauled Samuel down, leaving James and Nathaniel alone.

"They are damned, the churiphims. I can now see why they work alone," James said. "Come, she's given us no other choice."

The wall of fire blocking the ghouls at the door went out allowing the creature access.

"Go!" James shouted. Both raced down the stairs to the lower chamber.

"They're coming," Nathaniel yelled as they arrived at the bottom.

Leonette threw a torch on the stairs and flicked her wrist, sending a ball of fire rolling up the flight of steps, blocking off the ghouls. She looked pale, streaks of sweat streaming down her face. Her strength being stricken away with each power used.

Father Alrick and a few men pushed open a heavy slab of stone that raked the ground, revealing a hidden tunnel. The nuns rushed in with the children, followed by Father Alrick.

While everyone else filed in, Leonette traced another ward at the base of the doorway and quickly followed when she was done. James and Nathaniel helped push the slab shut and it locked in place with a loud clank of metal and stone.

"Wyman, what is going on?" Samuel clasped a hand to his head.

"The witch leads us into the forest, the fort is lost," Wyman said. Samuel only groaned a response, dazed.

Lydia and her siblings clutched each other, looking down the long narrow tunnel. It was illuminated by torches evenly spaced every few yards, the smell of earth and roots filled James' nostrils, and the warm air from the heat of torches pressed down on him.

Leonette walked ahead of everyone. "We must make haste."

Though with the fatigue painted on her face, her expression was unchanged, and her voice kept the same monotone nature through the battle. Do churiphims experience emotions?

"And why are we led forth by a witch?" Samuel snapped.

"Because for now, we have no other option," James replied.

"The witch burned the church herself, she forced us down here," Wyman added.

Father Alrick cleared his throat. "Gentlemen, perhaps it would better serve us to continue this discussion elsewhere, we have little time to waste, she is a churiphim and by that, she is deemed to take charge." He followed behind Leonette, who was a good distance down the tunnel, with the rest of the men following behind.

Samuel scoffed and followed.

Nathaniel shook his head. "She set the church on fire to force us to take the tunnel?"

"Yes," James said.

R

Another slab of stone groaned open revealing a small and sloping man-made gulch hidden by thick foliage and trees. The small company of hunters filed out with crossbows and muskets ready. Leonette was ahead of the group by the time James and Nathaniel stepped out.

"This way." She made for the thickest parts of the woods.

"You take us deeper into the wilderness, we need to head east," Wyman said.

She ignored him and kept walking forward, followed by Father Alrick and the hunters. Wyman's face flushed red, but he proceeded after them.

They walked for some time when Leonette stopped. James and Nathaniel had joined her at the front.

"What's wrong?" James asked.

"Be ready." She held a hand up.

"Ye are perceptive." Elspet stepped out of thick foliage and behind her at least twenty vampires, their eyes all gleaming faint greens and yellows. Howls followed and dozens of black wolves trotted out to surround the hunters.

"Ye left the protection of the fort walls. Verra bad mistake, ye have walked right into a slaughter," the red-haired vampire said.

The vampires charged in and the area exploded into movement, muskets blasting, crossbows hurling stakes.

Wolves rushed in, growling, and ripped into the hunters. The area was blanketed by the white mist of musket fire.

The nuns and Father Alrick crouched by the children in an attempt to keep them safe.

James swung his Machaira in one hand and a large dagger in the other. He brought down two of the wolves.

Nathaniel fired a stake into a vampire. It fell, paralyzed. More followed behind.

A wall of fire burst from the ground between the vampires and the hunters, a few vampires that were racing toward the group were instantly scorched by the flames and fell screeching and wailing.

Ghouls jumped out of the black foliage and joined wolves and vampires in the slaughter.

James spun around in time to dodge a swipe from one of the undead things. He chopped down with his Machaira and severed its arm, but it kept coming. Then its head bent forward and twirled to the ground, followed by the body. Nathaniel stood behind it with his weapon.

"Glad I sharpened it at the fort," he said.

"Watch out!" James yelled. He hurled his dagger. Nathaniel turned to see a large wolf plummet to the ground, the dagger lodged in its skull.

James grabbed a tomahawk next from his straps of bladed weapons. Three ghouls ran in the direction of Father Alrick and the children. James raced into them, spinning and arching his arm out wide and hacking off one of the monster's legs. He kicked another, sending it on its back, and stabbed his Machaira under the jaw and up into the brain of the third.

Nathaniel ran in and hacked down the two that James had dropped.

A blue glow washed over the area and James looked over at Leonette who held two swords lit with bright blue and white flames crackling furiously. He stood in awe for a moment, his reverie broken when she rushed two ghouls. Handling her flaming weapons with precision, both fell before they'd even swung a clawed arm. Her features were changed, animal-like. No time to ponder on it. Elspet landed by a group of hunters and hurled two toward a large gathering of ghouls, who swarmed in and shredded them apart, their screams becoming gurgled noises as their innards were pulled and stretched out by claws and teeth.

"Kill her!" James shouted.

The hunters fired stakes but Elspet was fast, dodging and twirling around each one. Her eyes were feral and focused. Hunters hands began to snap, arms bending. The sounds of bone cracking through skin flooded the battlefield. Men panicked as their comrade's screams tore through the forest. One hunter's head twisted completely around.

"What in the name of God—" Wyman said. "What is she?"

Leonette moved over to James. "Keep them moving west, I will give you time to run." She traced strange curved symbols on the ground and chanted.

What the hell good would it do? They couldn't outrun vampires. But, what choice did they have? The damned churiphim had led them into a trap. James shouted orders. "Withdraw, keep west."

When Leonette finished tracing her symbols, the wall of fire she had summoned grew streams of blaze that shot out, coiling around the hunters and setting the wolves, ghouls and vampires aflame. Strangely, James was thinking about that wall of fire; it hadn't set the foliage aflame.

"Leonette, no," Father Alrick said. "You are reaching your limit, you must stop."

What limit? James studied Leonette, indeed her features were changing. She was extremely pale, her skin taking on a milky white look, her eyes a bright yellow.

"Take them to the cave, I shall follow," she said in that monotone voice of hers.

After a moment's hesitation, Father Alrick nodded and led the nuns with the children into the thick woods. James followed with the rest of the group.

Leonette kept the swarm at bay with her churiphim craft, her muscles trembling; she was taking in deep breaths as tentacles of fire coiled and whipped about her, wrapping around their enemies. There were too many to keep at bay, and many ghouls trickled around her fiery circumference, chasing after the fleeing hunters.

The men fired muskets and stakes at the horde chasing behind them. Nathaniel wrapped an arm around Father Alrick to help him keep up. Men were clawed down one by one as the group ran, their numbers dwindling rapidly.

James came to a halt. A swarm of ghouls and vampires blocked their way.

"Damn that witch," Wyman cursed.

Samuel clobbered a ghoul with the butt of his Machaira. "All of them, one in the same." He lumbered on.

The vampires surrounded them. The churiphim had led them to their deaths. James looked back at Lydia and her siblings clutching to the nuns. Father Alrick bent his head down in prayer.

"Let us take as many of the bastards with us then," James said.

One of the vampires who moved in with lightning speed snatched a nun.

"Bare your crosses!" Wyman shouted. "Keep the demons at bay."

Ghouls and wolves swarmed on the hunters. Vampires made their way in attacking when a hunter's attention would set on a ghoul.

Lydia screamed. James turned to see four of the mindless things surrounding her and the nuns. James hurled his tomahawk and it hit dead center between the eyes dropping one. He ran for the other three. A vampire tackled him. It snarled as it tried to bite at him. James brandished his cross and the vampire leaped away, vehemently hissing at the Holy Symbol. The ghouls leaped at the children and James couldn't reach them. *God, let it be a quick death.*

The creatures were hurled away. The ghouls never touched Lydia and her siblings. Their bodies ripped apart in midair. Vampires stopped to witness this, confused.

Wolves turned on the ghouls, a moment of uncertainty fell over both vampire and hunters.

"Churiphim witchcraft?" Nathaniel huffed next to James.

"I don't know," he replied.

Ghouls dropped around them. A vampire screeched followed by its head twirling from its body. There was a blur of movement. Something was attacking them. It weaved in and out the trees, seeping out of the shadows to take down a vampire here, a ghoul there.

The vampires hesitated, their eyes darting, searching for what had attacked them, hissing in protest.

Alrick and the children also searched the darkness, only to see the image of a shadow after it had taken down another vampire.

The blurry figure stopped. Perhaps it was a trick. An illusion. But Nathaniel was looking at her with the same expression of surprise and doubt.

"Raven?" Nathaniel queried.

Raven leaped on a vampire, stabbing a stake into its heart, and ripping its head off with clawed hands. A swarm of ghouls rushed her, and they were hurled into the air by an unseen blast of power, their bodies torn apart by the pure force.

A hunter tried to shoot a stake at Raven. She caught it in her hands and vanished in a burst of speed.

"FOOL! Don't attack her, she's on our side!" James shouted.

Raven appeared beside James, a gust of wind swirling around him from the intense speed.

"I need a Machaira," she said.

James handed her his and he pulled a dagger. She disappeared again and another vampire's head flew. Every so often James caught a glimpse of her momentarily stopping to swing the blade at a surprised bloodsucker.

Further behind the line of fighting, flames burst around the battle. Leonette joined the fight. Perhaps Father Alrick's prayer had been answered. The tide of the battle was turning.

Leonette fought her way to James's group. She locked on to Raven and chanted.

"No!" James yelled

A stream of blue fire hissed toward Raven, but it never touched her. She appeared behind James.

"Raven is with us," James said.

Leonette stared at Raven. "She is a vampire."

"Who is part of the Order and hunts other vampires."

Elspet appeared in the middle of the dwindling fight. She narrowed her eyes at Raven.

"A vampire who hunts vampires, ye betray your awn?"

The hunters circled Elspet and aimed their crossbows.

"Kill her!" Wyman ordered.

They all fired, Elspet waved her hands stopping the stakes and holding them frozen in midair. The hunters were taken aback.

"Ye betray ye kind and cannae be allowed to live." Elspet hurled the stakes at Raven, who deflected them with her own unseen force and rushed the Lilin. They appeared as a ball of distorted movements when they collided, followed by snarls and growls. Elspet hurled Raven into a tree, snapping it in half. It fell creaking and cracking, landing with a loud thud and rustling of branches.

Father Alrick began a prayer and hunters flung Holy water on Elspet. She wailed in protest. The men brandished their crucifixes chanting, *"The Power of the Lord binds you. We are strong with the Lord and His Power."*

Elspet recoiled; Leonette rushed her, swinging both her flaming swords at her neck. The Lilin twirled around the attack.

"Ye willnae have my head today, perhaps if ye were a higher rank, little tyro." She fled into the trees.

Raven crawled out of the bushes to join the group. A large gash lined her chest quickly zipping together.

"Welcome back, demon child," Nathaniel winked.

Raven shook her head and smiled.

Only eighty hunters remained when the battle had ended.

"Keep moving, most likely, they shall send more. There is a cave ahead," Leonette said. She looked a pasty white as if on the verge of passing out and her voice was frail. Her eyes were a glossy yellow, not her normal black orbs, although her other features returned.

"You imprudent witch, you led my men to slaughter. We should have stayed at the fort," Samuel snarled.

"Keep moving." She walked past him, and he grabbed her by the arm, spinning her around. The loud crunch of his fist hitting her face caught everyone by surprise. Leonette's body whirled with the force and a huff of air escaped her lungs as she slammed face first on the ground. As she got to her hands and knees, Samuel kicked her hard in the stomach, dropping her again. James and Wyman rushed in to restrain him.

"What in God's name is wrong with you?" James said.

"Let go of me." Samuel wrestled himself loose. "I'm done." He walked off.

Nathaniel and Father Alrick rushed to Leonette's side. She was unconscious, drizzles of blood streaming from her nose and mouth.

"Who is she?" Raven asked, looking bemused.

They headed for the cave Leonette had mentioned. She was a churiphim, according to James and Nathaniel. Some elite hunter the Core Order used in the old lands, that was mainly considered a witch. Raven kept her control over the wolves and used them to scour the area for any surprise attacks while they weaved their way through the forest.

She recounted her story to James and Nathaniel who in turn did the same, though it was strange that no one knew of Gabriel. She explained her theory toward her strengthened powers, the effect of Gabriel's blood, and that it was only temporary.

Leonette was conscious by the time they arrived at the angled, black maw of the cave. *Was it the same one Gabriel had taken me to?*

The churiphim looked like she would pass out again at any given moment. Father Alrick stayed by her side.

Lydia was happy to see Raven again and walked with her along the way. She told Raven that she had prayed for her and asked God to send an angel to save her.

Is that what Gabriel was, an angel perhaps? Why would an angel help a vampire? It was too farfetched of an idea, yet the dream, the wings, they were clear.

Raven sensed the tension amongst the rest of the hunters and nuns, who were not happy having to travel with a vampire. She could hear their whispers of concern. *She will kill us in our sleep, she is a demon. What is Father Alrick thinking?*

As soon as everyone was inside the cave, Raven fought back a creeping sense of panic, her mind calling back the dreadful time she had fallen into the black crevasse where she was trapped for a day. She imagined the thousands of tiny spiders crawling over her skin.

"You alright?" asked James.

Raven nodded and kept walking.

Leonette pulled out one of her swords and spoke in a strange language. When she finished, coils of fire burst and wrapped in bright flames around the blade, bathing the underground chamber in shades of orange and yellows. Raven simply stared at it a long while, her trance broken when Nathaniel slapped a hand on her shoulder.

"Now you know what a churiphim is," he said.

Leonette led them deeper into the cavern, stopping at the end of the earth chamber. She passed the flaming sword to Father Alrick, traced the cavern wall with her hands, and pressed on a large stone that jutted out awkwardly. The wall rumbled and part of the rock slid open to reveal a large groined roof chamber created of stone and wood. Various runes and strange markings were traced on the floor and pillars upon which torches illuminated the area. Other openings led into more spaces; there was a sense of peace and awe as Leonette directed everyone in.

"What is this place?" James asked.

"A gathering point for the churiphim."

"Here the dragon lines of the earth meet. It is here the churiphim renew and strengthen their power during special times of the year," Alrick explained.

"Witch gatherings," Samuel muttered.

"While pagans follow the same cycles as churiphims, we are granted our power through the grace of God." Leonette stood at the door after everyone was inside, all except for Raven. Leonette blocked her way. "You are not welcome in here, Lilin."

Raven looked at James for help.

He stepped over. "She is with us."

"I'll not allow a Lilin to desecrate this ground." Leonette reached for the interior stone that would close the entrance.

"I have no place to go." Raven dared to move forward a step. Leonette snapped a glare on her that made Raven winch, and she dared not take another step.

"Listen, witch. She helped us; we would be dead if not for her. It was you who led us into the trap in the first place," said James.

Leonette looked ashen and trembled from lack of strength. She looked to pass out at any second. Her glare focused on Raven. "I suggest you use what time you have to find shelter."

"If you're not letting her in, I'm staying with her," Nathaniel shouted from the group and walked out of the chamber to stand with Raven.

"Foolish. You cannot remain outside, the Lilins may return." Leonette trembled out the words, fighting the weight of her eyelids, beads of sweat crawled down her face.

"But you would leave Raven out here." Nathaniel's eyes locked on hers.

"Yes," Leonette said.

"You are mistaken, witch. She is to enter so I suggest you invite her, or I'll make you." James stepped closer to the churiphim.

"Please, there is no need for this." Alrick rushed between James and Leonette.

Leonette's lips twitched to say something. Instead, she tipped over and Nathaniel caught her before she hit the ground.

"That settles that," Nathaniel said.

"She requires rest, her limit was about reached during the battle," said Father Alrick.

Nathaniel lifted her into his arms, carried her to the center of the large chamber, and gently laid her down, making a pillow out of tunics to lay her head. If Raven didn't know better, Leonette could have been a vampire, as white as she looked.

"What do you mean by her limit?" Raven asked.

Father Alrick stared at her for a moment, she wasn't sure if he was thinking about the question or simply didn't know how to answer a vampire. He realized what he was doing.

"I'm sorry, please forgive me. It is not often I speak to a... Lilin under relaxed circumstances. It is... strange, after all," he said, giving James a sideways glance. "All churiphims have a limit to the power they call upon. It takes an extreme amount of will to keep their minds disciplined. They must control their emotions or go mad. Churiphim believe that there exist elemental dimensions. Each churiphim has an affinity to one of the elements and thus can call upon it for strength against the Lilins. When their limits are pushed, a churiphim will take on the features of one of the denizens of these dimensions, and it will try to take over. Leonette's features were taking on those of a Fire Elemental and thus reaching her limit, becoming an Elemental herself and possibly killing us all."

"And I was standing right next to her during all this? Someone could have at least warned me," Nathaniel said.

"Most churiphim know their limits. I have not heard of many who have surpassed theirs. There is usually only forty churiphim at one time, each one ranked according to their limit and power declared by the pendant they wear."

Raven stared down at the medallion around Leonette's neck reading the Roman numerals. "She is the weakest. She is the fortieth ranked churiphim."

Father Alrick nodded. "Judith is ranked first and commands all other churiphim. She has unlocked the keys of King Solomon, thus positioning her as one of the most powerful and dangerous members of the Order."

"All witchcraft, it is the Devil's realm," Samuel hissed.

"Speak what you will of the churiphim, it is because of their help we are able to defeat true Lilins. They have been part of the Order of the Sons of Light since its creation. The hunters of the new world are not accustomed to the old ways and fear what they do not understand."

"I do not fear neither witch nor demon." Samuel glared at Raven, shooting invisible daggers at her. "Witches, churiphim, all are perverted beings, a mockery against God, created only by our misguided paths because of men who are too weak in faith, who believe God will not give them the power to stand against the Devil's minions. You cannot defeat demons by creating more demons."

"You forget yourself, Samuel. It is not our place to question the Order," Wyman reminded.

"I am a hunter, a protector of humanity. I have the right to question." He turned toward Raven and aimed his crossbow. "To kill these vile, grotesque things that feed on our families. On our blood."

"Samuel, restrain yourself." James stepped in front of Raven. Peter and Tabitha started crying. Lydia was holding on to them behind a nun.

"I will not. My men are dead. My family is dead because of these churiphim and Lilin filth. Step aside, James." He pointed the crossbow at James. "We have a churiphim, so we have no need of a Lilin, do we?"

Nathaniel flanked Samuel and aimed his pistol at his head.

Wyman interjected, "How dare you raise arms against your brethren! Lower your weapon, Samuel."

"Gentlemen, have we not had enough bloodshed?" Father Alrick stepped between James and Samuel. "A house divided amongst itself cannot stand. Please, we are all weary from the fight. Our minds are not right. This is not the will of God."

A long silence pressed on the room, Raven's muscles were like taut wire; she was ready to leap in front of James should Samuel release the stake.

"Nathaniel, lower your pistol," James said. Nathaniel hesitated but did as James ordered.

Samuel snapped back his crossbow. "I will see her burn in the fires of The Pit." He turned and walked off into another chamber.

The fires of The Pit, the words sent images of shrieking vampires into Raven's mind, chilling her nerves.

"When did the Order begin accepting lunatics?" Nathaniel shook his head.

"Father Alrick is right, we should all rest. I doubt ghouls or vampires will be getting through that door and

Leonette probably won't wake until morning," James said.

"And what of the vampire?" Asked Wyman.

Nathaniel rolled his eyes at him. "What? You too? She *saved* us. You think she did that to kill us in our sleep?"

"I do not need to feed, not for a few days, and I won't be killing another human," Raven said. She stared at James. He had lied to her. Made her kill when she hadn't needed to. She stifled a boiling rage.

Father Alrick turned to her. "I have your word you will harm no one?"

"I never have wanted to harm anyone. I never have wanted to kill or to be dragged into this fight. There is nothing I can say to make you believe me, to make you understand that I want things back to normal, but never will be. In the end, it is your decision to let me in and I hope you do." Raven was mentally jaded. "I am scared and lost, and I want to rest."

Alrick registered her words in silence, his expression not cold and his eyes warm. He smiled. "Come in, my child."

R

Dumitru stood stoically within the candlelit cavern, an exhausted Andreea by his side, holding gently to his arm. Elspet finished explaining what had happened, why the wolves he'd controlled were freed from his command, described her skirmish with the raven-haired little vampire who'd fought with the hunters, a traitor to their kind.

"You say you have never seen this young vampire, yet her strength was equal to yours?" He kept his voice low and calm.

"Aye, the wee lass possessed strength and speed only an elder could have," Elspet remarked.

Who was this vampire and when did the Order start using Lilins to hunt others in the new world? One so strong that she'd turned the tide of the battle. Intriguing.

The hunters had survived the night. His small vampire army was down to fifteen and Andreea was too drained for a second assault. The horde of ghouls was also dwindled down to fifty. He needed to replenish the numbers.

He kissed Andreea. "You did excellently."

He turned to the young girl who he had siphoned blood from the night before. She was pinned by three vampires. Her naked body arched at the back as one settled his head between her legs and tasted her. The heels of her feet pressed against her buttocks; the vampire forced her legs open. She tried to fight but may as well have been trying to break free from iron clamps. Her knuckles whitened as she fisted her hands and whimpered.

The other two vampires held her arms stretched out, each one suckling her petite nipples. She tried to hold back moans, her feet twitched as orgasmic spasms rolled over her body. A vampire's lust and power of pleasure were hard to resist.

He had promised her he would not take her virginity, and he had kept his promise, allowing his fledglings to only play with her. Besides blood, sexual energy was another form of sustenance. While blood healed and powered them, sex mended the mind and inner tortures of the curse.

Dumitru had come to know her name. Lucy. He walked Andreea over and both kneeled down by her. "Tomorrow night, we begin our journey north."

Lucy trembled as Dumitru pulled her arm and placed a knife above the old scar from which he had sliced before. Andreea set the silver chalice under Lucy's wrist.

"Leave us." He ordered the three fledglings. They were deep in the lust but obeyed, leaving Dumitru and Andreea with the young girl.

Elspet disrobed and joined them, lying next to the girl opposite Dumitru and Andreea. Lucy huffed out heated breaths, and beads of sweat gleamed her moist body.

"North, so ye mean to let the hunters live?" Elspet said.

"No, they shall follow us. The Assembly of Saints is destroyed, they can ill afford to let us live. We shall travel north replenishing our numbers; there is plenty of death from the war." He slit Lucy's wrist and the stream of blood poured into the chalice. Lucy squinted her eyes shut and turned away, biting her bottom lip.

"Aye, plenty of ghouls to be rising," Elspet said.

"And plenty more sanctuaries the Order has along the way. Each one shall burn."

Andreea took the chalice once filled to the rim and ravenously drank the crimson liquid.

"Please let me go." Lucy's voice was low and weak.

Elspet turned the girl's head with a lone finger on her chin. She licked Lucy's lips and nipped them with her teeth. Lucy whimpered softly. Elspet curled a leg around Lucy's and slid a shapely hip over hers.

Andreea joined Elspet and took one of Lucy's firm breasts, licking the top of her nipple and around the side to the pink areola. The girl's heart fluttered, her face was flushed red and tears streamed to the sides of her cheeks as she breathed hot air.

"Fear not for your life or your virtue. Unless you ask us to give you an eternal death, you shall live as our pet." Dumitru joined the girls and settled between Lucy's legs.

And the night continued as so until the undead slept at the birth of a new morning.

"Thank you, for letting me in," Raven said to Father Alrick, who was studying the runes etched into the walls of a smaller chamber.

"Raven." He faced her and smiled. "I couldn't leave a child to the wolves. Unbecoming of a Godly man."

"I suppose." Raven dropped her head to stare at the ground.

Alrick walked over and placed both hands on each of her shoulders. "Thank you, you saved us out there and we all should be grateful for that."

"I do not believe many agree with you. Samuel especially, and most everyone fears me, believes I will kill them in their sleep."

"Are you concerned about what they think?"

"Well... yes."

"Oh my." He lifted his hands off her shoulders, walked over, and sat down on a stone chair in the corner of the chamber. He patted the boulder beside him for her to join.

She did so. Alrick showed no signs of fear or tension, perfectly at ease being alone with her. Coming to him for questions didn't seem such a mistake after all.

"Do you think people's opinion of you is who you are?" Alrick asked.

"Not necessarily."

"You have doubts?"

"I am not the demon they fear."

"That's good," He smiled. "I believe we wouldn't be sitting here talking if you were. We would probably be dead or in Dumitru's army."

"Why are you not afraid of me?"

"Is there a reason I should be?"

Raven shrugged, staring at the ground again. "Father Alrick, why did God do this to me?"

Alrick contemplated awhile. "I was never one to believe that God gives us tests, for a special few perhaps, but not all."

"I do not understand," Raven mumbled.

"I don't believe He forces the bad of the world on us."

Raven glanced from the corner of her eyes at him.

"Then what would you say happened to me?"

"People mostly look toward God for strength, help, and guidance. They come to rely on that foundation and belief that He will protect them against all things evil." He shook his head. "The reality is, this is the mundane world; the world of the flesh and the realm of the Devil, the realm of human influence. Freewill is our greatest gift and when the world comes crashing in around us, it is our choice to bow down to the Devil or fight on. God is ever reaching out to us, but on the other side, so is Lucifer."

"I do not know. I am angry."

Alrick leaned in and captured Raven's gaze with his pale blue eyes. "God did not do this to you, Raven. He kept the curse at bay and saved your humanity. Are you going to let this curse consume you, or will you fight on, climb that wall and keep living? I hope you choose to keep living."

The sting of a lump formed in her throat. "I hate the Devil."

Alrick chuckled, "Rightly so."

"Raven, will you tell us a story?" Tabitha peeked around the chamber door, gaining both Alrick and Raven's attention.

"Looks like you're needed," Alrick stood.

Raven had more questions, but the look on Tabitha's big round eyes pushed them away. "Of course." Raven walked over and held one of little Tabitha's hands, a smile revealing a missing tooth.

"I want to hear the one about the princess." She clutched Raven's wrist with her other hand and pulled her along.

Raven looked back at Alrick as Tabitha led the way. "Thank you, Father Alrick, for the talk."

"Anytime. You can always come to me if you need to talk."

He waved at little Tabitha as she tugged Raven away.

CHAPTER 12

After Raven had put the children to bed, she confronted James about his lies, telling her she needed to kill in order to feed. He simply replied, "It had to be done," which of course made her snap at him, gaining the attention of the other hunters.

She let the matter go; making herself look like a crazed vampire wasn't the best idea. James promised her they would talk but she didn't expect it, and he most likely would be gone for the better part of the day.

Raven sat against one of the chamber columns and stared at the sleeping churiphim whose skin had returned to its normal tint. Glossy, black tendrils of hair covered half of her face. She was beautiful. Raven herself would never grow old. She would always be stuck in a child's body, unlike Leonette's, so wonderfully sculpted. It reminded her of the large paintings her father had made. She would never know what it would be like to age, to have a woman's body like the ones her father had captured in his portraits.

James stood at the far back of the chamber, deep in conversation with Wyman. They'd planned to go back to the fort as soon as the sun was up and left early that morning, taking Father Alrick and a dozen men with them.

Samuel stayed behind, lurking in the shadows of the chamber, glowering at Raven every so often with his steel-cold eyes. Thankfully, Nathaniel stayed with her. While he could be annoying, she welcomed a familiar face and there were many strangers, their eyes abundant with the burden of grief and fear.

The whispers continued from hunters and nuns. Their apprehension of staying in a closed chamber with a Lilin had them edgy with weapons ready. The nuns gave nervous looks each time Lydia walked over to Raven, whom they watched like a hawk. No doubt, they thought she had put some Lilin charm over the children.

Unable to take mounting pressure from the many cold stares, Raven explored the rest of the chambers. There were many smaller rooms linked together by arched earthways. Intricate runes were carved on the sides of each with flourishes forming beautifully intertwined patterns. She could feel strange warmth ever so slightly prickling her skin as she traced her fingertips over the symbols.

She found a small chamber lit by a lone torch. A round stone slab stood in the middle with smaller ones encircling it. The orange glimmer of the torch flames danced on the glossy surface of each. She sat down on one of the smaller stones to inspect more of the strange runes carved into the top of each table. Its smooth texture was cool to the touch and the heavy scent of earth was strong in the small area, giving her a feeling of aged existence.

Away from the others, she could feel the heavy press of loneliness fold over her. The talk with Alrick had helped. Nevertheless, what was she to do now? How could she live like this?

The realization was like a sudden punch that snatched her breath away. Her parents were dead, her brothers, dead. She'd derived strength to press through her tribulations because, she had told herself, she needed to get home. She needed to find her family, but in truth, it was denial. She had seen it with her eyes—her father's face frozen in horror as the demon ripped out his heart. Her mother's lifeless body on the floor and her brothers' screams echoing in her head.

Red tears splattered on the stone slab. She wrapped her arms over her belly and crumpled over. Her body heaved and convulsed as she burst into sobs.

Who would be there for her now? Who would take care of her? She was alone. James would probably leave her to fend for herself once he'd killed Dumitru.

Nathaniel rushed to her side, "Raven, what's wrong?"

She looked up at him trying to control her heaving, "They are all dead."

"Who's dead?" Nathaniel tensed, as he did a quick scan of the chamber trying to figure out what she was talking about. Perhaps thinking she had lost control and killed. He spun again.

"My parents, my brothers," Raven said.

He relaxed, understanding.

"I have no one." She sank her head onto her knees.

"I... I'm... sorry." He placed a stiff hand on her back. She sensed his hesitation.

"What am I to do?" She looked back up at him. He was staring at her. His lips twitched as if to say something. She could see he was searching for words.

"You don't care. I am nothing but a *demon* to you."

"Don't think that you have me all figured out. I can put up a pretty good act you know," he replied.

Raven straightened up. "It is true, is it not? Relief was probably in everyone's mind when they believed I was dead."

He sighed. "I wanted to go back, you know. I tried." He let his arm loosen and she could feel the press of his hand relax on her back. He sat down next to her on the stone chair.

"Then you were the only one," she said. A faint sense of ease lifted her spirit, knowing that someone cared for her. Her lips twitched a quick smile as she tried to wipe some of the tears off. She succeeded in smearing her face in red.

"No. James cared, though he won't admit it." He mopped her face with part of his tunic.

"You're going to dirty your clothes."

"I have enough blood from the battle, no one will notice," he smiled. "Though it would probably help if you stopped the crying. We have appearances to keep. What would people think, seeing a demon child cry?" He gave her a gentle swipe on the nose when he'd finished wiping.

Raven nudged him with her shoulder. "I am not a demon child."

"You have to admit, it has to be a little fun, throwing things by thinking about it, controlling wolves, running faster than a horse."

Raven stared at the floor, silent. Nathaniel nudged her back. "Admit it."

She smiled. "Well, maybe a little."

"Ah, I knew it, you are a demon child."

"Oh, be quiet." Raven shoved him off the seat. He held his hands up in surrender as he climbed back. She smoothed the folds of her tunic quietly.

Nathaniel stood watching her. "Well, let's have it, what are you worried about?"

She wasn't quite sure how to respond. Nathaniel was no one she'd had good and deep conversation with, but he looked genuinely interested in what she had to say. She wanted someone to listen, and all her worries began to spill from her.

"I feel angry, and alone." She studied him; he angled himself toward her indicating for her to continue. For the better part of the morning, Raven told her story, her fears and wants. She paused every now and then to hold back lingering tears and Nathaniel quietly waited for her to continue. He nodded and smiled at different points to assure her he understood her every word.

It was as though a tight knot in her chest had loosened, to have someone that would give this much time to her, to be there for her, listening quietly. When she was done, he smiled at her and to her surprise, came in for a hug. The last of her tears escaped. He cared. She felt safe with him, secure.

"You're not alone," he said, sitting back to face her. "I'm going to be here for a while, and James, he won't say it, but he is here for you too."

"He lied to me." Raven crossed her arms. "He said I had to kill to feed, and it was not true. Sometimes I think he sees me as a dog to be trained and used."

"James probably had a reason, he's blunt with everyone. Even if it's not something they want to hear." Nathaniel straightened his back as he stood. "When I told him you were left behind, his face went pale. Trust me; he cares."

"For me or for the loss of all he trained me for?" Raven kicked at the dirt. "I can see why James would pale at losing his one chance at catching his son's killer. I have come to understand him. He will do anything to further his goals. It is why he both saved and cursed me to Hell. A young fledgling he could easily sway and mold as his weapon."

"And he misunderstood your thinking, your ability to understand and master things. But Raven, tell me. If the tables turned, would you do any different if you had a chance to find your family's murderer?"

"Yes, I would ask before damning someone to Hell." *But he had asked me, hadn't he?* "I understand James, but when his search is over, will he protect me against the Order? Is he going to stay with me throughout my long years? When everyone I know is dead and gone and only the Order remains, what will I do?" That fear bore into her heart. The long years ahead, alone, watching people she would come to care about die.

"Learn all you can from James, from the Order. Hunt the one who destroyed your life; all our lives have been shattered by these vampires. You're the unique light born out of that darkness, Raven. You didn't change. You kept your humanity. Don't you see how rare a thing that is? You are special. Gain the knowledge you need, so that when the time comes you will be ready."

"Ready for what?" She looked up at him.

"For everything the world throws at you," Nathaniel smiled.

She contemplated in silence. Nathaniel was looking at her. "Thank you for listening."

"I know how painful it is to lose someone you love, to be left alone." He was spinning a thin silver bracelet around his wrist. His stare was distant. For the first time since she had known him, she came to see him in a new light. She had not paid much attention to his features, his smooth cheekbones, and strong chiseled jaw. Though he was around seventeen, his lean yet muscular frame gave him a much older look and only his boyish face gave him away.

A rustling and muddle of voices broke the silence. Samuel was shouting at someone. Nathaniel curled his brows. "What trouble is he stirring this time?"

"Whatever it is, he sounds angry," Raven said.

"I don't think that man is ever not angry." He held a hand out to her, which she took, and stood.

They made their way through the chambers, arriving at the main room to find Samuel and his men standing armed with their hand crossbows, each aiming at the churiphim. While Samuel's face was flush red with anger, Leonette's was stoic. Her thin lips were pressed together, but the rest of her face was smooth, with not a single crease to give away a hint of emotion. When Raven focused on her eyes, if vampires could have chills, she would have them now. Leonette's eyes were tinted silver and focused on Samuel. Raven could see the hidden fire locked behind those orbs. She could sense an inner power, a celestial power. Leonette shifted her gaze to meet Raven's. Unnerved, Raven looked away toward Samuel.

"You have no authority over me, witch!" Samuel shouted.

"I am the Order's weapon, charged with the authority to punish those who go against the high council, and thus God himself," Leonette said.

"I have done no such thing. Stand down before I send you to meet your true maker." Samuel spat at Leonette's feet.

"To threaten The Order's churiphim is to do so by pain of death." Leonette looked into each of the hunter's eyes, each holding a crossbow to her. "And all who conspire with the perpetrator shall follow the same fate."

The hunters tensed, a few looked to Samuel who was glaring at Leonette.

"That man sure can stir trouble," Nathaniel said, glancing at Raven. She looked around the chamber, most of the other hunters and nuns stood at the far end intently gazing at the churiphim and Samuel. Lydia was clutching her younger sister and brother, hiding behind two nuns.

"I wonder what this is about," Raven said.

Leonette took two steps toward Samuel and he adjusted his crossbow to her.

"One more step and you shall have a stake through your vile heart," Samuel warned.

She didn't seem threatened. She took a step and Samuel fired along with his dozen men. Leonette grabbed her cloak, flinging it in an arch in front of her. Every single stake flying at her pierced into the fabric and was held dangling there. Samuel's eyes widened.

"Witchcraft. Kill her," he ordered.

His men pulled out Machairas and rushed Leonette. Raven felt the heat before the blue flames appeared from the wall of fire that exploded in front of the churiphim. The hunters fell back, trying to scurry away from the flames snapping at them. Samuel was holding a hand to his eyes; he was blinded by the burst of light. Leonette walked through the blue flames unharmed and wrapped her fingers around Samuel's throat. She lifted one of her swords from her sheath, Nathaniel shot toward her.

"Leonette, what are you doing?" Nathaniel clutched her arm to keep her from swinging down on Samuel.

"Remove your hands from me." She lifted Samuel off the ground; he was clawing at her hand, trying to free himself from her grip.

Three of his men, back on their feet, rushed to help him. Leonette whipped her arm, flinging Nathaniel into them, and crashing them against the wall.

"Stop her, Raven!" Nathaniel yelled.

How could he possibly be asking her to stop Leonette? Though Raven was a Lilin, she wasn't thrilled at the idea of fighting someone who had the ability to wield fire—one of the main weapons used to kill her kind.

Leonette slammed Samuel on the ground and lifted her sword.

"Raven!" Nathaniel shouted.

Raven clenched her jaw and as Leonette swung her sword down, she sped over and stopped the churiphim's deathblow. Summoning her strength, she shoved Leonette off Samuel.

The hunters that were standing back joined the fight, but unfortunately, were aiming their crossbows at Raven.

Leonette unsheathed her other sword and bid flames wrapping around the two-edged blades she now held.

"Nathaniel," Raven called, as she backed away from the menacing figure.

Nathaniel rushed to her side holding a crossbow toward the hunters. "Maybe this wasn't the best idea."

Raven glared at him.

Samuel's men surrounded Leonette with their crossbows and Machairas ready. Samuel was on his feet, his teeth clenched and seething, his rabid eyes focused on the witch.

"I haven't the dimmest idea what is going on, but I think it would be better to settle this without blood being spilled," Nathaniel said.

"Blood shall be spilled, and it shall be the witch's," Samuel replied, "and if you care not to join her, I suggest you shut up, boy."

Raven could see the shadow of madness in his eyes. *How could someone like him be allowed to join The Order?*

"You stand at the side of a demon and follow a sorceress who has bewitched all of you," Samuel bellowed as he flung his arm wide, pointing a finger at everyone in the chamber. "The Lilin and the witch must die."

"The Lilin shall be dealt with upon completion of your punishment," Leonette cut in. "You are ruled by your emotions and have become unsound, placing your brethren's lives at risk. You have attacked a churiphim of The Order of the Sons of Light, thus attacking The Order and God himself." She gazed over Samuel's men. "You commanded your men to attack a churiphim condemning them to death in the laws set forth by The Order. Command your men to withdraw their weapons."

"I don't follow witches. I'll rip your tongue out and silence your mindless rubbish." Samuel aimed his pistol at Leonette. She looked at the hunters who surrounded Raven and Nathaniel and signaled them. Half turned their crossbows on Samuel's men.

"What is this?" Samuel said, taken by surprise.

Raven and Nathaniel stood in the center of the chamber, in the line of fire of both groups and Leonette.

The large stone that closed the entrance to the chamber rumbled open. Raven was relieved to see James, along with Wyman and Father Alrick, each one coming to a halt as they stepped into the chamber. A frozen look of confusion painted across their faces.

CHAPTER 13

Though she didn't like him, with Wyman back, Raven hoped he and Father Alrick would calm the situation before anyone was killed. The other dozen men that had gone with James that morning lurched to a stop at the entrance.

"What in God's name is going on?" Wyman demanded.

Father Alrick stepped forward in front of James and Wyman, his gaze falling on the churiphim. "Leonette, is this your doing?"

"Laws have been violated. Punishment will be carried out." Leonette said, turning to face Alrick.

"What laws?" Alrick asked.

"This man attacked me and as well threatened my life. His mind is clouded by emotions." Leonette didn't betray a hint of anger in her voice.

Raven had traveled with her father to the city many times and had learned how to read people by their body language. Even when people were smiling and conversing with her father, their body language and facial twitches betrayed their true sensitivities. People would fold their arms over their chest, or unknowingly pointed their feet to a door when they wanted to leave. Raven could always read a person's body language, but with Leonette, it was like looking at a statue.

"The laws of the old world are not as predominant here, Leonette. You have been here barely two weeks; you must be lenient with Samuel," Alrick said.

Samuel shot a hot glare at Alrick. "Lenient? She is a *witch*. How am *I* the one she needs to be lenient with?"

Father Alrick held his wrinkled hand out. "Samuel please, you are not accustomed to the laws of the old world, I am trying to save your life."

"Save my life?" Samuel growled.

"Shut up, Samuel!" Wyman ordered.

"Leonette, you cannot punish this man for disobeying laws he is not familiar with. Stop this at once. We have an army of undead after us; we can ill afford to fight amongst ourselves."

"As you command." Leonette faced Alrick and as quickly as the blue wall of flames had appeared, it vanished along with the blue fire that whirled around her swords. "I am under your charge and must obey your authority, but as a churiphim of the Order, should Samuel attack or try to kill me, I shall take his life."

She turned her back to Samuel and nodded at the hunters aiming their crossbows at him; they lowered them. Samuel's face flushed red and his eyes gleamed with rage.

"Lower your weapons, all of you," Wyman commanded Samuel's men. His tone left no room for argument. "That includes you, Samuel."

"We need to kill her and the Lilin. Have you all gone mad?" Samuel's eyes were wild. He pointed his crossbow to Leonette's back.

"If you do not withdraw your weapon, I'll strip you of your rank and have you locked in chains."

Samuel snapped his head to glare at Wyman. "You have not the authority."

"But I do," Father Alrick cut in. "Leonette is correct; you have lost yourself to your emotions. Samuel, do as Wyman ordered, or I shall strip you of your command."

James held his hand crossbow, ready to use. In the lasting silence, Raven could hear the racing heartbeats of the hunters. Samuel snapped his weapon up.

"Bewitched, all of you," he hissed. "You will all see, you will know the error of your ways. It is I that follow the ways of God, while you follow witches and demons. God will show no remorse for your betrayal."

He turned and pointed his crossbow at Raven. She tensed; certain he would pull the trigger. "And you, you will burn in The Pit, if I have to drag you there myself. You will feel the fires of repentance." Seeing the madness in his eyes, she took a step back. "I will hear you scream for mercy and forgiveness."

"Enough!" James snapped. "You've babbled long enough; we have the army of the dead to deal with, not your deluded mind."

Samuel bared and clenched his teeth. With a sneer, he turned and left into one of the other smaller chambers, muttering to himself. Everyone relaxed when the madman was gone.

"The Order needs to start filtering their people; the man is a lunatic," Nathanial said.

"The man has saved many and has lost his wife in doing so, this matter is dropped. I will hear nothing more of it." Wyman looked at the nuns huddling at the back of the chamber. "Get everyone ready; we're leaving."

Leonette stepped forward in front of Father Alrick. "The matter is not dropped. The Lilin, she must be destroyed."

Raven went stiff with fright when the churiphim's gaze fell on her. Why did Leonette want to destroy her? This was Nathaniel's fault, if he hadn't made her push the churiphim off Samuel, she wouldn't have to be staring into the chilling gold eyes focused on her.

"Now, hold on." Nathaniel stepped up to her. James grabbed his shoulder to hold him back.

"She works with The Order, I've trained her," James said.

"The Lilin should have been brought before the High Council. The Council decides if she is to aid us, and she must be bound in the chains of command. You have done neither with her."

"And how the hell was I supposed to do that? There is no council here."

"Not my concern." Leonette unsheathed her sword and fixed her steely eyes on Raven.

Raven stepped back against the wall. She had got used to fighting vampires and ghouls, but a churiphim's sole purpose was to fight vampires.

James stepped in front of Leonette, blocking her path to Raven. "I don't know how things are run or what the laws in the old world are. The Order is nonexistent here. You're coming into our battlefield, our homeland and trying to enforce your system upon us. The Order never sent help when the Lilin plague kept growing and slaughtering our families. Raven is *our* weapon. We'll use her to track the other monstrosities. With her, we gain an advantage. You will not be laying a finger on her."

"She will be insignificant when the other churiphim arrive."

With a scowl, Wyman turned to Father Alrick. "Others? There are more of them coming?"

Father Alrick's brow furrowed. "I wasn't aware of this."

"When they arrive, my kind shall track the vampires and hunt them all down. The council has honored your request for help. They sent us," Leonette finished.

Father Alrick stepped up to Leonette and stared her in the eyes. "Why did you not inform me? As the high cleric of this region, I should have been told."

"Your charge shall be taken by Mena; she shall lead the hunts."

A surprised look fell over Father Alrick. "Mena is coming here?"

"Who is Mena?" Nathaniel cut in.

"Second in command of the churiphim, student of Judith," Leonette replied.

One churiphim trying to kill her was frightening enough, but a group of them, and the second in command at that— If Leonette was the weakest of the churiphim, Raven couldn't even imagine the power the leaders could possess.

Leonette stepped to James's side and focused on Raven.

"Then we will bring Raven before your leader," James said.

"The churiphim do not speak for the Council. We only do as commanded." Leonette pulled her other sword out.

James gripped her arm. "Then we use Raven until they get here."

"Release my arm."

Nathaniel pulled out his Machaira. "You're not touching her. You'll have to get past me."

"Back down, you fool, she killed scores of the undead. What makes you think you would pose any threat?" Wyman placed a hand on James' shoulder. "She does make a point James. If more of Leonette's kind are coming, we have no need of the Lilin."

"Of course you would agree with her, as long as it means killing a vampire." James shoved Wyman's hand off.

"Raven saved us. If it wasn't for her, we would be dead. You think Leonette would have been able to keep the vampires at bay? No. Not by herself." Nathaniel walked in front of Raven, shielding her from the witch.

Leonette stared down at James' hand clamped on her arm. "If you do not release me, I shall make you."

"That is enough from all of you." Father Alrick had taken on a strong stern voice. "When is Mena to arrive?"

"Within three months," Leonette replied.

"Until then, we are outnumbered. You cannot defend us by yourself, especially now that we know Dumitru has an older Lilin with him. They travel north. No doubt they will be looking to replenish their numbers. We must follow in order to stop them, and we will need Raven and yourself to do so. Mena may take my charge when she arrives but until that time, I am the law and speak for the Council and by that authority, I command you to sheath your weapons." Alrick turned to James and Nathaniel. "Everyone."

Father Alrick's face had taken on such a rigid look that Raven had to wonder if it was the same old man she had met. James released Leonette and Nathaniel lowered his Machaira. Leonette was staring at Raven. All went silent, Raven could hear every drumming heartbeat in the chamber; James' was racing.

Raven felt she would crack under the tension but Leonette turned to face Father Alrick. "As you command." She returned her sword. "But if we are to go after the Lilins, we shall put the nuns and children in danger."

Raven's muscles felt like taut wire unwound. Her claws had dug into the hard rock behind her. She pried them loose and folded her arms, falling against the wall. She crunched her knees against her chest. Nathaniel came and sat next to her.

"Are you good?"

Raven pushed out a breath. "Never ask me to get in the middle of something like that again."

CHAPTER 14

There was only an hour left of sunlight and the nuns had left, taking Lydia and her siblings. Alrick sent the main body of hunters along to protect them, while Wyman and James would lead a small group after the Lilins. Samuel was included in the group. Raven and Nathaniel protested to James, but it was out of his control. Father Alrick had already decided he would be part of the tracking party.

Wyman ordered the hunters to lead the nuns southeast toward another of The Order's sanctuaries and away from the threat. The plan was that the best and most skilled of the hunters would track the vampires down. A small party would be easier to hide and avoid detection rather than a large group.

A lone messenger rode to the sanctuaries at the east in hopes of gathering more hunters to their aid.

Raven could already imagine Samuel's eyes bearing down on her with his icy stare, and there was the churiphim. Raven would not soon forget the gold tint Leonette's eyes had taken when she was intent on destroying her. Raven couldn't foresee any relief from an extremely taxing journey.

As soon as the sun had set, with much protest from the other men, Raven could safely go outside and the group started their journey. James brought two horses that survived the attack and Raven's carriage was left untouched at the fort. Unfortunately, everyone else would be on foot and Raven didn't like that one bit. *Why should the vampire have a carriage while hunters are forced to walk?*

By midnight, Raven had caught the slight scent of dead flesh. She led the group to a cave hidden deep in the forest. James and Wyman had their Machairas ready and Leonette's eyes took on their menacing glow.

"Do we intend to simply walk in and take on the army?" Alrick asked.

"No, the Lilins are long gone," James said," they must have set out the same time we did."

"Considering they travel as swiftly as if we were riding horses, they will be gaining distance on us." Alrick stared at the dots of stars that broke through the web of leaves.

Leonette walked to the mouth of the cave and chanted. A faint gold glow outlined numerous footprints. "They do not keep the ghouls with them, but they are moving north, as we assumed."

Raven and Nathanial both looked at the churiphim in awe. The bemused look on their faces was swept away by the sudden thunder of musket fire that grabbed everyone's attention. Raven couldn't smell the scent of human flesh. The battle was a distance away.

"The Devil means to grow his army of ghouls," Samuel growled.

"Of course, he makes way into the heart of the war. Plenty of ghouls to raise for his army of the dead," Wyman said.

James followed the trail of footprints, studying it. "Father Alrick, how many of the Order's sanctuaries are to the east of us?"

"There are at least a dozen up to Albany."

"Then I suggest we increase our pace; the tracks lead North East."

In the dark, Raven could see Father Alrick's face pale. The shock fell over the rest of the group. "Dumitru intends to attack each sanctuary, slaughtering everyone as he did at the fort," Alrick whispered. "Those sanctuaries not only house hunters, but women and children, orphans."

"Then, Father, we have better stop the demon before he carries out his plan." Wyman followed behind James.

James stopped for a moment and looked back at Raven. His eyes betrayed something more than a simple look to see if she followed. There was a concern and not for the mission. *What was James hiding from her now?*

R

There was not a sound as Dumitru maneuvered swiftly around the foliage of the forest like some dark phantom. Elspet and Andreea followed close behind, along with the rest of the small army of vampires. Dumitru meant to attack one of the Order's sanctuaries the next night and wanted to be as near to it as possible before sunrise. No doubt the surviving hunters were already hot on their heels, but without horses, there was no possibility for them to keep up.

With as much strength as Andreea would have to exert to have the ghouls follow, it was best to leave them. Though if the decision was based on her well-being or simply because it would slow their pace due to ghouls moving extremely slow, Andreea was left to wonder. No doubt Dumitru cared for her, but he was a decisive strategist first before a lover, and as much as she wished she were the first priority in his thoughts, over the years she'd learned not to press him.

Andreea could not ease her mind. Dumitru had crossed a line with his actions. Elspet warned him ripples would be made, powerful hunters called churiphim would come after them. *Why was he so focused, so bent on vengeance and dominance?* She loved him so much and feared so much for his safety and hers.

Andreea couldn't imagine losing him, if things should get desperate, she would do everything in her power to protect him.

There were at least a couple of hours left of the night when they arrived at the outskirts of the sanctuary. Dumitru had used his power over the creatures of the forest to search out another cave, unfortunately to no avail. They would have to dig their beds for the night. Dumitru and Elspet had grown immune to the Sun's light. She would stay awake to guard the group.

Dumitru sent Lucy further north with two fledgling vampires. He owned a large plantation and the fledglings would take her there safely upon which he had given them orders to give her new clothing and no harm was to come to her.

After much of the group had dug their beds, Andreea perched herself on a fat entwined limb of a tree. She was transfixed on the small sanctuary hidden by thick log walls, the point of a church roof poking out from the middle as if trying to pierce the night sky. By tomorrow night, the sanctuary would be no more.

She noticed Elspet sitting next to her, not sure how long she had been there.

"What be bothering ye? Since the start of our travel ye been in a silent mood," Elspet asked, looking at her with one brow lifted.

Andreea shrugged. "What do you think? Dumitru. I never thought the day would come that we declare war on the Order of Light. He has been talking about it for so long, but now that it's happening," she clenched her fists. "I'm scared."

"And rightly so; war be a scary thing." Elspet's words weren't exactly what Andreea was hoping to hear. "Dumitru is one of the finest strategists I have met. If any could see this war won, tis him."

"I wish I had your strength, Elspet. You and Dumitru don't fear anything."

"Dinnae think we are void of fear, we hide it verra weel," Elspet smiled. "I have seen many wars, all be filled with dread and fear, chaos and pain. Each one, I survived because I learned to control and use my fear for tis nae always necessarily our enemy, but is ever a battle for us to contain."

How many battles had Elspet seen? Though she looked every bit her eighteen years, she had been around as long as Dumitru. Sometimes, the way she spoke of things, it was if she had been around for many more years than she let on. Elspet carried with her a sense of strength and knowledge that was on par with Dumitru's, if not greater. It gave Andreea a sense of safety and assurance.

"The dawn is upon us, ye better be taking shelter," Elspet patted Andreea on the shoulder. "Dinnae worry, we'll keep ye safe."

Andreea nodded and gave Elspet a strong hug before heading off.

R

Dumitru stood at the edge where the forest ended, opening into a wide expanse of flat grassy land. He was motionless like a statue bathed in the yellow morning sunlight. The sounds of roosters crowing resonated through the trees and the sweet smell of human blood filled the cool air. The sanctuary sat on the lush green land, its walls out of place in the beautiful surroundings. After tonight, Dumitru planned to leave a different view for the hunters that pursued him.

"Ye have the look of the Devil himself scheming of the night slaughter." Elspet moved next to him, her eyes penetrating his.

"The Devil is who these humans will see tonight as I rip their entrails out and feed upon them."

Elspet raised an eyebrow. "A bit over-dramatic, are we?"

"Will you be up to the task tonight?"

"The hunters and the little churiphim shall be upon us by midnight, I can hear their heartbeats like whispers in the air."

Dumitru turned a curious eye to her. "How is it that you haven't ceased to surprise me with your abilities?"

"A girl has to hae her secrets."

"The hunters, I heard them call you a true Lilin. What did they mean by that?"

"Ye have other worries, dinnae waste ye energy on futile efforts."

"Futile? Why should they be futile? Why put barriers against me Elspet? We fight for our survival, yet here you hide your abilities from me. Abilities that can possibly give us an advantage."

"Aye lad, I stand with ye, but the secrets I keep, I dinnae hide them from ye. Do ye think that The Order be the only one with a watchful eye upon us, especially now?"

"What do you mean? Who else besides The Order would we have to war with us?"

"Ye never ventured and explored much of the old world. The elders would never contact the children of Dracula."

"Elders? More of the firstborn to Dracula?"

"No," Elspet giggled and turned to leave. "I'm going to check on our sleeping army."

Before Dumitru could ask another question, she was gone. He was left more than a little irritated with her and her half answers. Why was she dodging his questions? Who are these Elders she mentioned? Indeed, Elspet was years older than him. The days he spent studying her had assured him.

The question now was, why was she helping him? Vampires normally did not follow others of lesser power, or younger for that matter. This meant he was being used for her plans, for vampires always had plans.

He would keep careful watch of her. She was not any normal vampire. She could prove to be a threat to his position, though she had shown no intent to challenge him, for leadership at least.

Tepes had mentioned the Lilins to Dumitru, the first true vampires born from Lilith, putting Elspet at anywhere between six thousand and four hundred years of age.

At present, the focus must remain on the strategy at hand. The pieces of the larger picture were falling in place as he'd planned.

CHAPTER 15

A cool breeze of the evening rolled over the blanket of grass that surrounded the sanctuary. It looked like a green ocean of water rolling to the wind. The walls of the sanctuary created long shadows that draped over the swaying grassland. Dumitru and Elspet stood within the darkest shadows created by the trees where the forest ended.

The people in the walls of the sanctuary sensed something amiss. They felt the evil intent emanating, the calm before the storm. The inky dark clouds that Elspet summoned engulfed the last light of the evening, and encircled the setting sun, like the enormous maw of a dragon.

Children ran, seeking shelter inside the soon to be destroyed church.

"Awaken the others. It is time," Dumitru said to Elspet.

Elspet nodded.

R

The storm clouds coiled above Raven and Leonette. Knowing that there was no way they could reach Dumitru in time, James presented the idea for Raven and the churiphim to go on ahead of the group. They needed to reach the sanctuary in time to warn the people of the impending attack. Raven sensed they were near; she could feel an eerie vibe lurking in the air.

The churiphim hadn't said a word since their departure. Her eyes focused ahead, she kept pace with Raven with supernatural speed, and the surrounding was a blur as mixtures of greens and browns flashed by. Churiphim were amazing and frightening.

"I can sense something, the same feeling I felt back at the fort," Raven said.

Leonette nodded and leaped into the trees. Raven came to a stop, watching the witch climb the top of the highest one. She was scanning ahead and found what she was looking for, then leapt down and started her run again. Raven followed after.

"Did you spot the sanctuary?" Raven asked.

Leonette ignored her question, as she had all others through the whole journey. Raven's attempt at befriending the churiphim had been a futile effort. She wasn't sure how much she should press, fearing Leonette may try to slice her head off for bothering so much.

Lightning sliced across the sky, followed by a roaring boom of thunder that shook the ground. The smell of damp earth and rain filled the air. The forest ended and they came upon a roaring fire and crumbled walls. Walls of the sanctuary.

"We are too late." Raven stared at the rubble of wall being devoured by simmering fires.

The churiphim kept going, leaping over the licking flames of the fallen walls. Raven was a little more than hesitant to follow but did so anyway. The hot sting of the flames bit at her skin as she leapt over them.

When Raven landed, Leonette was standing battle ready on the other side, swords in hand, blades glowing with the magical blue fire. Bodies were scattered about, entrails and limbs along with them in bloody pools. Though the sight of it was horrific, Raven felt a tinge of yearning for the sweet blood oozing from the shredded flesh and bone. She shook her head to banish the wicked thoughts.

The church doors were tattered; the bodies of nuns lined the steps. A scream drew Raven's attention; Leonette was already on the move. Raven rushed after her and came in behind at the entrance of the building. An older nun was on the floor, half her throat ripped, a vampire crouching next to her, parts of her flesh hanging out his mouth.

It stood and hissed, making a dash at Leonette. The vampire slashed with his claws. The churiphim ducked under and sliced the demon in half at the torso and immediately beheaded it once its upper half hit the floor.

Two doors were at each side of the nave, where out came more creatures. Six in total advanced toward Raven and Leonette.

"This is hallowed ground. They should not be able to walk here," Leonette said.

"Ay that it was, but nae anymair. I claimed this unhallowed ground for myself." The red-haired vampire Raven had battled with stepped in through the entrance behind them. "They sent ye ahead little churiphim, with the newborn?"

"I shall grant you a quick death if you beg forgiveness from God." Leonette pointed her right sword toward the vampiress. The blue flames came to life, becoming animated, reaching for her.

"Elspet. At least call me name when ye be throwing futile threats. And what be yer name little one?" Elspet swept her gaze to Raven.

Raven looked to Leonette who had her eyes locked on Elspet. The other vampires were circling around them.

Elspet smiled. "Ye have nothing to fear, ye be one of our kind and we look after our awn."

"I'm not your kind, you killed my family, killed these people," Raven hissed.

Elspet laughed. "Child, ye yerself have nae killed? Ye are as much a killer as we. Poor young thing, ye been led astray to be used by The Order who dinnae care if ye live or die. What do ye think they will do with ye once they finished with us?"

Before Raven could respond, Leonette charged forward and was on Elspet in a fraction of a second. The tip of her blade came within an inch of the vampire's throat, but she circled her hand clockwise around Leonette's wrist, deflecting the thrust. With the same fluid movement, she stepped forward, wrapped her arm around the churiphim's neck and sent her flying.

Leonette slammed into the floor by Raven's feet and rolled with the momentum, tumbling next to three vampires.

"Nae much fir conversation that one," Elspet shrugged.

The churiphim was a whirlwind of blades, shredding one of the trio near her which made the others halt their advance. Her eyes had taken that pure gold tint; she was possessed once more by her conviction to kill.

Elspet stepped out, nonchalant, as if nothing were happening. This vampire did not fear the churiphim.

Raven made a running leap for her. Elspet sensed her and spun around snatching her swing. Her grip was intense, and she whipped Raven up and over, slamming her on the ground with a loud thud. Elspet crouched down, keeping her hold.

Raven snarled and swiped at her attacker's face with a free hand. The crimson-haired vampire dodged and grabbed. Now both Raven's arms were seized and Elspet crossed them over each other using Raven's outstretched arm as a bar, then pressed the other down, hyperextending her elbow. Raven let out a screech with her joint at the point of cracking as Elspet pressed harder.

"Ye have great strength and speed I give ye that, but poor fightin' skills," Elspet smiled.

Through the wrenching pain, a scream weaved in from the distance. It was familiar. Focusing was hard; Raven's world swirled, and the moist streak of blood tears escaped her eyes pooling under her lids, the tendons around her elbow were being stretched ready to snap. Raven tried to twist her body using her legs, Elspet sat on top of her, bending her arm. Raven screamed.

"No struggling. I hae questions that need answering." Elspet bared her fangs and licked the points with the tip of her tongue. "It may be a bit unpleasant fir ye." Elspet then crunched down on Raven's wrist with her teeth, both her fangs piercing through flesh and bone, sending a web of burning venom cutting up her arm.

The burning did not paralyze her as before when she was human, but Raven did not dare to move lest her bone crack. Leonette grunted inside the church, fighting the vampires. She probably didn't care to come and save her; Raven was alone against this powerful demon.

There was a scream from the distance again. The pain blurred her mind, playing tricks. Raven knew that shrill. She recalled playing with her brothers, but they were dead. James said they were dead. It couldn't be Matthew.

A second scream. She recognized it as well, was sure of it. *Phillip's?*

It rang clear, Phillip was calling after Matthew, it shot a surge of realization through her. *Her brothers. How?*

Her vision was a red blur, but she turned her head to look, searching in the direction of the screams. There they were, her brothers. They were frantic, they were running. Matthew turned and saw her. He stopped.

"Selah!" He stood for a moment with a look of uncertainty.

Phillip latched on to him, trying to pull him; both were snatched up by their assailant. The vampire lifted them, one in each hand.

The pain didn't matter anymore. The chemical reaction in her brain pumped instantly into her muscles, the snapping of bone and the tearing of her skin was not important, not her elbow popping and bending, only her brain working, judging the distance, and clocking the speed she had used before. She had a fraction of a second to be at the vampire that was baring his fangs down on her brothers, using her now free arm to dig her claws into Elspet who was probably surprised to find herself hurled through the air, crashing into the side of a burning building.

Raven stood using her one good arm and in a blink was behind the vampire who stared at the clawed hand protruding through his chest, holding his heart.

Phillip and Matthew dropped, landing on their backs, faces ashen pale, eyes wide and focused on Raven.

More of the monsters came around the corner of the church. One in particular stood taller than the others, long blond hair pulled back and tied neatly behind. He stood firm, clothes clean and tidy. The group followed behind him. This vampire was the leader, possibly Dumitru.

Next to him was a beautiful vampire girl with dark brown eyes and black coal hair.

Elspet walked out of the crumbles of the building Raven had thrown her through and came to stand by the man.

"This is the young vampire you spoke of?" the man asked.

"Jonas be the one that turned her," Elspet said.

He furrowed his brows, his eyes becoming serious and focused on Raven. "Jonas created her? You know this for certain?"

Elspet wiped a dribble of blood off her lips. "Aye, and she be strong, her blood is invigorating. Look at how her arm heals already."

Raven had not noticed the dwindling of fever-hot pain; indeed, her arm was mending at a rapid pace. She had to adjust her snapped bone, pain wrenching as it was, before it came together deformed.

"Intriguing." The man rubbed his chin, staring at Raven like something to be studied. His eyes were unblinking, and his pupils contracted a dominating trait.

"Dumitru." The girl who stood at his side moved with wicked speed and shoved him.

Leonette leaped through the burning church window, her sword's mark was Dumitru, but the girl took the hit instead.

She screeched as the churiphim's weapon plowed through her gut. Leonette kicked her, sending her rolling in flames.

"Andreea!" Dumitru charged to her, trying to grab the girl with his hands, which he snapped back from the raging flames engulfing her. "Elspet help her!"

Elspet held her hand toward Leonette who was hurled into the air. As Leonette fell, a wall of fire materialized behind the vampires. Leonette was trying to trap them with her powers.

Through the roaring flames, Raven could hear Elspet chanting something. Andreea's flames went out. "Take her away," Elspet commanded. The vampire continued chanting and the wall of fire disappeared shortly after.

Dumitru lifted Andreea into his arms, coils of smoke escaping her burnt flesh. "Kill them and bring me the churiphim's heart!" He burned his stare into Leonette then leaped into the air, and the darkness of the night swallowed them.

The last eight vampires surrounded the women. One looked to be a British Captain. In fact, all of them looked to be British soldiers, or at least used to be. Their garb ripped and stained in the dried crusted blood of their victims, no doubt.

"I claim one of the boys; I want his sweet blood," remarked one of the creatures, his eyes sunken, his skin like cracked leather tight against his bones.

Raven hissed at the advancing demons, hearing the vampire set her aflame with rage. "You will not a lay a finger on my brothers." She concentrated, summoning deep from within her mind the invisible power that sent the four closest demons flying, flesh ripping and bones snapping. They crashed on the ground wailing and grabbing at shattered bones and sliced flesh.

Leonette chanted and stabbed one of her swords into the ground, tracing a fiery circle that formed around Raven's brothers. "Within the circle you are safe, stay," Leonette commanded.

The churiphim bolted toward the remaining four who stood with a look of incomprehension.

"Benton, ye take the little vampire and I'll do away with the churiphim." Elspet said to the vampire. He nodded and pulled his saber then leaped like a cat at Raven.

Raven dived low under the captain's swipe and summoned her unseen force. It burst forth, ripping into Benton's body, shredding his clothing and ripping his saber from his hand. He twirled away from her, slamming and sliding face first into the dirt. He was sturdier than the other vampires. He stood, webs of streaming blood upon his skin. He hissed like fire at her.

Elspet was casually walking toward Leonette, who had already downed two of the remaining vampires, both swords raging with blue flames. Raven didn't have time to look on, as Benton came in swishing with his claws, but he was out-matched. The blood that Gabriel had given Raven coursed through her. She leaped to the side, raking down the side of Benton's neck with her left hand. Blood spewed out, slapping the ground.

She jumped on him and by pure instinct grabbed his throat and ripped off a hand full of flesh. Benton grabbed at the wound as if to stop the burst of blood projecting forth. Unable to bear the gurgling sounds, Raven plunged her clawed hand into the ribs, shattering bone and crushed his heart in her hand. He fell knees first, then body, with a heavy thump.

Leonette finished cutting down the last vampires. Elspet stood but a few feet from her. The four vampires that Raven had sent flying earlier with her power were back up. After seeing the others downed so quickly, including their captain, they made no move to attack.

"Go to Dumitru, see to his safety ye cowards. I'll stay to finish this," Elspet said, her gaze never leaving the churiphim's.

Elspet advanced toward Leonette, a ghoulish grin painted on her face. Leonette squeezed her grip on her swords. Her muscles became taut.

"Ye have not fully recovered ye strength lass. Ye sure tis a fight ye want?" Elspet took two more steps toward Leonette. They stared at each other in silence for some time. Raven could only guess each one was waiting for the other to make a move.

Leonette broke first, swishing her blade at Elspet's mid-section. The vampire twirled, dodging each attack with such grace it looked as if she was dancing. Elspet moved her arms in circle patterns, hooking her bent wrists around Leonette's and locked the churiphim's right arm with her own in a similar fashion as she had done with Raven.

Leonette, however, knew how to escape such a maneuver and leapt into a somersault, swiping with her left sword. Elspet once more blocked it with a slap of her now free hand. Using the momentum, she grabbed Leonette's arm and tossed her over her back, slamming the churiphim supine to the ground, lifting a cloud of dust.

The vampire had both her hands wrapped around Leonette's hand and wrist, making a slight twist that made the churiphim grunt, dropping her sword.

The witch stabbed with her left, making Elspet release her hold to dodge the attack, allowing Leonette to kick her legs up and out to flip back to her feet.

Elspet waved her hand, and the sword Leonette had dropped went flying into the abyss of night. "Dinnae think ye be needing that."

Leonette leaped up with a flying kick, which the vampire turned in a complete circle to avoid, coming to face her opponent in time to slap away a high kick and block another from Leonette's second sword. Elspet wrapped her right hand around Leonette's left arm and under her elbow, lifting her to her tiptoes. She forced her to drop the sword. Leonette shouted in Latin, and her body flushed with the blue fire that had covered her swords.

Elspet let go and thrust away; her hands scorched. "Ye have tricks. I suspect that takes a bit of strength, strength ye have nae recovered."

The flames went out as fast as they had appeared and Leonette's breathing had become labored. Beads of sweat peppered her face. She lunged in at Elspet with a spin and kicked out, aiming at her gut, but Elspet swiftly dodged. They both entered a strange dance of kicks and punches. The fight was not equal; Elspet kept pushing the churiphim back and forced her hands into another lock, then swept her off her feet.

The protective circle that Leonette had summoned for Raven's brothers went out. The vampire was going to kill Leonette. Raven had to act. She mustered that force once more from deep in her mind and concentrated on Elspet.

Thin lesions appeared on the vampire's face, forcing her to let go of the churiphim.

Elspet glared at Raven, who felt an intrusion in her mind. The vampire was mentally assaulting her, a loud chiming blasted in her head, forcing her to her knees. Raven screamed as if to let the pain flood out.

She fell, writhing. "Stop. Please." Raven clenched her head; the chiming was a pulsing white heat throbbing against her temples. Then it was gone.

Elspet stood over her shaking her head. "Ye have been gifted with dark powers, yet ye have not the knowledge to draw on them correctly, lass. Come with me and I can show ye better our ways."

"No, I do not want to know your ways. I am not your kind, you tried to kill my brothers, you killed my father and mother." Raven shot back.

"Was not I lass, the one ye seek is Jonas."

Jonas's image flashed in her memory along with her dead father and mother, the blood pool, her father's crushed heart.

Leonette came in from behind Elspet. The sword she had dropped was back in her hand. The swing would have sent Elspet's head flying, but the vampire turned as Leonette thrust in, catching the churiphim's outstretched arm.

Elspet drove her right hand into Leonette's elbow, snapping it. Raven could feel the break as it echoed off the empty buildings.

Leonette screamed. Elspet twisted the broken arm and plunged the sword into the belly of the churiphim, letting her drop on her back.

"No, leave her alone!" Raven lunged on Elspet's back, trying to rake and bite, but the vampire was amazingly skillful and gripped Raven's fingers in her hands. Elspet crunched them together, sending flames of pain up Raven's arm. Raven felt herself swung over Elspet's shoulder and smashed face first on the ground next to Leonette.

"I can snuff the both of ye like a candle flame." Elspet held Raven down with a hand. Leonette grunted, gripping the hilt of her sword with a trembling hand, fingers white as paper. Raven could see she had no strength to force the sword out.

Raven bled tears from her eyes; she was trembling, the cold edge of terror piercing her heart.

Her brothers were going to be killed by this demon, and she wouldn't be able to stop her. Even with the power she'd been given, she was powerless against Elspet. Of course, she couldn't hope to beat her; she had been here for hundreds of years, a thousand according to the hunters. *How could something like that be defeated? Not even the churiphim could stand against her.*

Matthew and Phillip clutched to each other, curled up in a ball, tears filled their big round eyes.

No, not again, I will not lose them again. I have to fight, have to compel my strength to come, my mind to call upon the power of force.

In one sudden move, she let out every ounce of the gifts she'd gathered and propelled herself up, shooting the invisible force, hitting Elspet and shredding her clothes and skin as she was flung away into the sky.

She vanished into the night as if Raven had dispersed her into the blackness. Raven's legs trembled, the heat of bile rising in her throat, nauseated from the lack of strength. Even vampires suffered certain ailments as humans.

Laughter resonated off the walls of the buildings that shot a jolt of desperation through Raven's core. "Now, that be the way to use the dark powers. There is potential in ye. We shall hae to finish this the next we meet, young vampire."

Raven searched the night sky for the voice but there was no sign of her. She was gone.

She ran over to the churiphim who was, surprisingly, alive and trying to extract the sword from her belly. Raven kneeled next to her.

"The wound is mortal, I cannot treat this," Raven said.

"I do not require treatment; remove the sword." Leonette's voice was weak but held that monotone nature. "Now."

Raven gripped the hilt with both hands and slid the sword out. Leonette grunted through a clamped mouth.

"My wounds will heal, though not as quickly as yours. I need to stop the bleeding, or I will die."

Raven understood, and indeed the gash was already healing, but Leonette would bleed out before it could fully close. Raven ripped a chunk of her tunic, wadded it up, and pressed it against the wound. "Matthew, come hold this."

Matthew and Phillip sat in silence for some time, fear captured in their eyes. "You're one of them," Phillip said.

Raven understood they believed her to be a monster.

"I am not one of them, I am your sister. Please, help me or she will die. I need to set her bone and I need to make a splint."

Uncertainty flashed in their eyes, but Matthew eventually came and pressed down on Leonette's wound, holding the ball of now red-soaked tunic over the gash.

Raven started on her broken arm, adjusting the bone so that it would set properly. Leonette's muscles were taut from the shifting that caused her immense hurt, and eventually, she passed out.

Raven fashioned a stilt from nearby debris and fit it around the arm. She moved on to the gash and her brothers had found a sheet to dress the wound with. When she was satisfied with her work, she laid the churiphim's head on her lap. Her brothers sat across from her and they waited in silence.

CHAPTER 16

"What happened to you?" Phillip asked after a long while of silence. The twins had been giving each other looks and Raven wasn't sure how she would explain everything that had happened to her. The last few of months had been like some horrible dream.

"I was dying. That thing that killed Mother and Father—"

"Vampire," Mathew said.

"Yes, a vampire. He bit me and I would have become one myself."

"You have teeth and claws and you can do things with your mind," Phillip said sharply.

"But, I am not one of them. James stopped it. He stopped the curse from taking my mind and spirit. He showed me how to hunt vampires, so that I could find the one who killed Father and Mother. That is whom I have been with in training, and we meant to warn everyone here, but arrived too late. I never imagined I would see the two of you, I thought you were dead. I didn't think I had anyone left." Raven lifted her gaze from Leonette to the twins. "I've been so alone. You don't understand how awful it has been. Nightmares every night, your screams, Father and Mother—"

"You're not alone, not anymore," Matthew smiled. Phillip had his knees tucked up to his chest, arms wrapped around them. His gaze fell on the ground to avoid looking at her. A squeeze of hurt swelled in Raven's throat.

"How did you come to be here?" Raven asked.

"Your friend James also rescued us. Well, him and the other hunters. They sent us here, said we would be taken care of. They told us about the vampires, wanted us to become hunters when we got older." Matthew pointed to one of the bodies. A priest. "Father Mark. He made us read about the vampires, about their weaknesses. He was nice to us."

"They were training you two to be hunters? James knew you were alive?" Raven felt anger flaring inside her. James had lied to her again. All this time, he'd known her brothers were alive when he had told her otherwise.

Matthew noticed her sudden mood change. "What's wrong?"

"Nothing. James should be here soon."

"He's coming here? Will there be more hunters?"

Raven nodded. They spent the next few hours talking. They talked about their parents, their good times and bad, their journeys the past months. They laughed and cried. Phillip joined in here and there but mostly stayed silent and distant, cold toward Raven. But Raven felt joy in finding her brothers; she wasn't alone anymore and nothing would separate her from them.

Leonette stirred from her sleep, her eyes slowly focusing on Raven.

"Your wound is healed, and your bone mended. We were not sure when you would wake," Raven said, as Leonette sat erect.

Leonette examined her body, unwrapping the dressings and stilt Raven had used to keep her cracked bone in place. "You are skilled," she said in her usual dry and monotone voice. She stood and scanned the area. "You are the only survivors?" she asked the twins.

Matthew grimaced. "They killed all the hunters. The red-haired one could control the weather. Phillip and I were hiding under the basement floor when they attacked. Everything went black. We couldn't see nothin'. The hunters couldn't see. We were all blind."

Leonette swept her gaze over the rubble that used to be the sanctuary. Ravaged bodies were scattered in pools of red. "We must behead each body. They will rise as vampires tomorrow or be summoned as ghouls."

Leonette walked over and picked up her sword from where she had dropped it then moved to the nearest body and with one quick whack, hacked the head off.

"Why?" Matthew asked, turning away. "Raven came back fine, why can't they?"

Leonette said nothing and proceeded with more hacking off heads. Raven scowled, wanting to ask the same question, but then the feeding, the killing, the hot coal pain of turning ran through her mind. Mostly the voices urging her to let the evil of the curse take over and destroy everything she was. The cold emptiness of it had tried to devour her essence.

"They will not come back; they will be something else," Raven said.

"But you're still you," Matthew wrinkled his brows.

Leonette threw a Machaira at Raven's feet. "To let them come back as vampires is to damn them. There is no place before God for Lilins." Leonette bore her gaze on Matthew. "Only damnation. Do you wish to damn these people to Hell?"

"What about my sister? Will she go to Hell?"

"Yes." Leonette left him silent and turned back to continue her business.

Raven too was quiet, replaying those words in her mind. Damnation. Hell. She could no longer enter into the Kingdom of Heaven. She would burn for eternity. James knew this. James knew he would be damning her by letting the curse complete. Fury flamed inside her; she picked up the weapon and unleashed it on the bodies.

As the hours passed, Raven's mind whirled with words, words she would release on James. Questions she would demand he answer. The twins had succumbed to exhaustion and were sleeping soundly huddled in each other's arms.

Leonette stood, arms crossed, staring into the thick dark of night. "Something has happened," she said. "Wake your brothers. We shall head back to look for the others."

She was right. It surely was at least two hours past midnight. James and the others should have arrived by now. Could they have been attacked? Raven's mind stormed with too many possibilities. She woke the twins quickly and soon they were on the march. Concern gnawed at her. Why was she worried? James had lied to her after all. The image of Nathanial popped into her mind; he had been honest with her, listened to her, was there for her when she was alone and she had come to like his company. It was fun when Nathanial was around, compared to James's serious attitude. Nathanial was reason enough to worry.

Raven sensed the dawn nearing and as the teeth of anxiety started nipping at her, the beating of hearts emerged from the forest. The smell of human flesh was familiar.

They came upon the group; Wyman and Nathanial came out from their hiding places of foliage and trees, each with crossbows aimed toward Raven and Leonette's direction. They lowered them once they recognized the women, relief in Nathaniel's eyes and Wyman's, which was strange.

Leonette rushed past Raven toward the others. Something had happened; Raven saw new bruises on Nathanial's face and Wyman's garments were ripped. There had been a battle.

"What happened?" Leonette asked. Raven noticed her voice had taken a different tone. She was agitated. Raven saw what she referred to when James stood, revealing Father Alrick on the ground. His breathing was forced, making him wince.

"We were attacked by that red-haired bitch," Samuel said.

Leonette crouched next to Alrick. Her usual expressionless face showed a nuance of worry. She turned his head, revealing a deep gash where Elspet had bit him on the neck. Blood flowed through his robe. She stood and turned to James. "We must hurry to the easternmost fort. We use the vampire's carriage to carry him and quickly."

The group gave her hesitant looks. Wyman said, "What of the sanctuary?"

"He will die and be turned if we do not," she replied. "The Sanctuary is lost."

"Lost? What do you mean lost? What of the people?" Wyman asked.

"Dead, all except Phillip and Matthew here," Raven said, clasping a hand on each twin's shoulder.

Samuel thrust his Machaira, wedging it into a tree. "Only two children from an entire sanctuary? What the hell did we send you there for?"

"So, our little group was going to do better, yet they took out the entire sanctuary. I can see that working out well for us," Nathanial chimed in.

"Shut up boy, I'm done putting up with your cynicism," Samuel sneered.

"I call it truth, or did you miss the fact we barely survived an attack from only one of them?" Nathanial shrugged. "Then again, you are the crazy one here."

"Enough! We head east," Leonette shouted, silencing them.

"Our mission lies north on the heels of Dumitru, that is our command and duty," Wyman said. "Father Alrick is bit at the neck, the curse has spread through his body. We cannot save him, but we can save the people from the same fate before Dumitru reaches the other sanctuaries."

Leonette's face contorted. Father Alrick's eyes fluttered open and he rolled his face to see her better. "It is too late. I won't make a journey east." His words were a whisper.

"We can seek help, keep the curse at bay." Leonette wrapped an arm under Alrick to lift him. "James, come help, my strength is worn."

"No, Leonette," Alrick said sternly. "Would you have me damned to Hell? I have been bitten, there is nothing to do. You are a churiphim, a warrior chosen by God and you must stay true to your convictions. You must head north and stop Dumitru." His voice cracked and he went into a spasm of coughing.

Raven could see the hidden strain of muscles in Leonette's face. She was churning inside, fighting to keep her composure. Father Alrick meant more to her than she had let on.

"I will find this demon. I will find the one who did this." Leonette's eyes took on their silver shade.

Father Alrick smiled. "I know what troubles you, but you are not alone, child. Your father, your mother, they are always with you, and so am I." His voice was gentle again. He placed a hand on Leonette's cheek and smiled.

"I do not know what I should do." A tear escaped her and rolled down Alrick's fingers.

"You'll do your best. You're God's warrior and you will fight for all that is good and just, in this creation of His, and when your work is done, you come join your loved ones who will be waiting. That is what you will do."

With an annoyed glower, Samuel walked over to Wyman. "So, the witch delays us. We should get this done and be moving before the demon bitch sends friends to finish her job."

Wyman snapped a look at him. "Quiet man, have you no respect? We shall be on the move soon enough."

Samuel grumbled something under his breath and stomped away.

Alrick breathed in deeply and then let out a couple of low raspy coughs. "Leonette, you know what must be done, it is time. I feel... cold." Alrick placed his hand to his chest. "Heart, then head." His eyelids slid closed and with his last breath he said, "I love you."

"Grandfather—" Leonette's lips quivered, tears escaped.

Leonette stood and rushed to Raven's carriage, grabbing the reins and pulling the horses over.

"Leonette, stop!" James put a hand on her shoulder; she shoved it away. "He's dead!" he shouted.

"No, we take him to the sanctuary." She kneeled and slid her hands under Alrick and lifted him, her legs still wobbly from the fight. She fell. Everyone watched as she tried again, tears dripping.

She put up one wobbly knee. "Help me. Now." No one moved. Alrick's limbs dangled lifelessly. Leonette's knee gave in and they both fell to the ground. Wyman shook his head at James. Samuel marched out of the trees.

"To hell with this."

He pointed his pistol and put a lead ball through Alrick's head. The blast shredded the night. Everyone jumped. Leonette screamed.

"What the damn hell?" Wyman shouted. Leonette growled a screech and lunged at Samuel. James tackled her as she swung her sword, slicing the side of his tunic.

"Damn witch," Samuel jeered. "The problem is solved; now can we get going?" He marched off.

Wyman cracked Samuel with a right fist, sending him on his rump. "You damn idiot."

"I did what no one else would. Alrick was already dead." He stood and spit blood on the ground. "Get the fuck away from me."

"You ever do something like that again—"

"You'll what?" Both men glared at each other. "To hell with you." Samuel walked off.

Leonette's eyes beaded with tears. James let her loose. She crawled over to the priest, laying her head on his chest.

When the last tears fell, she sat on her heels, silent, staring at her grandfather.

Everyone gave each other silent looks and shrugs. James slumped his shoulders and stepped to her.

He pulled his Machaira. "I have to do this."

"Stay away from him!" Leonette lashed out, her eyes taking a silver hue. "I will do it myself."

The churiphim stood, her fingers white on the hilt of her sword. For a long while, she resembled a statue. Her hands started to tremble; her nose flared. She took in a deep, heavy breath.

Leonette plunged the blade into Alrick's heart and with a final swipe, she severed his head. Slowly she turned to face the hushed group, walked to the center of the cluster and looked at Wyman.

"We head north." Leonette's voice had taken its uniform tone, no emotion, though to Raven's ears, she could hear the undercurrents of pain in her words. She said nothing more and walked north, oblivious to what anyone else was doing.

James glanced at the twins, but did not say a word, and followed after Wyman.

"So, who are they?" Nathaniel asked, nodding toward the twins.

"My brothers," Raven said as she walked off to join the group.

"Brothers?" Nathanial furrowed his brows.

Matthew waved and ushered Phillip forward behind Raven.

CHAPTER 17

Raven escaped the light of the morning sun within her carriage. Phillip and Matthew had joined her inside and slept on one of the small cushioned seats at the side of her bed of earth. Matthew had stayed awake for a while longer after his brother dozed off. They talked until he joined Phillip in slumber.

Raven longed to have a conversation with Phillip but he mostly stayed quiet and remained distant from her. She would give him time. He had been through so much. For some, grieving could take many months. Years. Raven hoped that wouldn't be the case with Phillip.

Her mind was wild with thoughts that fought to keep her awake, which was another annoyance carried over from the human life. Nathanial walked at the side of the cart. Raven had attuned herself to his steps and smell, and could easily find him without the use of sight. James sat in his usual spot at the front. Raven hadn't said a word to him, instead waiting for the right time to unleash her anger. She could no longer play his game; she had a family to look after. Her brothers were alive, and being the eldest, it was now her job to look after them, to protect them, and not let them be pulled into this dangerous world. In fact, she was pretty angry at the whole idea of her brothers being taught to hunt vampires.

The journey that day was an uneventful one. Raven fell asleep sometime in the late afternoon. Phillip and Matthew were walking outside with the group when she awoke. Nathanial was laughing at something Matthew had said, which involved Raven. More than likely some embarrassing account he would use against her. Raven stepped outside before Matthew spilled more secrets she didn't want Nathaniel to know.

"The demon child is awake," Nathanial said, then smirked when Raven stepped out. The stars blanketed the sky. She could feel the ghost of heat left from the day. James was walking with the horses, which Raven was happy about. She didn't want to have to start any conversation with him, not until they were alone. Raven hopped off the carriage and gracefully landed next to Nathanial and shoved him into nearby branches.

"Did I not say to stop calling me that?" Raven arched a brow.

"But you look so cute when I do." There was that smirk of his again, that etched deep dimples on each side of his smile.

"What were you two conversing about?" Raven rustled Matthew's hair.

Matthew pushed her away. "Nothin'."

The smiles that Nathanial and Matthew were giving each other meant completely the opposite. Phillip was also walking, though a few steps behind them. He wasn't paying attention to them; he was walking by simple automation. Matthew joined him and they both jumped on to the carriage, climbing to the top and sitting down to dangle their feet over the side. Matthew was playing with a small silver knife. Phillip was lost in thought, watching the ground.

"He loosened up some, got him to smile at least." Nathaniel had noticed her looking at Phillip.

"He's changed so much. He used to smile all the time. Father would take Matthew into town most days and Phillip and I would have to come up with things to do around the house to keep us occupied. Phillip was the younger brother and I was a girl, so we did not get to go as often. Mother tried to keep me inside. She was always trying to teach me womanly things. Things that would make me a good wife someday."

"I did not care for it. I never wanted to be a wife anyway. Phillip always got me out of the house one way or the other and we would go exploring, playing games. We always had fun. Now he does not want to be around me." Raven forced out a breath.

"Your brothers have been through a lot. Seen things no other ten-year-olds have. Hell, you don't see your parents' hearts ripped out in—" Nathanial looked at Raven. "I'm sorry, didn't mean to bring that up."

"I'm fine. But you are right, I should not be complaining, my parents are gone but at least I have my brothers, and it is my job to look after them." She lowered her voice. She didn't want James or any of the other hunters to hear. "I do not want them trapped in this world of demons. I do not want them to be hunters."

Nathanial's face became serious. "They've seen this world, to become hunters is the only option for them, or join the Order as priests when they are older. Trust me, priests—not the best option; you haven't been bored 'til you've tried a month of that."

"I am going to leave and take them with me. I want you to come with us."

Nathanial stopped walking. "That's impossible, Raven. You can't—" He rubbed his palms against his face. "You shouldn't be saying that."

"Lower your voice." Raven nudged him on. Wyman stared at them a few yards behind. Worry tugged at

Raven. Maybe it hadn't been the wisest choice to tell Nathanial of her idea.

Nathanial continued walking. "Raven, you can't leave; you're a vampire."

"I am a person, not some dog that is kept by a leash," she scowled.

"That is not what I meant." Nathanial tightened his lips. "They're not going to let you leave. The only reason you're alive is because of James. You're able to walk freely because of him. No other vampire could have been given that privilege."

"Privilege?" Raven gaped at him. "It is a privilege for me not to be kept locked up like some animal?"

"No. Stop twisting my words."

Raven felt the heat of anger rising. She had to push it back before she gained the attention of the others. She shouldn't be getting so riled; of course Nathanial wouldn't understand. He had been raised as a hunter, taught to kill vampires and treat them like demons. It wasn't his fault; she shouldn't have asked him to come. After being around him, the one thing about Nathanial that always stood out over any other of his traits was his convictions.

"I am sorry, it was wrong of me to tell you." Raven let out a heavy breath. "I need to be alone." She walked off the trail into the hilly plateau they were currently traveling through. A medley of flowers and grass pressed against her legs as she pushed through the untraveled ground.

Wyman came up to Nathaniel. "What is she doing?"

"Walking off to think of ways to kill us in the night." Nathanial shook his head and followed after Raven, leaving Wyman glowering.

R

Raven had confided in him and he'd completely acted a perfect ass. She had been avoiding James and he had meant to find out why, but instead Raven had trusted to tell him of her plans. Nathanial felt horrible; he was never any good with words. He needed to explain himself.

She fell into a casual walk and he caught up to her. They were a good way off from the trail.

"Usually when one needs to be alone, it means no one else around," Raven said, as he walked up next to her.

"I'm sorry, Raven."

"Well, you are here now."

"I meant I'm sorry about how I acted. I'm not that good at expressing myself and I have a tendency to mess up what I mean to say." Nathanial fought to find the right words; he didn't want to blunder a second time. "You want to leave; I understand that and would probably want the same myself given the situation. You have to protect your brothers but you're only looking at one perspective."

"Not one. All. I know the ideas and thoughts of everyone, I know their beliefs. I know I will not simply go to James and tell him I have decided to leave." Raven stopped to look up at the sky. The breeze washed Nathanial with her scent, her fragrance was sweet down his throat. The half-moon poured its light down, giving Raven an ashen color to her skin. Her transformation gave her a beautiful complexion. It was smooth and clear. She had been a beautiful girl for her age and the dark curse accentuated her prettiness.

"Before all this, I thought that there was already something wrong with me. I saw the world differently than other children my age, even adults. My ability to gather knowledge was further advanced than any normal girl my age. I'd thought it a curse. The mundane studies of school and daily things become repetitious; my only escape was the study of the world at large, the workings of the laws that bind us in this world. Studying numbers was my favorite past time. Numbers are a language that, if studied and learned well, can open to you answers to mysteries of human thought."

"What do you mean? You can read people's thoughts with numbers?" Nathanial looked at Raven, confused.

Raven smiled. "No, but I could tell you the probability in percentage the outcome of a situation given all the variables in play."

Nathanial's head was starting to hurt, which Raven noticed. "I am trying to say that I know what you mean. I am a demon in their eyes. They no longer see me for a girl. As for you, you are honorable for holding in your convictions to the Order of the Sons of Light. I was the one at fault for bringing my emotions to the open with you. I should not involve you in something I know would put you in conflict with those convictions and the morality of the situation."

But he wanted her to open up to him. She was not alone. He knew he wanted to be there for her, let her know he knew much more than his words expressed. The soft cool touch of Raven's arm against his skin gave Nathaniel realization of his proximity to her.

He curled his fingers around her chin and turned her to face him. She searched his eyes. Her look told him she was also surprised at his nearness. "Raven, I do want you to open up to me. But I'm worried for you; that's why I acted a complete oaf." He pulled her in close.

She hesitated, placing her hands on his chest. Her fragrance made him hunger for her. His heart throbbed, his head whirled. Her touch sent sweet tingling sensations up and down his body. He kissed her.

Raven felt the soft caress of his lips pressed against hers. Her body burned with the delightful sensation; his smell was intoxicating. She felt as if she was floating, losing herself in his embrace.

It was wrong. Her throat burned. A flaming hunger boiled deep in her core. Something was terribly wrong.

"Stop." She pulled away, but Nathanial kept his hold, kissing her on the neck, grabbing at her hips. "Nathanial, stop. Something is not right."

He wouldn't listen. "Everything is fine. You're beautiful." He placed a hand on her breast.

"Stop." She pushed him away.

He fell down and his eyes showed confusion. "What the hell happened? What did I do?"

Her throat felt like hot coals. "Something's happening to me." She felt her fangs growing; the voices in her head rang. Kill him, take him, feed.

Raven fell, curling into a ball screeching. "James. James!"

Through her own screams, she could barely hear the footsteps of James and the others running to her.

"What did she do? Did she attack you?" Wyman shouted.

"No, I don't know what happened," Nathanial said.

James knelt by Raven. Her screams shattered the night silence.

"Kill the damn thing before she has an army upon us," Samuel commanded.

James grabbed her arms and turned her face up. "How long since you last fed?" His words were barely breaking through the wall of white heat burning under her skin. It stole her breath; she tried to tell him but only mumbled squeals came out.

"She has not fed for three days from my account," Leonette said.

But Gabriel said his blood would sustain her a few days, had it already been that long? But she didn't feel hungry. Why didn't she feel the hunger? Why did it come upon her so suddenly? The chorus of voices blasted in her head. Feed, kill, kill them all. Her mind was tearing apart, one half to let herself succumb to the voices, the need to feed, the delicious blood. The other fought for control, to remember who she was and that her brothers were here.

"It's too sudden, she should have felt the hunger building," James said.

Nathaniel knelt on the other side of her. "I'm not sure what happened, I... I kissed her and then all went to Hell. I couldn't control myself."

"Idiot boy, her pheromones have increased. She charmed you without knowing it. Her vampire body is built for seduction and is at its highest when she is near starvation," Wyman said.

More pounding of feet, too many to count.

"An army approaches," Leonette said.

"Raven, we need to get you into the carriage." James grabbed her by the arms, trying to hold her down. It was no use. It was as if her body was moving on its own. She tried to claw him. Nathaniel jumped in to help, grabbing hold of her other arm. The flaming hot pain and voices throbbed in her head.

She felt the sharp stab of a stake going through the side of her ribs. The pain was added onto the already coal-hot sting of torment lashing through her body. She was paralyzed, unable to scream or move.

Her mind became hazed. Leonette was muttering something, a chant. Raven felt rolling darkness swallowing her. The voices moved further away, the sting of the stake and the pain of hunger was cooling. The darkness dragged her down into sleep. She welcomed it.

I have her. Samuel whipped the horses. They protested with snorts, but their hoofs pounded the ground, dust swirling as they raced forth. Fools. What damn fools. It was by luck that a group of Continentals had come upon them. James and Nathaniel had left Raven confined in the carriage while they handled the Continentals. God always provided. Samuel smiled.

He could see the anger and surprise on their faces when he whipped the horses into a full sprint. James called after him, Nathaniel tried chasing; fools all of them. They would thank him for freeing them. They would see, they would see indeed.

He had the demon. She would burn in The Pit, burn and scream.

He had told her, hadn't he? He'd told her she would burn in The Pit. He would keep his promise. That little bitch of a demon would release them all from her witchery.

R

A sliver of rattling sounds stole Raven from her dark sleep, the bite of the stake lodged into her heart kept her paralyzed. She was in the carriage and it was moving rapidly through bumps and rocks. A voice ushered the horses faster. It wasn't James. A wave of panic took hold of her. The voice was Samuel's.

She tried forcing her fingers, her feet, to move, but they wouldn't obey. It was if a large weight pressed down on her, keeping her from moving. The sense of time was lost; the tug of dread made her press harder. Raven commanded her body, her finger twitched. A slim ribbon of hope weaved its way through her panic.

A shriek cut through the sounds of the rattling carriage. The banging of metal resounded outside, entwined with more cries and screams from both men and women. Where was she?

The carriage stopped. The door opened. Samuel stared at her; a man crazed. His eyes were animated with pure hate. Another man came into view, a giant man, his gut round, his arms thick and hairy.

"All the way from Pennsylvania for one vampire?" the man asked in a gruff voice.

Samuel narrowed his eyes. "Don't let her fool you. She seems a little thing, but she bewitched my men. Bewitched them all, including James and Wyman."

The bear of a man grabbed and effortlessly lifted Raven from where she lay. "She won't be using any witchery on me, I tell you that."

Panic washed over with terror as the man brought Raven out of the carriage by her throat. Large walls of both wood and stone encaged them within what she could only think of as Hell on earth.

Pits of fire filled with the remains of people had been dug at every area of the ground. Burnt bones, skulls, hundreds of them littered the ground. Flames licked at the air as smoke coiled and escaped into the sky, blurring the stars. Men and women hung nude from various torture devices. Some were pinned by glowing hot metal pickets. Raven understood where the screams were coming from.

Men hammered down red glowing stakes into the hands and feet of these people. No, not people. Vampires. They were all vampires. By each torture device and cross, there was a furnace where the metal stakes were heated. How the vampires twitched and wailed at each slam of the hammer driving pickets into their hands and feet.

"Her blood is all but drained. The demon has no strength," Samuel said, as two more men took Raven and ripped her clothes to shreds. She wanted to cry out, to lash out. Her muscles twitched, her fingers moved but not enough. After the men finished stripping her of clothing they pulled and bound her hands behind her with wire, and did the same with her feet.

"It's secured. Let's hear her sing, boys." The large man hissed. He ripped the stake from her heart, releasing the paralyzing hold. Raven screamed.

Where was James? Where was Nathaniel? Why was this happening? How could they let this happen?

"Throw her in the cage; she burns tomorrow after the night's cleansing." The man wrapped his grubby fingers around her jaw forcing her to look at him. "Tomorrow, little demon, you will be cleansed. You will repent your evil ways and face God's judgment."

Air raged out into a hiss, she tried to bite him, but she had no strength and the man's grip was like iron.

Two men carried her into a tight passage. Stairs made of hard earth led them to a large underground dungeon. It was made from murky, slimy limestone, and pungent with a rotting flesh smell. A lone torch fought a losing battle against the dark.

They threw her into a cell. Raven landed face first on the hard, wet floor where she was greeted by shadows, and could see the outline of a man curled against the corner of the room. His bright yellow eyes glimmered as his gaze moved to her.

"Welcome to The Pit, little vampire." His voice was low and deep. "You shall join me in painful death tomorrow. At least I will not suffer alone, after all." His laugh bounced off the empty walls.

Only the wails and screams of the vampires outside accompanied the silence afterward.

CHAPTER 18

"You are much too young to fend for yourself. Who is your master? Who turned you?" The vampire's voice sounded distant. The fire of hunger, though not as immense as when it had been before, suddenly came on biting at Raven's insides. Her mind was hazy; spurts of lucidity would come and go, and time moved quickly, and yet not.

Flashes of James and Nathaniel popped in her mind with her brother Matthew. Continental soldiers had found them. She couldn't piece the puzzle together, but she had been moved into the carriage, and somewhere in that time, Samuel had taken it.

"You've not learned to control the hunger; you must be a fledgling. How saddening to die so young in both life and after death," the vampire laughed.

Her vision cleared. She could see her cellmate, his legs and arms bound by large iron shackles, wrists to ankle which made him crouch forward, knees to his face. He was studying her, and she felt exposed, she scooted to a wall and pulled her legs in to cover as much of herself as she could.

He laughed again. For death soon to be upon them, this vampire was laughing and enjoying himself considerably too much.

"What is your name, fledgling? Mine is Victor," he smiled. Indeed, a handsome man, he couldn't be more than twenty-five or so in human years. Long strands of soiled hair fell across his face. His features were sharp yet proportioned.

Raven could see other cells in the large oval room, other vampires lingering in shackles.

"Don't be shy, this is our last night ... well, yours perhaps. You see, I'm only visiting. I don't intend to die. I was simply curious of the stories I hear of this Pit. Truthfully, I didn't expect for them to be real, but alas they are, and here we are; two strangers naked and bound in a cage waiting for eternal slumber. Well, not for me."

"You can get out of here?"

Victor laughed. "So, I have your attention. Perhaps now you would give me the courtesy of your name?"

"Raven."

"How old are you, Raven? Not more than sixteen, I would say." His gaze fell over her, probing, and she tucked in her knees tightly, feeling vulnerable.

"Thirteen, I just had my birthday."

"Your master must have been fond of you to turn you. Most vampires your age don't make it for long. Well, I suppose you didn't make it far in this afterlife either, since tonight you will go through the cleansing and meet a painful death, I should say." He smiled.

"Why are you doing this? I have done nothing to you. Why do you torment me with such words?" Raven's voice trembled.

"Oh my, I've been rather foul, haven't I? Very well, I shall refrain from mentioning anymore of the doom that shall soon befall you. What is it that you would rather have a conversation about?" Victor wrinkled his brows.

"I do not want to talk. I want to leave this place. You said you could get out."

A befuddled look washed over Victor's face. "Did I? My, I don't remember saying that at all."

"You said you did not plan to die."

"Oh yes, I do remember saying that, though I didn't say I could get out. No, no, no."

"Then how do you plan on not dying here? If you are only visiting, you must plan to leave," Raven said.

"Yes, yes I do, for I would not want to die here. Well, I would rather not die anywhere, but most certainly not here."

Raven felt a pinch of frustration. Victor was playing with her, or he had gone mad from being in The Pit too long.

"How long have you been here?" Raven asked.

"A couple of interesting days. I've learned a bit about this place. The place is hidden by churiphim enchantments. I suppose that is why vampires could never find the damn thing." He let out another boisterous laugh. He focused back on her. "Tell me, little fledgling, of your story, for I so do love the tale of every vampire I meet. Tell me and I shall tell you how I plan not to die in here."

Raven didn't trust Victor—his eccentricity—but there was no other choice if there existed a chance to escape. Besides, what would it hurt?

The next two hours she recounted her journey, her father's death, her mother's, how she'd believed her brothers were dead, all of her fears and pains, her loneliness.

Victor would say a few words here and there, recounting something from his past, similar in nature to what she'd described. He was interested in her recount of Gabriel and the blood he'd given her, the powers she'd gained.

She felt herself getting weaker. She could feel her body eating away at itself. It was like fevered heat under her skin. Footsteps resounded off the walls, they were coming down. The clutches of panic swept in and gripped her.

"Ah, alas, it is too late to tell you my tale. My plan to live. They have come for the cleansing. The sun is set. The time is now. Deep the darkness has come and we to The Pit shall go." Victor looked as if he was daydreaming.

"No, take me with you, please. I told you my story, do not leave me." Raven fell. Her body chilled from the dread of being burnt.

"Time for cleansing. God's judgment falls on you tonight, demons," a lanky man said; his face painted with a layer of soot, hair scraggly. His eyes burned into Raven, they were filled with pure disgust and abhorrence. "You will confess all your sins, you beasts, by the blessed fires of our Lord. You will suffer your sins. Take them."

One of the men opened the door and carried a long pole with a noose at one end. Raven tried to stand but fell on her side. One of the men latched the noose around her neck and dragged her out the cell. Victor was dragged by another man in the same fashion.

The rope burned into Raven's skin. It was Wolfsbane. She tried to scream, to hiss, but the noose constricted her throat like some serpent wrapping itself around her neck. They dragged her up the steps, each edge scraping into her sides, back, arms and legs.

Outside, they held Raven and Victor down with the noose while others brought large crosses, dropping them with a loud thud next to them. They took off the binds releasing their arms. Raven tried to lash out, but the men held her down. She had no blood, no strength and was weaker than when she'd been human. The men lifted and bound her outstretched arms to the cross.

They did the same to Victor. How was he planning to escape? Was he actually mad? There was no escaping this; she would die tonight. The last of her strength fled from her. Hopeless nausea ate at her insides.

The cross was lifted and carried over to one of the angry, flaming furnaces. The heat bit at the side of Raven's body.

"Time to confess your sins," a tall muscular man said. His beard was heavy and thick. His old face was also covered in the black soot. With a thick iron tong, he pulled out a vicious red-hot metal stake.

"No, please do not do this." Raven shook her head. "Please, I have helped the Sons of Light."

White searing heat ripped into her clenched fingers, forcing her to open wide her palm. Flames flickered from her singed skin. She let out a scream that shot out all the air in her lungs. Another man slammed a hammer down on the stake, piercing it through skin and bone and wood. There was not enough air in her lungs to keep screaming, she savagely sucked in more air that was relentlessly stolen by another of her screams.

Victor was laughing hideously as stakes were pounded into him. No, there was no escaping this; they would die, and painfully.

Why did God do this? What of her brothers? The fire in her hand brought her back. She couldn't escape into her mind. The last of any blood she had poured from her eyes.

"Confess your sins demon. Confess them or shall we continue with the other hand?" The man's face was close. She smelled garlic and other mingled spices from his breath.

Raven couldn't think, the searing pain was endless. "I... I did what I was told—please, I am not like the others."

Another rip of white heat pierced her other hand. Raven's body felt like wire about to snap as she wheezed in air that exploded out in another scream. Her throat felt like it was torn to shreds from it.

The man held another stake above her stomach.

Raven's body quivered, her muscles aflame from the stress and her words coming out in broken sentences. "I... I fed on a rapist... I killed a soldier. God forgive me, please."

The white heat poured into her stomach as a stake drove through, and the screams came again. This went on for an eternity. She could not fall into the sweet sleep, that cool darkness that had taken her before. The wicked heat kept her there in the moment. She couldn't escape into her memories, couldn't escape into any thoughts, only the angry red heat.

Wolfsbane and whippings followed, the leather biting at her naked flesh. This would be how her death came. Oh, God, what if this was her eternity? She would die here and suffer in Hell. God had forsaken her here, so would He in the afterlife.

Waves of black did come when all her strength had gone. In the dark abyss of pain, she could see all the vivid colors of the fire that burnt her, hear the cracking of the whip against her skin.

R

Samuel watched her naked body squirm, watched her beg and plead and somewhere deep down in the dark recesses of his soul, he liked it. He knew it was her witchery. She was trying to yet keep a hold on him. He could feel the lust burn in him for her moist naked body on that cross.

He was smart, though, smarter than the fools he had saved from her charms. That stupid boy, he had fallen deep in the witchery.

Samuel stared on and the anger rose in him. Go on with it, burn her eyes out, burn the sin. She was trying to charm him, that bitch. How dare she, how dare she toy with his mind?

"That be a sight," a woman whispered into his ear. He flinched back, almost falling.

A cold dread slid down his spine. The red-haired vampire stood but a couple of feet from him. On this hallowed ground. She stood on the hallowed ground. Her smile was wicked and terrible.

"You desecrate this ground. YOU DARE TO DEFILE—"

She was at him. He whimpered when her claws ripped through his breeches and wrapped around his manhood, digging into his flesh.

"Shhh, ye are a noisy one aren't ye." She licked the tip of his ear.

"You Godda—" he whimpered again as she squeezed harder.

"Ye love to spout ye mouth. Now, look what ye did." Hunters were running to them. "Weel, this is inconvenient for ye."

She tightened her grip, Samuel's eyes widened.

"No, don't--"

She ripped his manhood, his flesh tearing and blood streaming. With a boisterous scream, he fell, cupping what was left of his privates.

R

The screams of men mingled in with red, blue and yellow spots, like a small sliver of noise weaving its way through all the colors of this endless agony. Her eyes would be staked next, Raven knew. From all that was told, she knew what was next. But time passed, the sizzling pain calmed—only a bit, but it did.

She peeled opened her eyes. Her vision was hazy. It was empty, the men had gone; only the angry crackling of the furnace flames lingered. The ground was layered by the dead bodies of her torturers. The red-haired vampire was there, her vision was misty, but Raven knew it was her. Elspet was releasing Victor from his bonds. He let out his boisterous laugh.

"Elspet you wicked, wicked girl, you had me worried," Victor said. "You had me believing you had not followed me."

"Ay, ye be thinking I forgotten ye?" Elspet hugged him. They smiled at each other and turned to walk away.

"Please... let me free." Raven's voice was a whisper. "Please—"

Elspet turned, surprise painted on her face.

"Raven my dear, you're awake." Victor came and kissed her on the cheek.

"Ye ken this one?" Elspet walked to the other side of where Raven laid on top the cross.

"Yes, we were cellmates. She told me of the little fight you had, quite exciting," Victor smiled. He stood naked and Raven could see he had also been staked many times over, his bruises barely healing, his skin webbed with black veins, from the Wolfsbane. He was resilient to be standing after so much damage.

Raven turned to Elspet. "I beg you, please." Each word was sucking the last strings of strength.

"You think she will live? The sun is peaking," Victor said.

"She be special this one, to survive this as a fledgling." With a wet sound, Elspet pulled out one of the stakes. At least twenty or so lined Raven's body up and down, and each one as painful when pulled, as the next.

After the grunts and moans, all the stakes pulled and arms and feet freed, Elspet lifted Raven off the cross. The pain was over, by some miracle she was freed from it by one of the vampires she had meant to kill. It didn't matter right now. There was no fire, no red-hot agony.

Her arms fell around Elspet's neck as the vampire cradled her. Raven's body convulsed uncontrollably as she clutched on to her dark angel, and then came dry cries.

"Get the others and meet us at Dumitru's main sanctuary," Elspet said. She lifted into the air, gliding across the sky at a remarkable speed. Raven cried herself into the black ocean of sleep. Elspet crooned to her in that sweet blackness.

R

The waves of darkness flowed through cracks of hazy visions, like a faded dream and sometimes nightmare. There was the cracking of her bones as a stake drove through, the resounding metal sound vibrating in her eardrums. She would wake, clawing at the man and then swoon back into the black depth of her mind. "Mother," she would call out and dry heaves would follow.

The gentle embrace of her mother eased her fears, but her mother was dead. She was dead, someone else was caring over her. The scent of the woman was familiar, soothing and fresh and sweet. She had seen Elspet in one of her cracks of vision; she had been crying and Elspet had been cradling her, saying comforting things. It was all one long ocean of visions and dreams. What was real and what was a dream, it was hard to discern. There were others somewhere; she could hear the mummers of voices, some angry, some confused, women and men. Raven recognized Elspet's and the deep and commanding voice of Dumitru.

It had been days since Raven had been freed from The Pit. Elspet had poured blood into her mouth. "Drink or ye body shall eat itself, little fledgling." It had driven Raven mad, but Elspet had easily held her down and the darkness rolled in. More days drifted by.

The low simmer of voices woke Raven out of the cool ecstasy of slumber. Her eyes fought her a while before peeling open. Flowering out before her was a beautiful, heavenly white room filled with white and red curtains hanging from brass rods. Heavy framed paintings hung from the walls, a purple velvet coverlet enveloped her, along with the white bed and velvet pillows she slept on. A beautiful white dress was laid out on a red velvet chair next to her. Someone stood at the corner. Elspet walked out of the shadows.

"Ye wake, ye been sleeping fir two weeks. I had Victor go back fir ye carriage. Ye needed your soil." Raven looked under her covers and sure enough, a thick layer of soil was there, though she was also in need of clothing. She pulled her covers tight.

Elspet smirked. "Dinnae be shy, I've looked after ye fir those weeks and we both be women; nothin' I've not seen before."

Another woman walked in, she was young, at least eighteen or so. Behind her stood two men. Raven could tell by their skin they were vampires but the girl... No, she was human. Raven felt the hunger rage inside her, like fevered heat through her body.

"Is she the one, madam?" the young girl asked.

"Aye, she be the one," Elspet replied.

The girl made a motion to walk to Raven.

"No. Get away, get her away. She cannot be here. I cannot control—" Raven shouted, clutching her stomach as it rumbled viciously for that sweet liquid.

"I'm here to take care of you, don't worry now," the girl said in a cooing voice, trying to calm Raven.

"Please get away from me." Raven rolled out of bed, gripping the blankets around her. The sweet scent of the girl inflamed her stomach, every particle of her body wanted to leap, jump, claw at her. She needed to dig her fangs through the girl's skin, needed to drink the delicious blood that her body was craving, that it so desperately ached for.

The girl moved around the bed to reach Raven. She froze.

"I said get away from me," Raven hissed through fanged teeth.

The girl screamed and turned to run, Elspet clutched her by the throat, lifting her off the floor. The girl was wide-eyed, and she flailed helplessly. Her neck cracked and she went limp.

Elspet walked over to Raven and laid the girl at her feet. "She be alive and suffering. She will die a slow death if ye do not feed on her and end it quickly."

The big blue eyes of the girl pierced into Raven's, she could see the fear, the horror in them. Spasms shot through the girl's body. She was suffering.

Elspet sliced the girl's jugular with one sharp nail. The blood poured. Raven was frenzied. She bit in, drinking the luscious nectar. The lustful sensation sent waves of ecstasy down her muscles, energizing them, her limbs tingled with the sweet refreshing liquid, as her heart pumped the blood to the thirsty tissue. Her mind was floating in that sensual abyss of flowing elation. Elspet was gone, the vampires were gone, the girl's death didn't matter. Only the beautiful taste, the evaporating hunger, the cool refreshing feel of her throat.

When the girl was emptied of the last bit of liquid, Raven stood, certain the girl was dead, and breathed in deep, her chest sinking in and out. It took her some time to come back into the moment, back to the room where stood Elspet and the other vampires and Dumitru.

"Have you had your fill?" he asked.

Raven looked down at her naked body, smeared in the red liquid.

The young girl had been mangled. Had she done this? In her frenzied state, had Raven ripped this girl with her claws?

"What did I do? How could I... why?" Raven fell back against the wall.

Elspet walked around the dead girl and held a hand out to Raven. "Ye not eaten properly fir two weeks, probably more. 'Tis amazing you survived this long on the little blood ye drank." She pointed to a silver goblet sitting on a desk to the side of the bed.

"Most do not return from the maddening. Vampires that have not fed past four days usually become rabid creatures, killing anything either living or undead,"

Dumitru said. "You seem to have luck on your side, fledgling." He walked off with the other vampires in tow.

Elspet remained, holding her hand out to Raven. "Ye be needin' a bath. I'll have one prepared."

Raven took her hand and lifted the covers off the floor to wrap herself with. She followed Elspet out into the cavernous hallway. Dark wood floors shimmered with the bouncing warm lights of the candelabras. Elspet led her to the back of the huge house and to the bathroom, where a clawed foot bathtub rested. The fresh clean water was inviting. Raven needed to clean her body of the girl's blood.

"I'll be outside. I'll have your dress brought to ye." Elspet closed the door, leaving Raven to herself in the large room.

CHAPTER 19

Raven opened the door and Elspet stood outside waiting for her. She regarded Raven with a smile. "Ye look a perfect porcelain doll in that dress."

Raven was working her mind, not sure how to respond. She had been tracking Elspet and Dumitru and now here she stood, saved by them. They had trusted her into their home.

"Come, Dumitru is waiting for ye," Elspet said after a moment of silence.

"What does he want with me?" Raven didn't move.

"To understand ye, tis the way the mon put it." Elspet glided down the hall. After a few hesitant beats, Raven followed.

They came upon a vast open room with a high-beamed ceiling and various velvet couches splayed over the dark wood floor. More gilt-framed paintings covered the walls and a fireplace completed the immense room. Dumitru stood by a large window, staring out at the property incased by thick trees. Even in the darkness, Raven could see the outline of the land.

Dumitru turned to regard Elspet and Raven. "You are a beautiful young lady. I take it you know who I am?"

"The one murdering helpless families," Raven said icily.

A tight-lipped laugh escaped him. "Oh, I doubt they are helpless, these humans." He was analyzing her. "I understand." He nodded. "You have barely come into the dark life; you think yourself part of their world. You think yourself human. Though, I could not fathom why you would."

"I would rather cling to my humanity than become murdering monsters like you. You killed children. You tried to kill my brothers. I will never be like you."

"I see, *monsters*, you call our kind. You think us monsters, for what? For feeding on humans? Do you want to die, Raven?"

Raven tensed and stepped back. "No."

"Calm yourself. You would not be here if I meant to bring harm to you. I do not like to kill my own, though the need to do so arises sometimes. In this case, I simply wish to understand you. You have branded us enemies without hearing our side. You follow blindly those who have hurt you, while we have only the wish to protect ourselves from them. The human hunters."

"Your kind killed my father and mother. It is because of you monsters that I am cursed to be this, this evil thing." Raven stared daggers into him.

"You fascinate me. Your mind should have adjusted to our ways, yet here you stand, defending the humans after they tormented you, helpless and naked upon a cross. What an amazing creature you are." Dumitru sat down on one of the elegant red and caramel colored couches and extended a hand toward another, inviting Raven to sit. "Let us talk and perhaps you will open your mind and understand our side. Your kind. Perhaps you will not think us such rivals."

Raven looked at Elspet, who smirked and shrugged. "Weel tis a reasonable request."

"Fine." Raven walked over and sat on the couch opposite Dumitru.

"I never chose this curse, Raven. I never chose for my wife to die burning and suffering at the hands of hunters. I never chose to kill and feed on blood. It was forced upon me. While there are others who searched out the dark gift, many were turned against their wishes. But I did learn that it was not such an evil thing."

"How can you say that? You kill innocent people; you slaughter whole families. You massacred a town."

"We are at war, Raven. What do you think is happening right now between the Continental army and the British? You are delusional if you think they do not feel the same. You hold humanity on a pedestal of innocence. Yet throughout history, they have been the most violent race. They look for the weakest among them to enslave, to kill and rape. Look at what they did to you. Do you think they haven't done the same to human children? Remember the Inquisition, the witch burnings, the cruelty of Medieval times? Oh yes, we have an unquenchable thirst for blood, but humans have an endless evil ever-lurking in them. Ever are they looking for justification in their religions, their wars, their hate, and their lust."

"Do you believe it was God's wish to have women tortured, their breasts ripped, their sexual organs shredded by priests? What do you think? No, Raven, they are led by their inner demons. All humanity is a disease upon the earth. They were flushed away once by a great flood, and according to their beliefs, they will be again."

"You are twisting truths, there are good people—"

"Let us all die then, tonight. Let us set this house on fire right now. Let us end this evil life of ours. Elspet, get the torches."

Raven jumped off the couch. "No, I do not want to die."

Dumitru stood. "What? You are making no sense, Raven. We must die here, tonight. There are good people out there and we are killing them. You are killing."

"Stop, you are trying to trick me."

"Trick, what trick? Do you want to feed, or do you want to die? Do you want to kill so you can live, or do you want to die?"

Raven shook her head. "I want neither—"

"Impossible, it is one or the other. It is that simple."

"No." She screamed.

"You are a confusing child, you are damning us for the want to live, yet it is perfectly fine for you to go on."

"I did not say that."

"What then, what are you saying? Tell me, I wish to understand."

"I did not ask for this, I did not ask for my father and mother to die, I did not ask for the curse—"

"Yes, yes. Neither did I, neither did many of us, but it is upon us, and there is nothing to be done of it. You are not telling me what you want."

"We do not have to kill to feed. I have drunk blood from a chalice. Elspet has fed me—"

"A snack. It serves to keep the hunger at bay for an hour or two. A day or two. Then it will madden you. The life energy. The spirit of the blood directly from a living human is what sustains us, our empty, lifeless shell. A goblet of blood here, a goblet there, but eventually, this shell will tire of the tease and you will go mad. The bloodlust will come, and you will probably slaughter many a human before it is done."

Raven's mind worked feverishly, but deep down, she did not want to admit it. She did not want to die, she feared it, feared suffering an eternal Hell or vanishing from existence. But how could she live like this? How could she solve this riddle?

"Why do we kill the innocent? Why women and children? Why families?"

"Details. You are one for details, aren't you? The intricacies of it all. Does the wolf ask the same when it kills? Does a lion ask? We are hunters, the highest of hunters. But some of us do have our penchants. Some of us acquire a taste for the rich, some for the poor, some for rapists, others for warriors. Each has a distinct taste."

"That does not answer my question, why do we need to kill children? They could not sustain us. Why kill the innocent?"

"Why does a man rape a woman? Why does a mother kill her own child? Vampires are individuals; we have our minds, our pains, our dreams, and hopes. We all want to live, same as a human who would be stranded and starving. Would a human choose to starve or kill a doe or a fawn if it meant life or death? While a human's body may sustain a couple of days, vampires starve every night and will bloodlust within three days of not feeding, during which everything that comes across that vampire's path will die."

Raven's head pounded; she took in a deep breath and stood silent. Dumitru's eyes probed her. "Your mind is in a quandary; you are trying to solve this puzzle of life and death. You had simply known one side of the story and now you know two, each with their own reasons."

Raven was flustered. Dumitru had cornered her for every question, and worst of all, his answers had reason behind them. The moral conflict would be her own now. It had grown to encompass these other cursed beings. "It makes no sense. Is God this cruel?"

Dumitru scoffed. "Amusing entertainment for him, vampires and humans fighting for survival. Each side seeking vengeance for lost loved ones, each side fearing for their lives. Each side as cruel as the other, but we are the ones censured."

Raven rubbed her temples, shaking her head. "No, this is wrong; there are options."

"What options? Tell me, I wish to hear them."

Silence. Raven had no words, her mind worked, but no answers came.

Dumitru towered over Raven. He draped a large hand over her shoulder. "You have much to think about. Feel free to walk about the land, you are welcome to return. I hope you would not betray our location to any hunters should you decide to leave."

"I have questions."

"The chess game is over for the night; I have learned what I needed." He stepped outside and was gone. Raven let out a huff and headed for the door forgetting about Elspet who stood silently as a wraith behind her. She followed Raven.

Outside, the property opened vast and wide, patches of trees hid the house in a wall of foliage. The house was tall and sturdy, built from limestone, a beautiful two-story home.

"Most of the first-generation vampires have accumulated wealth. Dumitru possesses both wealth and connections in the human world. He's obtained other shelters like these up in New York," Elspet said.

"First generation vampires?"

"Aye, the firstborn to Dracula, they are the most powerful, and blessed wi' more than one gift on rare occasions." Elspet led Raven around the property. Other vampires lurked in the shadows, eyeing Raven as she followed. "Much as yourself. Strength, speed, animal control and telekinesis. 'Tis strange for a second generation to be gifted wi' so many abundant powers."

"I am a second generation, Jonas is first?"

"Jonas is the most powerful of the first-generation children. None have seen the full potential of his powers but 'tis said he is gifted wi' many. He was the first child of Tepes," Elspet stopped, "and ye be the first child of Jonas. 'Tis probably why ye have gifts... and why Dumitru have interest in ya."

Dumitru had interest in her? Raven now knew why she hadn't been killed. Of course, he would have an interest. It had to be linked with Jonas. Elspet was telling her of Jonas, which meant there was a connection to Dumitru's plans. Powers. Raven was gifted with many powers and Jonas was the strongest of the vampires. A meeting to join forces that had gone wrong. Yes, that must be it. Raven's mind worked as it usually had when she was human. Connecting the missing links to puzzles, to mysteries, equations of life.

Elspet held her gaze on Raven.

"Dumitru wants me to join with him. Jonas did not share his vision. Since he heard word of me, I am the next thing to Jonas he could use," Raven said, when her brain had finished its piecing of the puzzle.

Elspet wrinkled a brow. "So, ye also read minds."

"No, even before I was cursed, I was different than other children my age. My mind is quick. Father used to call me a sponge for knowledge due to my quick study of things." It was Raven's turn to study Elspet. "So, it is true? That is why Dumitru kept me alive?"

"It had crossed his mind upon our encounter at the sanctuary when I first told him of ye creator."

"I will not be used by him, not by anyone. James wanted me for hunting vampires, now Dumitru would use me the same to hunt humans." Raven wrapped her arms around her chest.

"Weel daen't be too hasty to tell him, 'twas I that swayed him to let ye live lass. After ye friend the churiphim attacked his beloved, Dumitru sought retribution."

The churiphim, Leonette—what had become of them, of Nathaniel and most importantly her brothers? "I have to get back; I need to find my brothers. Do you know what happened to them?"

"Our trail went cold fir them, thanks to me. I followed them fir a few days. Once they lost hope of finding our trail, they headed north-east toward New York."

"New York? George Washington has lost New York. The British occupy it, why would they head there?" A sliver of worry escaped through Raven's voice.

"The other churiphim will arrive early," Elspet said.

"They knew about the other churiphim. How?"

"The Sons of the Order of Light have immunity from the dealings of the mundane world. The church sees to that." Elspet gestured for Raven to follow.

Raven trailed behind her, around the large plantation and to a patch of thick-knotted foliage. With a flick of Elspet's hand, the plant life split apart to reveal two limestone double doors carved into the ground. Elspet effortlessly pulled them open, which was a spectacle considering her tenuous looking frame. They both followed winding steps down to torch-lit earth and stone-framed hallway. The moist soil filled Raven's nostrils and the press of the heat made her wince. Flashes of her torture blinked in and out.

They came upon an enormous, finely sketched-out chamber created of limestone frame, heavy dark wood and stone pillars. A black marble floor spread out before Raven like a dark ocean where floated a large, thick-legged table.

Vampires, many of them, at least fifty, glared at Raven. Raven froze at the entrance, hesitant to keep following Elspet. She could hear the whispers: *Vampire hunter, she kills our own, kills her own kind, traitor*. It reminded her of the nuns back in the cave. They'd whispered similarly, though their words were tinged of fear. These vampires whispered with undertones of hate. Raven's stomach whimpered, her muscles tight and trembling with the need to run, to get out of this room.

Elspet stopped and turned back. "'Tis fine lass. They are ye kin and ken better than to harm their awn."

Before Raven could counter, Victor stepped out from the crowd. "Raven!" He squealed with excitement. "How is my beautiful cell friend?" He wrapped an arm around Raven and pulled her forward into the grunting multitude of vampires. Raven was sure one of them would plow their fist into her chest to rip out her heart. Nothing of the sort happened, and Victor pulled out a chair for her at the large table that stretched at least twenty feet long.

"What is she doing here?" One vampire asked.

"She will give our secrets to the hunters," another growled.

"What? Raven? No, she is my cell friend. Why would she ever do a thing like that?" Victor pulled a chair next to Raven and plumbed down, kicking his feet up and slapping them on the table's edge. He leaned the chair back and looked toward the vampires. "She is our kind after all, and we look after our own. She was simply misguided by the dreadful Sons of Light. Terrible, terrible ordeal, I should say."

Elspet came and sat next to Raven on the opposite side of Victor. A simmering chorus of voices erupted from the ghastly crowd.

"Silence." Dumitru's voice resounded not from the room but from within her mind. The room quieted. One of Dumitru's powers. Did it also mean he could read minds?

Dumitru sat at one end of the table. "This chamber is one of three we use as meeting grounds in the western world," he regarded Raven. "You see, vampires don't usually gather but only rarely, in particular when a great threat to our secret world arises or new laws are decided upon by the elders and most powerful. Other than that, we usually travel with one companion, claiming our territories, or traveling the world as nomads." He turned his gaze to the vampires. "But we have always struggled against our one great enemy. The Order of the Sons of Light."

"And Victor has informed us they have sent a large group of their witches to vanquish all vampire life from the western world," a vampire said. "They come because of your blatant and rash attacks upon their safe havens. You dared to kill the head priest of this territory. You have enraged them and focused them. You have set them on course for that one single purpose. Fool." A wave of gasps rolled in the group.

Dumitru's face remained unchanged. "Jonas."

Jonas. Raven's body jerked at the name. Her limbs tingled with a flaming sensation. Jonas, the one who did this to her, the one who killed her parents, was here. Everything else faded into the background—the vampires, the smells, the voices. Her legs felt wobbly, her fists clamped, nails digging into her flesh.

From the crowd, Jonas stepped out; Raven recognized that face. The evil yellow glow of his eyes as he'd watched her dying, teasing her with that wicked smile of his.

"You took my invitation? I am pleased," Dumitru said. Jonas slithered down into the chair at the opposite end of the table. Soon others joined, sitting around the table. Raven could only assume they were the eldest of the group. Twenty vampires joined them while the rest lingered around.

It didn't matter, only Jonas did. This devil would die tonight.

"It seems you have brought war upon us," an older wrinkled vampire started.

"There was no choice in the matter. I had to draw your attention, and this was the only way to do it. The old ways are not working. We are being dwindled down while the hunters grow in numbers in the New World. We must claim this land. We must hold our ground against this inferior race. Safety in numbers. Strength in numbers. Never has such an assembly of powerful vampires come together, we have the upper hand, the surprise. Victor has seen ten of the churiphim led by their second, Mena." The vampires flooded the room with talk upon the mention of the name.

"Mena? You are pitting us against the second in command of the churiphim. Have you not heard the rumors of her power?" A lanky vampire shouted.

"Have you not witnessed ours? Alone, we the elders have taken dozens of hunters down. Imagine what we can do together," Dumitru countered.

"I remember a time when there sat forty elders at this table." This time a younger looking vampire spoke, at least eighteen years, black wavy hair framing a rugged and handsome face.

"My point, exactly. The old ways shall be our demise," Dumitru said. "And with our own army, we shall turn the tide," he stood and waved his hand in an arc directing everyone's gaze behind him and to a cavernous arched hallway. "Andreea."

The vampire Leonette had stabbed at the sanctuary stepped out. She was fully recovered and as enchanting as when Raven first saw her. From the shadows following behind her was a multitude of vampires, both Continental and British soldiers, priests and nuns, and others that looked like normal farmers. There were a hundred or more at least.

"You bred an army," Jonas smirked. "And not just any army, I sense."

Dumitru gave Jonas a thin smile. "Your reputation precedes you, Jonas. Andreea and I have been culling this army and weeding out the ones without gifts."

"And what did you do with the unfortunate ones?" Jonas cocked his head.

"The Order of Light believes we sacrificed my army to destroy villages and their own sanctuaries. They follow a cold trail, thinking we will continue attacking, and I will oblige by sending cannon fodder to attract their attention. We, on the other hand, will head far north; our quarry is in Washington. Victor has seen that this human will obtain victory; he will be the first president of this free nation. Our president. For I intend to give him an eternal existence."

"Thus, holding sway over the government and laws, banishing the hunters from the New World," Jonas chuckled. "Your mind is as sharp as ever Dumitru. This plan of yours may work. Yet, you have broken many of our laws devising it."

"I only hold loyal to one law: survival. Those who wish to live will follow it. There is no turning from this war that is coming. I have locked us to it. We needed action, not promises or sophistry from the elders. Words are meaningless without action, and since I knew this council would not agree with me, my hand was forced."

"You risk death—"

"I risk nothing. This army holds loyalty to me and there is no elder in this room I could not persuade to my side should the need arise." Dumitru and Jonas locked icy glares.

"When this war is done, Dumitru, you and I will have a private chat," Jonas said evenly, though that would never happen since Raven would be killing him that night.

"Of course." Dumitru stood, towering over the table, his face half in shadow, his eyes challenging Jonas.

"Fight or die. That is what is presented to you. The army of hunters arrives in three days' time. They will track every last vampire down, these churiphim. Track every vampire and wipe them from this new world, unless you join me in battle. Choose your fate." Dumitru sat down.

The time crawled. There was more debating between the elders, but they all agreed to join Dumitru in war. Something that apparently had never been done before. The great gathering began to disperse, and Jonas made his way out. Raven shadowed him.

A black carriage waited for him outside. He stopped to talk to Andreea and Victor. His back turned, Raven's muscles snapped into action and she was at his side. She swung her claws aiming to rip his throat; there was only air. The edge sharp cut of pain at her back brought her to her knees screaming. What happened?

CHAPTER 20

Two weeks, no leads, and no new attacks on the Order's sanctuaries. Two weeks and nothing. Raven was gone. James had planned to beat the life out of Samuel, but when they had arrived at The Pit, the place was a massacre.

Nathaniel was certain Samuel would have taken her to The Pit, and he was right. Samuel had been found impaled upon one of the crosses they used to torture the Lilins, along with his penis nailed to his forehead.

They had met with a couple dozen other hunters sent by the New York territory. They'd been informed that Mena would arrive earlier than planned. It had been foreseen by the churiphim that The Pit would be attacked, and a large number of vampires would soon siege the main headquarters of the Sons in New York—the House of Filius.

The House of Filius was built to be the ruling head of the Sons of Light this side of the world. The house of Pater was the ruling house in the eastern world, and the house of Spiritus Sanctus, located in Britain, was the third house. All were ruled by the main, the house of Scutum Fidei in Rome where the secret orders of the churches met in discussion regarding the war on the Lilins.

Other secret societies also joined forces, two being the Bavarian Illuminati and Masons. James had been a member of the Masons, which granted him certain privileges of knowledge. The Illuminati worked deep in the shadows, however, and even he didn't have access to their secrets—all for the greater good of God and humanity.

Nathaniel rode behind James and Wyman, keeping his horse at a slow trot. The kid was taking it pretty hard. He had grown close to Raven. But hadn't he also? James felt a bit of regret. Raven was different, wasn't she? She had fought on their side, returned to them instead of running. James squeezed his fingers around the reins. He could have been gentler with her.

"The idiots did not listen to the pleas for help and now a full out war is brewing." Wyman broke the silence. "Ten churiphim have been sent, the strongest of the Core. No normal endeavor to send that much power to the New World."

James smirked. "People of the old world run differently than they do in the colonies. The Core Order has their witches at their disposal and also any Lilins they capture."

"They will try to force their power here," Wyman said.

"Then they are more foolish than I thought," James shook his head. It was a different war in the old world compared to here; the church was more influential and commanded authority.

"This is big, really big." Nathaniel was looking up at the sky. "Never heard of so many hunters called to one area before. Could the vampires have amassed together? Has Dumitru been able to bring the demons together?" He asked.

"That is unheard of," Wyman shook his head. "Impossible."

"No. All the rules have been broken, it's a new fight," James said gravely. Dumitru had spilled his evil into the world.

Wyman scoffed at him. "Your need for retribution seems minuscule now. Raven is probably with Dumitru; he's more than likely convinced her to join her kind. She is now another of the demons. And you released her into the world, any deaths she brings is your responsibility."

"She's not like that," Nathaniel interrupted.

Wyman scowled at him. "Fine, keep believing that. It is all meaningless in the end. She will die with the rest anyway."

"So be it, but shut up, at least around her brothers," James said.

The twins had taken it harder. They had found their sister only to have her ripped away from them again. Phillip had become more stoic, while Matthew was certain Raven would return. The twins rode in the cab of one of the many carriages that belonged to the Sons of Light that had joined them on the road to New York.

They would join the Order and become hunters. They would be taken back to the old world and taught in the house of Spiritus Sanctus, which was the main house for combat training. After all they had seen, there was no other choice in the future for them. The secret world of vampires, and the Sons, had to remain a secret.

What a fool he had been; he should have killed her that night. Raven had been a good daughter to her father and mother, had a good life. Why had he let her become this thing? He had condemned her to Hell. If she had joined with Dumitru, he would hunt her down, he would have to kill her, he would rectify this mistake. She would burn in Hell, there was no place in Heaven for such things as her. Her soul had been consumed by the demon. A damned fool, he had let his hunger for vengeance send a young girl to the path of Hell and in the end, it was all for nothing. Raven was meaningless, her training had been meaningless. The churiphim were coming, the most powerful of them. No vampire could hope to stand against them. Along with the churiphim came a hundred hunters armed with Machairas and the Sword of the Spirit Armor. The armor was called Sword of the Spirit since it had been blessed by the highest clerics of the Order, blessed with the word of God to both protect and attack; a skintight armor that would burn any vampire that touched the hunter.

Yes, this was something serious, to send the strongest Sons to the New World. James stared up at the wavering primary colors of stars. But maybe, just maybe, he would see Dumitru. Maybe it would all be worth it.

"We camp here." Leonette raised her hand, signaling everyone to stop. "We will continue in the morning. We travel by day from this point forward."

Hunters nodded in agreement. Wyman shook his head, not accustomed to the witch giving orders, but the Sons that now joined them were from the old world. They followed the order of churiphims unless a cleric deemed differently. Churiphim only answered to clerics or the Knight Commanders of the Sons of Light.

Nathaniel hopped off his horse and was approached by Matthew. "Have you dreamed of her?"

The muscles of Nathaniel's jaw tightened; he had been having dreams of Raven. No doubt she had unknowingly created a link with him. A vampire's link to its prey was one way they tracked humans they had been stalking. They could track from around the world in some cases.

"Not lately," Nathaniel replied.

"Do you think she will come for us, in New York? Do you think she will find us there?" Matthew pressed.

Nathaniel went down to one knee. "I don't know, it'd be pretty dangerous for her. These—" His eye flickered to Leonette and back to Matthew, "other hunters we're meeting, they don't like vampires. They wouldn't want to be friends with your sister, because she's not like us."

"Why? She helped us, helped Leonette, she—"

"She is not our sister anymore. It's not Raven." Phillip's words had stung Matthew, who glared back at him.

"Yes, she is. Take that back." Matthew shoved Phillip, making him fall on his rump.

Nathaniel pulled Matthew away. James tried to help Phillip to his feet, but he pushed away and stomped off.

"Hey, what'd you do that for?" Nathaniel held Matthew, letting him go only when he'd calmed down.

"He shouldn't have said that. Raven is our sister; we're the only family she has." His bottom lip quivered. "If she doesn't come to New York, I'll find her myself. She is my sister and I'm not going to leave her; family doesn't do that."

"No, I suppose family doesn't." Nathaniel patted Matthew on the shoulder.

R

Nathaniel watched the open heavens and the wavering stars blinking in and out as if they were whispering to each other in that vastness of darkness. He stood at the outskirts of the camp, contemplating. A cool breeze rustled the branches and licked the side of his face. The east winds were chilling, signaling the changing of the season. He pictured General Washington. He wanted to be part of that war, part of the creation of a new country. America. Home of the free. All meaningless in the greater scheme of the world. The rebels fought for freedom from King George and the Sons of Light fought to save the world at large from the enemies of God.

Was Raven an enemy of God? She was good at heart. Nathaniel had only seen her intentions as good. Hell, she didn't even like feeding.

He walked the perimeter of the camp. The hunters sat in groups, talking in hushed whispers, laughing, playing games. He had seen similar scenes in his travels with his mentor, though instead of the Sons of Light, they were Continental soldiers.

How different their worlds were, their war. The Sons of Light were apart from worldly dealings; they were the warriors of God and thus detached themselves from those wars, those politics. Theirs was a greater call.

He tried to push back the memories of his dreams, the memories of Raven. How had her power gripped him? This longing to hold her had stolen his thoughts at night. The sweet smell of her was like a warm whiskey warming his blood. He needed to hold her again, kiss her. James had warned him, explained the power of a vampire link and the charm it came with. Was that what this was? Had she accidentally linked with him, charmed him? What a cruel curse.

Leonette stood further away from the camp. A sculpture staring upwards, her lips hinting of prayer. He came up to her. A faint radiance of the moon washed down over the countryside and he could see the glitter of drying tears under her eyes.

"You have a question?" She looked at him.

"Reaching out for your grandfather, up there somewhere?" He pulled his gaze up.

Silence.

"I remember that night my house was attacked, my mother's scream woke me and I heard my father running for his musket. Fat lot of help that did. I was eight when I saw my parents sucked dry. Saw the vampire who'd done it too. After that, I kept my feelings bottled up, figured no one could understand. I hated it though, hated the loneliness."

"I do not feel loneliness." Leonette's voice was monotone, but he could see she strained to keep it so.

"Everyone feels loneliness—"

"What is it that you want from me?" Her voice cracked.

"Nothing, I'm here as a friend, to talk."

Laughter turned him around to three hunters walking past, probably to go relieve themselves in the trees.

"Foolish, lad. Churiphim don't like to talk."

"Maybe he's charmed by her. He's in love," the second said.

"He loves Lilins and witches." The third gave a wry smile.

They shook their heads and made their way past the trail into the foliage. Nathaniel felt his cheeks reddening. He had woken a few times the past nights screaming Raven's name and had gained the attention of the hunters. Nathaniel, a hunter charmed by the Lilin.

Leonette was staring at the sky again; it was hopeless. Fine. If she didn't want to talk, he wasn't going to push it. To Hell with it. He turned back to the camp.

"He was the last of my family." Her voice was quiet and gentle, stopping him in mid-step. "I came here to protect him, to be his guardian." Her face was no longer hardened, taking on softer features. The mask of the churiphim was gone and before him stood the true Leonette, small and lonely. Her dark hair danced to the breeze, a few strands tickling the sides of her face. "After my family was slain, he became my new father. Now I have nothing."

"I wouldn't say that. You are part of the Order, brothers and sisters of the Light. I trained with many others my age, sure they are in other territories now but during our schooling and training, they became like family, brothers. We keep in contact through the years and when opportunity allows, we meet as a family."

"In the churiphim Order, we only have purpose, we're trained for one cause. Taught to kill our emotions, our want for companionship, taught to only fight and die."

"That's why you're taking it so hard? Seems your training faltered." Her eyes narrowed and he smirked. "Giving me that look only proves my point."

"Churiphim live a long time, our leader is over three hundred years old and the one before her was said to be nine hundred," her nostrils flared. "I am only on my eighteenth year of living. I am the youngest of the churiphim, the Blood of the Virtues given to me at the age of eight. I've only been a true churiphim for ten years." Her eyes had started to take on a tinge of silver.

Nathaniel threw his arms up in surrender. "I'm sorry; I wasn't trying to get you all riled up or be offensive."

She froze her eyes, widening as if realizing what she was doing. She relaxed. "My apologies." She wrapped her arms and stared far into the dark horizon of rolling green landscape to the left of the camp.

"So, what is this Blood of Virtues?" Nathaniel asked, wanting to change the subject to a more inquisitive nature.

"The blood given at birth to a child born of a churiphim. The blood entrusted to the Sons of Light after the great flood and abolition of the Nephilim. It is the blood that gives us the power to fight the Lilin plague. Power of the angels granted to us by infusing their blood with that of humans."

"If that is true—"

"I am not a true churiphim or institution. I was given the blood at eight by request of my grandfather. Only by his influence and friendship of the Core Order was I granted the privilege to join. Yet, my age made my training difficult, my emotions hard to control, I falter much. I am the weakest of my Order."

Weakest? Nathaniel had seen her take scores of undead down, and use her fiery magic and create wards. She stood her ground against a true Lilin without having fully recovered her powers, and she was the weakest?

"Fine. To Hell with the Order and training. You're not going to be alone Leonette. It's not the way of things, we all need someone there for us and you can bet I'll be that someone for you."

She frowned, flicking her eyes at him. Nathaniel continued. "Ignore me if you want, but I know what it is to have all your family snatched from you and what it does to you inside."

"Why? Why do you insist on this, this bond you wish to build with me?"

Nathaniel had to think on it a moment. Why indeed. "Trust. We need to trust someone to hold us together in those dark times that could break us. Reason for the fight I suppose. Isolate yourself and you forget what the fight is for; you forget that sometimes you need help to pull you through such times as these. You're human, deep down inside, you are human, and you can't deny that. Without a link to someone you can trust, without anyone at all, you break yourself by yourself. I know, trust me."

"You as well hide two sides, Nathaniel," she tilted her head regarding him for a few silent beats "So you wish to be my friend so that I do not break myself?"

"And... for a churiphim, you're an interesting person to carry long conversations with."

She stared him in the eyes and said nothing, simply nodding. The whisper of a smile shaped her lips.

"You are a strange warrior Nathaniel," she turned back to the camp. "Thank you."

She left him standing alone smiling to himself. His thoughts roved to Raven. Where was she? Was she lonely right now or had she found new companionship? Would she come looking for her brothers? Two days and they would be at the Gulf of the Delaware River, where they would take the boat to New York Her brothers would be shipped off on a six-week journey to England to be trained. Raven wouldn't want that, but what could he do? He let out a heavy tired breath and walked back to the camp.

CHAPTER 21

Jonas squeezed his claws deeper, Raven screamed as her flesh ripped by their sharp edge points. His strength was astounding. Dumitru and Elspet appeared in front of her. Victor and Andreea stood with shocked surprise.

"Who is this young vampire?" Jonas hissed.

"What a question to ask. You are the one who sired her after all. I would think you would know your children," Dumitru said.

Jonas retracted his clench, freeing her from the agonizing grip. She let out a gasp of air and fell to all fours trying to steady herself. Laughter, taunting and mocking, erupted from Jonas. The wretch stepped in front of her and crouched down, the wicked smile etched on his face.

"I remember now, those beautiful eyes, that lovely youthful face, so innocent, so fragile. They should have killed you," he tilted his head; his yellow eyes were unnerving. So near to her face, the evil chill emanating from him sent prickles through her skin. She didn't realize she'd been slapped until she hit the ground. "You shouldn't be alive. I'll rectify the mistake."

"So quick to dispose of our kind? We have a law against such things," Dumitru said. "You said so yourself."

Jonas placed one foot on Raven's chest and pressed her down, pinning her. She tried to push him off, but some power held him firm, weighing down on her. "She is too young to fend for herself. She is a liability, never to be sired. She was simply dessert."

The points of his fingers elongated, and he raised his arm to strike. Raven could see the intention in his eyes, but his face had contorted into an expression of both anger and confusion. His arm twitched, but it was if some invisible force held it from striking. His glare fell on Elspet who stood with arms crossed and a smirk playing at the edge of her lips.

"Elspet. That is your name, isn't it?" Jonas lifted his foot off Raven and turned to face her. "You are the mysterious red-haired one. The one exiled from the old world. You should be wary you do not end up confining yourself to some wretched place."

"Aye, I left the old world for new possibilities and to do that, Dumitru be needing Raven alive. I cannae allow ye to do her harm."

She had lost her smirk and both her and Jonas became rigid, the air around them energized. Though Raven didn't understand it, there was an invisible battle happening.

"The girl is under my command. Live or die, I choose what her fate is. It is within our laws and you cannot deny them," Jonas said.

Elspet tilted her head. "Not my laws, the old ways or new, I follow neither."

Jonas narrowed his eyes. "You forget your place here; you tread on my realm. You play your little games in this domain only by my permission. Dumitru has no power here."

Dumitru's gaze quivered slightly. "You are not a lone king here, Jonas, no matter how true you believe the fantasy, it's nothing but a far-fetched dream," he commented, his tone even and steady.

Jonas's wicked smile returned. "Your ego is damaged. You have always been the little pup trying to play with the big dogs. Perhaps if you were the first born of Dracula, you would have been ruler of this new world. Perhaps if you were the first to travel here, to hunt here, perhaps if you had the power to challenge me... but you are a pup and this game of yours will be the end of you and your flock."

Jonas turned away from them and stepped into his carriage. "Keep her, perhaps my new-found daughter of the night will survive, she would make a nice pet to keep my company." He winked at Raven, closed the door, and the carriage was down the dirt path and gone.

The crowd of vampires who had stopped to witness the interaction soon dispersed and were vanishing down the road in their own lavish carriages. Only the main group of Dumitru's flock remained.

Andreea stood over Raven and offered her hand. Raven ignored it and climbed to her feet.

Raven didn't want to admit it, but her pride had been singed through her defeat by her family's murderer. Why had she been training with James? All of it had amounted to nothing in the end. Jonas had slapped her down like an insect. She had believed herself special, had special powers, but it was futile.

She wanted to be alone, needed to think. Her emotions threatened to drown her into a dark place; she couldn't let herself succumb to it. She was among the demons she was supposed to kill. They had revealed their plans, their intentions, and their reasoning for them. They considered her one of their own. She didn't trust them. She fled into the shelter of the woods; its dark pressing confinement gave her comfort.

Raven found a large thick branch high off the ground where she could see the open expanse of stars floating past the curtain of inky foliage. She lost herself within her musings. She needed to find her brothers, if nothing else; that was the one thing most important. She wanted Nathaniel as well, wanted him to go with her. She would take him and her brothers far from this war, far into the west, further into the lands beyond.

She closed her eyes and pictured Nathaniel. Was it by some charm that he had kissed her that night? Could it have been her unchecked power that caused his need to want her? An image of him played in her mind; it was so clear as if she was there with him in a valley of lush green grass. There were tents and other hunters, her brothers were sleeping, James stood by alone far off in the distance by a trail. This image, it was real, she felt the wind, the sweet smells of the land. New York. That's where they were headed. That's where she needed to go.

Raven felt a presence. Below stood Elspet, watching her. "What do you want?"

"I ken what ye think. Ye yearn fir ye brothers and intend to find them," She said, her voice low, yet firm and polite.

Raven was on her feet. "You read minds?"

Elspet smiled. "I read the language of the body. It tells me the secrets some wish not to reveal, the truth of feelings. Go to them. Find them before Dumitru's army attacks."

Raven registered those words: army, attacks, and brothers. His army meant to attack the hunters, his *cannon fodder* as he called them.

"Ye brothers will be caught in the battle. Dumitru intends to destroy the Son's headquarters," Elspet said.

Raven's claws crunched into the thick branch. "Why are you telling me this?"

"We are not enemies young one, ye are kin, be it by accident or by ritual, it matters only that ye are now of our kin and we protect our awn. Ye may not believe it, nor accept it, but it is our way as it has been for hundreds of years." Her easy tone soothed Raven's fears, yet she couldn't trust this demon. Not after what they had done, not after what they meant to do.

"You speak of hundreds of years, but you have seen more." Raven was as much a study of body language as

Elspet. She had learned to let her brain read the micro movements, the patterns that declared what people felt toward her or her father when they would travel to town. She could tell when people meant the opposite of what they said. "You hid your true feelings from Dumitru, your intentions. You have no stake in this war he ignites."

Elspet furrowed one brow, a twitch of shock rolled over her face. "Ye be possessing an astuteness. We'll have many dances you and I." A silence fell as both stood to study each other. "Go, find ye brothers and when ye do, find ye awn way. Be it to stay with the hunters or return to us, it matters not. This, this is one event, a simple ripple in the river of time that will be forgotten. Ye are young and the dark immortal life ye have been born into is yours to embrace. Live long or die. Love, lose and sire, this be the fate ye make fir yourself." She turned and walked into the blanket of foliage. "Ye carriage shall be ready and waiting fir ye. New York is a week's travel by carriage, but ye possess powers of an elder, speed that ye have not tapped into. Learn to summon it and ye can be in New York in half a night, though, I'd take a satchel of ye native soil. We can roam a little over a hundred miles from the place of our birth before we begin feeling the effects of unrest." Elspet sped into the dark and vanished, leaving Raven to her pondering.

Why? The question pressed in her mind. Why were they so, human-like? They were supposed to be monsters, demons, yet they had not harmed her. Only Jonas, the murderer. Raven covered her face with both palms, shaking her thoughts away. Only one thing mattered, she needed to get to her brothers, needed to be reunited with them, her family. She would no longer be used for either side, she would be the one to choose her fate in this dark life. Hunters, vampires, she would create her own rules and live apart from both. Her brothers and maybe Nathaniel would go with her to the west, to new lands.

R

Raven arrived at Dumitru's home. Her carriage waited in front, Dumitru beside it. Victor, Andreea, and Elspet as well.

"You said I was free to leave," Raven said to Elspet.

"And indeed, you are. Go and find your way little fledgling," Dumitru assured her.

"We are accompanying you, cellmate." Victor walked over and enthusiastically hugged Raven.

Raven pushed him away. "Why?"

Victor looked sincerely hurt by her question. "You pain my heart to ask such a question. After all that we have been through—the danger, the pain, the torture—we are like brother and sister." He waved his hand dramatically over his heart.

Elspet stepped over to another carriage that waited, ready for travel. "We are leading the charge on the Son's headquarters."

"What? You can stop the attack?" Raven's voice raised an octave more than intended.

"There will be no stopping, the attack will proceed as planned," Dumitru said.

"My brothers will be there."

"Which is why you go to retrieve them. Do so, reunite with your family and leave, you have time before the attack. But I warn you, the churiphim will have already arrived; retrieving your brothers will not be your only obstacle. Whether we attack or not, they will be shipped to the old world where they will be trained as hunters. Conditioned to hate you. You will never see them again until they return to kill you. Our attack provides you the opportunity to retrieve them; a distraction if you will."

The churiphim. The most powerful of them. Raven shuddered at the image of Leonette when she was intent on killing her. One of the churiphim leaders would be in New York.

Raven had no misgiving that they would target her. Leonette was considered the weakest, yet she had slaughtered groups of vampires and fought Elspet without regaining her full powers. Dumitru indeed was a strategist. He had planned this, timed it; he wanted Raven to join him. He'd seen something more in her that she did not herself see, and he was doing anything he could to make her sympathetic to his side. It would not work.

Dumitru walked up the steps to enter the large lavish house. "One other thing, your brothers may be shipped off as soon as they arrive," he said before closing the door.

This had turned into a race; she would not be separated from her brothers again.

Victor gave her a big smile and joined Elspet in her carriage. Two carriage men sat and waited for him to close the door and ushered the horses forward once he did. There were also two men waiting for Raven at her carriage. Andreea too, waited there.

Dumitru indeed was a cunning strategist. But how would he fare at a game of chess? The game would never happen; she didn't intend on seeing him again.

The groaning and creaking of the moving carriage faded into the background. She could feel the light of the sun emerging outside. An hour later she succumbed to the sweet desire of sleep. Andreea slept on the opposite side of her.

CHAPTER 22

James had only been to the outskirts of New York twice, to the small wall of forest that hid the headquarters of the Sons of the Order of Light. The House of Filius stood ten miles north of New York City and was surrounded by homes of the families of hunters, protected within the tall thick stone walls blessed by the Order's priests. An elaborate church sat at the northernmost wall, which was nothing compared to the architecture and elaborations of the House of Filius itself.

The house stood three stories high with two-story high pilasters. The house was lined with pediment windows and dormers and roof balustrades lining the edges, that protruded out of the parts of the gabled roof. Stairways led up to the arched doors of the raised foundation, the entrances styled with beautifully symmetrical rectangular transoms. Though mostly Georgian in style, the house was long, with corner towers that resembled something like a castle. All this was built on Holy ground and the main houses of the Order were heavily guarded by the Knights Templar and the Knights of the Shield.

James was awed the first time he had come to the place before he was shipped to England to be trained and taught the ways of a vampire hunter. Now he was here again, this time with the threat of an attack on the house itself. Dumitru had done what no other vampire had.

Leonette led James, Wyman, Nathaniel and the group of hunters up the stairs and into the House of Filius. Inside, the great hall of the house greeted them with a view as elaborate and elegant as the outside. The hall was mammoth and cavernous, lined with dark wood and gleaming black floors. There to greet them was Archbishop Archer and four of the Knights of the Shield. Behind them stood the churiphim—rigid, silent and emotionless. Their piercing silver eyes made the back of James's hair rise.

Leonette was a normal looking girl compared to these creatures. Mena commanded the room, her presence emanated through the area, clutching everyone's attention. She was taller than the others; her red cape was covered in Celtic symbols.

"Warriors, hunters of the dark, welcome to the House of Filius," Archer greeted them with a gentle voice. It was a voice that seemed out of place with his sculptured physique and firm face framed by short brown hair. He was in his mid-forties, but his presence was not forgettable. Mena stepped past him and set her glare on Leonette.

"You have much to explain. We shall speak after preparations are completed." Mena's voice was tempered but the cool fire of ire was twined ever slightly. "The attack is soon upon us. Archbishop Archer, we leave you to your business." Mena nodded to Archer and proceeded down the hall with Leonette and the other churiphim clicking boots right behind her.

"Friendly ladies," Wyman said.

"They are churiphim, they only have one propose in life: to kill Lilins. No other can match them in that skill, which is why they have been summoned here," Archer explained as he gestured for them to follow him. "Most of the northern hunters have arrived in preparation for the attack, foreseen by one of the vampire's own, their most powerful Seer. We do not know the numbers, but we do know that it will happen tomorrow night."

He led them to a large chamber where other leaders of the Order sat in the elegant furnishing that lined the large room. The other hunters left, leaving only James and Wyman. Nathaniel was escorted elsewhere by one of the maids, along with Raven's brothers.

It was well into the night by the time the meeting was adjourned. Nathaniel sat outside on one of the many wood-carved benches waiting for James. Phillip and Matthew waited with him.

"They're moving out all the families tonight and shipping the new recruits off," James said, nodding at the twins.

Phillip sobbed. "I don't want to leave. I don't want to go, I don't."

James stared down at him. "What are you going on about?"

"I was mad is all," Phillip said through half breaths.

"I don't wanna go either, they can't make us," Matthew joined.

"Not much we can do about that now. You two boys know too much, seen too much," James said, plainly.

"What the hell are we supposed to do, let them take Phillip and Matthew? Raven will come for them." Nathaniel thought he could take them himself, leave to find Raven. He knew he wouldn't though, not when vampires would be attacking.

"I didn't mean what I said before, about Raven. She is my sister. I didn't mean it, I was mad, but it wasn't her fault." Phillip began crying again. "I don't want to go."

"The Order won't simply let you be," James repeated.

"James, Raven will come for them, I know it," said Nathaniel.

"She will die if she comes here. The churiphim will kill her. The knights and hunters don't see her for one of us. Hell, I don't know if she is even one of us." James shook his head.

"I know she is. Raven won't become one of those monsters, not with the hate she has for Jonas, not the person she is." Nathaniel had come to know Raven well enough to believe his words.

Matthew walked up to them. "We are not going and that is it. They can't make us go against our will."

"They can and they will. You are orphans—"

"We have Raven." Matthew cut James off.

"Even if she were not a vampire, she is young."

"She is our sister; they won't break us apart. We'll fight if we have to." Matthew's eyes burned with determination. Phillip nodded in agreement, both crossing their arms simultaneously.

James heaved out a breath and shook his head. "Fine, I'll take it up with the Archbishop," he looked at Nathaniel, "but I doubt I'll sway any decision."

"Doesn't mean we can't try," Nathaniel said.

The boys both nodded in agreement.

R

The carriage popped and squeaked as it rolled on. Raven stared out the side of the cart from the window she had opened. The black shadows of the forest greeted her.

Andreea sat quietly for some time across from her. She kept probing Raven with her eyes.

"What?" Raven asked.

"You hate me being here with you."

Raven didn't know how to respond to that.

"It's not a question. I know that you do."

"You are about to kill innocent people, women, and children."

"I don't want to, not really."

Raven turned to regard her.

Andreea let out a small laugh. "I love Dumitru. I'd rather he didn't do this. But they are not all that innocent, these *people* we war against."

"Children? They are innocent. What have they done to deserve death?"

"I suppose." Andreea looked out the window. "What do children know of evil things? They know not what they do when they rip a butterfly's wings, when they hang a cat by the tail and torture it with sticks. What do they know of evil things when they beat or bully others? When they push and pull and throw temper tantrums."

"The nature of growing. It is why parents punish them, show them right and wrong. What Dumitru does is true evil. He knows of sin and death and murder." A low rumble carried in Raven's words as she stared into the depths of Andreea's eyes.

"You're right. There is no denying evil."

Again, Andreea left Raven without words. She looked out the window, her eyes distant and lost. "I fear death. When I was human, it was a different fear. Fear of not knowing what waited beyond the shroud. I know what waits for me now. Punishment, terrible and eternal. And everything I brought to myself, my own fault, but it is a mistake that is irrefutable. I took Dumitru's offer of life eternal so that I could be with him, love him, help him. I threw my soul away for him. If I could go back and change it, it would be fear that would make me turn his request down if it would be possible. Fear can be as powerful as love, I suppose. Tell me, what should I do Raven? What can I do now?"

"I—" Nothing. Raven had nothing to respond with, only anger. Anger at not knowing how to answer these infernal questions.

They rode in silence.

R

Green and browns streaked from trees and earth as Raven raced behind Elspet. They had long ago left their carriages behind with the coachmen. Andreea and Victor kept pace behind her. At this speed, they would be at the headquarters of the Sons by midnight.

This was one large chess game of visions, as Elspet had explained. Miruna was a powerful vampire seer the Core Order had captured; her powers to tell the future were unrivaled. Victor, however, was Dumitru's secret weapon. While he only had the ability to see sketches of the future, he could project prophetic visions, visions he could alter. This gave them the surprise attack tonight.

Raven felt herself being split, like two halves of her clashing against each other, twisting and fighting. She would be with her brothers again, but at what cost?

Innocent people were about to be killed by these demons. But Elspet hadn't been a demon to her.

It wasn't her war; it wasn't her fate, Raven told herself. Only her family mattered, let the vampires and hunters have their fight, she belonged to neither side.

The hunger was peaking, the burning deep. Her core was rising into her throat like tiny ambers clutching to her flesh. Elspet explained that only the eldest vampires could accomplish this type of speed. She, however, was unique, having acquired the gift of speed from Jonas, along with others such as strength and animal control. These powers meant that blood would be consumed quickly.

It was close to midnight by the time they arrived at the edge of the Hudson River.

James had taught her that rushing water was considered pure, used to baptize. Vampires could not cross running water and the Hudson River was pretty wide. How could an army of vampires cross?

The rustling of foliage and the thudding of hundreds of feet came not long after. Not until the vampire army emerged from the thick curtain of forest did Raven grasp the size of the force. Not a hundred, but hundreds of vampires. There had to be at least a thousand or more.

When the entire army emerged, it came to a stop by the edge of the water.

"Elspet, let's cross the river shall we, I am so excited to see." Victor squealed with laughter.

Raven watched Elspet in confusion as she walked to the edge of the bed and chanted. It was a strange language. She raised her arms high above her and increased the intensity of her voice. The ground began to shake, slowly at first. Then it rumbled and cracked. The waters of the Hudson River simmered and lashed out violently and rose. Raven stood in complete awe as the river parted and opened like two curtains pulled apart.

"Go now!" Victor yelled.

The army rushed forward into the great opening. Elspet remained where she stood, her face strained, her arms trembling. Blood oozed from her clenched teeth.

"We must go, the full power of the river falls upon her, her strength will wane." Andreea beckoned for Raven to follow into the opening.

How strong was Elspet? How powerful to hold the force of the river at bay? The power of a true Lilin.

Nathaniel looked over the large hedge that grew at the side of the entrance to the House of Filius. Matthew and Phillip ducked behind him. The ships that would take them back to the old world were soon to set sail and James had failed to make the Archbishop reconsider them staying. So here they were, trying to find a way past the guards at the entrance and after that, a way to open the gates.

"I don't have a plan here." Nathaniel hadn't thought this far.

"We have to hurry, they are going to find out we're gone," Matthew squeaked.

"I know, let me think."

"You should know the wall is shielded by our runes and glyphs. Your presence is easily discovered, young hunter." A cold rigid female's voice jolted them. Behind them stood one of the churiphim, the symbol on her necklace revealed number fourteen.

"They don't want to be hunters." Nathaniel stood and stepped between her and the twins.

Another statue, she didn't blink. "The laws of the Order cannot be broken. Follow me."

"Not happening, we're leaving... and we need the gate opened." Here we go, all or nothing. What the hell was he doing?

"The gate is to remain closed at night. No one enters or leaves except those boarding the ships. Come with me."

Nathaniel shook his head. It was like talking to a wall with these churiphim. Behind number fourteen, Leonette approached. That was it. There was no way he would be able to keep the twins here now. What was he going to do?

"Leave them be," James said, coming down the entrance trail. "The boys will remain with me, I'll teach them. It solves our predicament."

"You hold no sway, hunter. Bring the children," Number fourteen said.

Nathanial looked to Leonette. "They can't do this. They can't force them to go, to leave their home. Say something, Leonette."

She stood quiet, weighing his words. He could see she had changed. Her eyes were animated with a hint of life compared to the other churiphim. She walked over to the twins, grabbed them by their collars, and dragged them forward.

"What the hell, Leonette?" Nathaniel was wrong. She was a churiphim at the core.

"Sound the alarm bell, the attack is happening tonight. Nathaniel, take them to safety," Leonette said, pulling the twins.

The other churiphim had taken a more fearsome look. Her eyes were complete silver and a glow of gold shimmered fiercely around her pupils.

"How?" James was on alert scanning the walls.

"Go now," Leonette commanded. "Sound the alarm, we are under attack!" she yelled, grabbing the attention of the guards.

The earth trembled and an explosion roared through the courtyard. The entrance doors of the great wall had been disintegrated and everyone was thrown down.

CHAPTER 23

Raven witnessed in shock as the doors of the great wall obliterated.

Victor clapped his hands, squealing with laughter. "My command of power is as strong as it ever was. I haven't used it in years, well, I mean on such large objects. Yes, yes, large indeed, this is wonderful."

Andreea stepped up to him. "Yes, we have their attention. Now make them scurry out of their holes." She went into a trance, her eyes closed, and the muscles of her jaw strained.

Already the shouts of men and screams of women issued out from the two ships that were docked on the Hudson. The ships were exposed outside of the walls and the horde of vampires swarmed in for the kill. Raven bit her bottom lip. The wail of children came.

"My brothers!" She screamed at Elspet who stood next to her.

"Be within the walls, I ken their scents," Elspet reassured.

"Dumitru said I would have time before the attack to find them."

"Aye, take that up with Victor, the idiot need learn restraint." Elspet shot her glare at him.

"Oh, but I could not wait, the smell of revenge licks at my core. The sweet scent of food tugs at my hunger. I cannot ignore it." He burst forth, his eyes glowing a sickly yellow, the form of his face sunken.

"Fool," Elspet yelled.

Victor sped through the door and fell to all fours. His skin simmered at the touch of the soil. He shrieked, trying to crawl back out.

Elspet was by him, grabbing and hurling him out the entrance. "The ground is Holy, ye cannae enter."

The horde of vampires hissed and stopped at the entrance. The trumping of hundreds of feet echoed in the night. To the south, a horde of ghouls emerged out of the veil of blackness. The vampires meant to use the same strategy as before. Raven had to find her brothers before the ghouls reached the entrance.

R

James shook away the swirling in his head, trying to regain his bearings. The red-haired Lilin that had killed Father Alrick stood by the entrance. Apparently, Leonette had spotted her too, and was trekking toward her with a deathly glare. Nathaniel and the twins were dazed from the blast; they scrambled to their feet as Leonette passed them, swords in hand, already angry, with flames.

At the entrance a swarm of vampires snarled and clawed at the wall, the Holy ground keeping them at bay. The alarm bell sounded and the commands of the Knights Templar and of the Shield poured out from the buildings. The House of Filius came to life as warriors flooded out.

James crawled back to his feet, unsheathing his Machaira, and moved toward Nathaniel. Leonette reached Elspet.

Elspet turned in time to dodge a swing that would have surely decapitated her. "Little churiphim. Ye want to dance again." The vampire shouted something in Latin that hurled Leonette back and tumbling to stay on her feet.

Nathaniel, Machaira in hand shouted, "The ships are unprotected!"

"Fear not, four of our sisters guard the ships." The rigid drone of Mena's voice made them turn. She stood with five churiphim behind her.

"Do you see how many vampires are out there?" Nathaniel pointed to the entrance. Mena took no notice of him and moved toward Elspet.

"Sisters, punish these sacrilegious heathens for their desecration." In a speed only equal to the Lilins, the churiphim vanished with movement and were at the entrance within the time of a blink. Their bodies were covered in various colored flames, swords swiping down vampires, blasts of fire washing over the horde, winds roared down on the demons and the snarls soon turned to yelps and screams of confusion. The vampires tripped over each other, recoiling from the deadly witches.

James and Nathaniel stood gaping at the spectacle. It was overshadowed by the sudden thunder that roared through the yard, making the earth and buildings tremble as if they were cowering.

Mena was enveloped in circular discs hovering and whirling around her. On the ground appeared blue hissing light, circular in shape, and strange symbols wavering within it. Mena stood in the middle of it.

The air tingled with energy, an immense power that made James shudder. It was both powerful and threatening and sent prickles of hair to stand down his skin. He'd never felt a deep fear like this; a terror resonated within him.

Mena's eyes were a pure black shade, a sickly black aura covered her. The discs that whirled around her launched into the sky and arched over the walls outside, more thundering issued, lightning exploded from the area where the circles landed. Three of the discs flew at Elspet, discharging their full might. She was quicker and leapt into the air.

R

Raven retreated a few steps back maneuvering out of the way of vampires with missing appendages.

Explosions thundered and lit the night in every direction. The churiphim were shredding down the vampires. Raven knew she could easily be one of those undead beings cut down so effortlessly. There were blasts and screeches coming from the ships, the vampires' attack had slowed. More churiphim, probably.

Andreea was in her trance. The ghouls had reached the battlefield and moved toward the entrance. They were drenching wet, giving them a slimy appearance. They couldn't have come from the other side of the river, not with the small amount of time Andreea had to summon them. Dumitru had a way to dump and keep the bodies hidden in the Hudson. Had he accounted for the power of the churiphim?

She had to act. Raven sped to the furthest wall south. They were blessed against vampires, but could she climb them? She had been turned in a church, and Holy ground hadn't harmed her in the past.

She dug her claws into the stone, nothing lashed out at her. She climbed. Up at the top, she could see the courtyard, see the entrance and Leonette. Nathaniel and James stood near her, but Raven's attention was on her brothers.

Behind them, a brigade of hunters rushed toward the entrance. Raven wouldn't be able to get to her brothers, not just yet. She looked around. The area had enough buildings and shrubbery to allow her to hide in wait for the right moment. Raven leapt down. Again, nothing lashed at her or felt aggressive. She sped from building to shrub, a blur in the night.

By the time the mass of hunters had reached Nathaniel and James, the undead ghouls had trickled in past the churiphim that fought off the vampires. More blasts erupted; chunks of wall rained down.

Victor was using his power to create other openings. The churiphim that stood by the entrance began to move forward. Lightning and blue discs whirled around her, disintegrating the undead creatures swarming in.

No doubt about it, this had to be Mena, she was giving orders to the hunters who had joined the fight. Beyond the entrance, Raven could see the attackers had stopped their advancement, a pile of decapitated bodies and severed limbs encircled the five women that guarded the opening.

R

Andreea felt the tearing of her mind as she fought for control of so many undead. The number was double that which she had before. She opened her eyes to witness the battlefield. Her ghouls were being dispatched as quickly as they entered the courtyard. One of the witches was fighting her way to her. At this point, she couldn't hope to defend herself and keep control of the ghouls. "Elspet, where are you? Elspet!"

The churiphim lifted her flaming sword, but then the ground below her exploded, launching her into the air and crashing into a swarm of vampire and ghouls.

"Close one indeed, pesky churiphim they are. Oh dear, I've angered her." Victor grinned behind Andreea.

The churiphim's body unleashed its full fury of red fire that covered her, catching any vampires that grabbed her aflame. Her sword chopped down the ghouls. She rushed, appearing behind Victor, and swiped down her sword. He grabbed her arm, stopping her attack, and let out a screech as the fire licked at his flesh.

"Damn you, witch!" He lashed out with his other clawed hand, but the churiphim was quicker and clutched his wrist, sending the flames flooding up his limbs and enveloping him. He fell rolling and wailing.

Above them, Elspet hovered and chanted. There was a crackling of energy that rumbled the earth near them, and the flames vanished. Only the coiling smoke from Victor's singed skin slithered into the air.

Elspet landed by the churiphim who swiped her sword, dodging its blow by swirling away and clutching the witch's arm. The churiphim's fire also trickled up Elspet's hand and arm, covering her in the red flames, though she was unaffected by it. Andreea barely registered the churiphim's arm separating from her shoulder. Elspet sliced it off with a blade of her own. The witch didn't scream or show the slightest twitch of pain. Elspet hurled the churiphim away, crashing her into the wall.

Her four sisters looked over, two of them started for Andreea and Elspet. Victor was looking dumbfounded at his skin and started giggling to himself. "Elspet, sexy little vixen, you never cease to amaze me with your witchery. No never, such beauty and power, sexy little vampire."

"We have not the time, Victor. You have to bring down the wall, now," she commanded.

"Oh yes, yes, of course, of course." Victor vanished in a blur toward the far north of the wall.

Elspet moved toward two approaching churiphim.

"Get them out of here!" James shouted.

Nathaniel nodded and pulled the twins with him toward the main house. Leonette sliced down a few of the ghouls that had made it through the entrance; she focused her attention past the main battle. Another blast rocked the ground, the northern part of the wall crumbled and more of the undead crawled through. Leonette rushed them.

Three zombies moaned at James who kicked one and split the brains of a second with his Machaira. A Knight Templar finished off the third. Both men moved toward the main fight.

Raven moved from shrub to tree and closed in on her brothers. Nathaniel led them back to the main building. As they neared the house, Raven rushed out into the light.

"Nathaniel."

Nathaniel turned, surprised.

Matthew darted to her, embracing her in a tight hug. "I knew you would come. I knew it."

Raven kissed him on the top of his head. Phillip stood by Nathaniel. He took a step to her and hesitated. She walked up to him. "You are my brothers. I will never leave you. From now on we stay together as a family."

A tear rolled down Phillip's eye; he sniffed and nodded and gripped her tight.

Nathaniel looked around and grabbed her hand, tugging her to the shadows.

"How the hell did you get in here? If they find you—"

"I was not about to leave my brothers, not ever."

"We have to get you out of here." Nathaniel pulled her, leading her to the back of the house, deeper into the shadows.

"Where are you taking her, hunter?" They froze. Leonette stepped out from the side of the building, both her swords at each hand.

James beheaded another of the ghouls. The Knights Templar and the Shield had advanced out from the walls, baring crosses and using Holy water to weaken, then hack down the vampires. The hunters covered them by taking down the ghouls. They came, vampire after vampire, endlessly. James' arm burned; his grip was weak on his Machaira, but he pushed on. Had to.

Dumitru had dared to attack the House of Filius. The Order had to show their true might, make the demons suffer for the murder of so many innocent people. To show weakness here would open them up for more attacks.

Mena ordered the knights forward, pushing back the vampires. More of her powerful orbs appeared, lashing out and disintegrating ghouls and vampires alike.

James stopped momentarily, taking in the scene; hundreds of vampires surrounded the hunters and the knights. The fear of churiphim funneled them over to the less dangerous targets.

James struck down two more ghouls and shoved his Machaira into the back of a vampire, piercing through bone with the blessed Holy power of his weapon. The knight who'd missed a biting thanked him for the rescue.

Mena started etching runes into the earth and finished some incantation. The ground rumbled and a flood of black and blue radiance burst around her and flowered out into the wave of ghouls. The air charged and then a thick pressure swept through the area. Somewhere in the distance, one of the demons wailed, her screams piercing his eardrums. The ghouls fell lifeless, every single one.

Andreea clutched her head. The power that swept through the air pierced her mind and made her release the hold over the dead. It burned her brain into lave. Dumitru had underestimated these churiphim.

The pain subsided but her vision was a haze. Elspet was in front of her, the two churiphim rushed in, stabbing their swords deep into her chest. Elspet clutched the flaming blades, holding them in place.

Yet another Elspet appeared suddenly behind the two witches, piercing one with her blade and slashing at the other with claws.

One churiphim went down, the other turned, a shield of lightning formed around her like spider webs wrapping her and blasting Elspet.

The vampire was flung back and she tumbled to a crouching position. The decoy Elspet blinked away. "Ye command the power of lightning weel. Shall we see how I do?"

Elspet flew into the inky black night. There were low clouds hovering above, and lightning bloomed through them, illuminating the battlefield. Corpses from both sides littered the ground, the swarm of vampires and hunters swirled together in bloody pools like some black cyclone of bodies.

The churiphim that had been stabbed by Elspet pulled the blade out and stood, her silver eyes focused on Andreea. Not boding well at all, Andreea crouched low, ready for the attack.

A thundering explosion stole her and the churiphim's attention. A large chunk of the northern wall had been blasted apart, pieces of debris rained down on the field. Victor had blasted down another section of wall.

Andreea felt the white-hot pain of fire as the churiphim pierced her heart. She crumbled to the ground, paralyzed. This is how it would end for her. She would never see Dumitru again. She would die here at the hands of this witch. The churiphim raised her sword.

Lightning crackled and flooded Andreea's vision in a white heat. The witch bawled out and the smell of burnt flesh swirled in Andreea's nostrils. The witch was flung away. Elspet landed and pulled the flaming sword from Andreea's chest and waved the flames away with her power.

Raven shielded her brothers from Leonette and stepped back. Nathaniel stepped in between them. "Raven is here for her brothers."

"Her brothers are to be trained as hunters; they have seen part of the hidden world that must remain shrouded from the mundane," Leonette replied.

"We are leaving here. We will head west, far from the colonies. Leonette, I want to be with my family. Let us go," Raven pleaded.

"The rules of the Order cannot be broken by any churiphim." Leonette inched forward.

Nathaniel drew his Machaira. "Leonette, I want to be your friend, but I won't let you harm Raven. I won't let you split her family apart like the demons did." He lifted his weapon and took a defensive stance. "I don't want us to fight, for God's sake, we fought together!"

A long silence lingered. Too long for Raven's nerves. The thumps of rushing footsteps beyond the bushes broke the quiescence.

"Please, we don't wanna leave. Don't make us go." Phillip clutched to Raven.

Raven hugged both her brothers close as if to protect them from the fury of death around them.

Men were coming around the building, their footsteps nearing.

"Leonette, please." Raven's lips quivered. She wanted to cry out in hopeless despair.

The men were rambling and shouting commands. They came around; only the shroud of trees and wall kept Raven and this small group of hers hidden.

Nathaniel stepped forward and Leonette brought her swords up. "Damn you, churiphim," he simmered out a whisper.

"Follow me. I can cloak us from human eyes." Leonette sheathed her swords and uttered a few Latin words. "Quickly."

A great relief washed over Raven on hearing Leonette's response. Her muscles twitched as a surge of weakness rolled over them.

The group followed Leonette to a large opening on the western wall. Leonette led them and were all taken aback at the site of the battlefield. "My cloak will not work on vampires or other churiphim, you must head out from here, then make your way west."

Three vampires rushed out at them. Leonette struck two of them down. Nathaniel threw Holy water at the other and severed its head while it clawed at its bubbling skin. More swarmed in. "Help us," the vampires beckoned to Raven.

They were chopped down by two more churiphim, who focused on Raven. A flash of lightning streaked overhead. One of the churiphim rushed to Raven's side.

Raven barely crouched under her large broadsword. Again, the churiphim lifted her weapon effortlessly, as if it were a feather, and swung down. It clanked against Leonette's sword. "Sister, what are you doing?"

"This vampire is not our enemy. She is part of the Order." Leonette shoved her back.

"She is not recognized in the Order." The second churiphim approached. "Destroy the demon."

"No, that is a command I cannot follow. Let her pass," Leonette said coolly.

"Disobey a command and you will be brought before the Core Order for punishment. This vampire must die." The churiphim shot forth.

Raven felt her skin torn but there was nothing touching her. She screamed as blood squirted from the incisions that appeared across her body.

Leonette jumped to shield Raven. The clanging of swords reverberated off the wall, but Raven could not see the weapons. Leonette and the churiphim were moving so quickly, the swords were faint shimmers of movement.

Leonette had taken on sharper features; her eyes were feline and glowing gold.

"Behind you!" Leonette yelled. The other churiphim leapt at Raven for the kill. Nathaniel jumped in front of her. The attack was stopped short a hair from his face.

"Foolish boy, do you want to kill yourself?" The witch lifted Nathaniel by his throat and hurled him out of the way. Raven's brothers each grabbed the churiphim's legs. She slapped them away and the heat of rage rose in Raven.

Raven shot forth her invisible power, pushing all her might into it and sending the assailant swirling away, her armor and cloak shredded by the sheer force.

The churiphim fighting Leonette retreated, aghast at Raven's display. "The vampire's power broke through the blue flame shield."

Leonette was on the whisper of a word when a tremendous surge erupted in an explosive show of blue and black swirling light, forming like a cylinder shooting skyward. The earth opened at every place where vampires stood. Fires leapt out like serpents engulfing them and pulling them under, sealing them within.

James watched, frozen, as Mena raised her hands to the air. The black aura around her whipped out with many tentacle-like appendages, setting aflame any vampires it touched. Those near the light that burst forth disintegrated, and others were sucked under in pits of fire. Hunters and Knights fell back, aghast, shrinking as far from Mena as possible.

"What has the witch done?" The men shouted.

"I open the Gates of Solomon. Befall my enemies," Mena yelled.

Black wraiths flooded out of the circular openings that appeared from the earth. The things grabbed and shredded the vampires, lifting some to the sky and raining down blood and flesh as the wraiths diced them to pieces.

"The witch has gone mad," Wyman said, standing next to James. "She summons the minions of Hell to do her bidding, this is blasphemy."

"Where the hell have you been?" James remarked.

The winds swept in, and lightning struck at the House of Filius, setting aflame the roof.

Another explosion from the wall knocked a group of knights down who'd been fighting at the south side of the wall.

James spotted the vampire creating the destruction.

Mena moved with such speed that her after-image made it seem two of her existed. She appeared next to the vampire.

She had two Claymore swords at her back and drew them both, cutting the vampire down. Her speed was beyond words. Vampires stopped and many retreated upon seeing this. James never imagined that the magnitude of the churiphim's ferociousness was ghastly.

Andreea was at her feet by the time four more churiphim joined the battle. The wound to her chest wasn't healing as quickly as normal. Lightning shot down at the witch closest to her, but two more advanced. She tried running, but the witches' speed was uncanny. Elspet landed in time to kick one and send her tumbling away.

The other churiphim charged in, Elspet blew some kind of black dust into her face, blinding the witch.

A stake pierced Andreea's chest, collapsing her to the ground once more. Elspet turned and herself was pierced by two stakes to the chest, she hissed ferociously at a swarm of hunters encircling her and the other fleeing vampires. The black wraiths swooped in for the kill, grabbing her, but they were disintegrated upon touching the Lilin.

To Andreea's amazement, Elspet took on a shadowy black form herself, the stakes falling from her. The hunters halted their advancement.

A churiphim swung her sword, which was trapped as it sliced into Elspet, who in turn plunged a shadowy hand into her attacker's chest and ripped out her heart, letting it drop with a wet splat. The churiphim crumpled.

Elspet's eyes flushed a fiery glow and focused on the hunters that surrounded her. They turned on each other until all were slain.

"Strengthen your minds; she uses her witchery on us," the Knights shouted to each other.

Six churiphim charged forth. Elspet took physical form again and took the fallen witch's blade. She met the group dead on. The clamoring of edged steel rang out.

Above, the clouds swirled, and the wind roared with a wave of anger that made the earth tremble and the trees bow.

R

The silhouette of a twister formed behind the House of Filius. Elspet must have summoned a storm to destroy the Order's headquarters.

Raven grabbed Matthew and Phillip's hands, pulling them with her, fighting the thrashing wind. Nathaniel and Leonette pushed against the wind following after her, moving away from the wall. The two churiphim blocked their way.

"Sisters, I do not wish to fight you, but you give me no choice," Leonette growled.

"You give no choice, you will die." Both women rushed in. Flames crawled up Leonette's skin and her swords crackled vehemently in the wind.

Her sword was precise, and she sliced through the wrists on one sister, sending her to her knees, shrieking and clutching her severed stump. Her hand fell, clutching her weapon.

The other held two swords. "Foolish. You call upon the elemental power, you will reach your limits. You will endanger everyone." This churiphim took on a green tint to her eyes. They clashed swords, but it was evident that Leonette was outmatched. She could not equal the potent vigor of her sister.

"We have to help her," Nathaniel said.

"Take my brothers. Get them safe. I'll help her." Raven handed the twins over to him. Both Nathaniel and her brothers hesitated. "I will find you, I promise. Go, hurry."

The howl of the twister convinced them. Nathaniel kissed Raven on the cheek. "We'll be waiting."

As soon as they disappeared into the trees, Raven focused her attention on Leonette and the churiphim.

The second witch attempted to lift her fallen sword with her left hand. Raven shot forward, commanding her muscles to obey, charging every particle of her body as she slammed into the churiphim, sending her flying and tumbling yards away. Indeed, she had untapped strength, as Elspet had explained.

Leonette was now holding ground and increasing in speed against the churiphim she battled. Their swords were a blur of movement and metal shrieking. Raven hesitated to move in. There was no time. Raven focused her mind, concentrating on a small area, calling her invisible power. The churiphim's face whirled to her left as if she had been punched. Raven's idea worked, she directed her power into a single point releasing it, an invisible punch.

Leonette crunched the butt of her sword to the churiphim's skull, knocking her out.

The other witch returned, but Leonette had already claimed her weapon and hurled the blade over the wall.

"You will answer for this. The shame of a traitor shall befall you Leonette. You attacked your own." The woman's tone dripped venom.

"I accept the ramifications of my actions." Leonette burst forward, swinging the flat of her sword and landing a hit to the side of the churiphim's head. She was out cold. Leonette looked to Raven. "Go."

"What about you?"

"I have a battle to finish."

"Thank you, for this."

Leonette nodded and turned back.

R

James grabbed on to a large chunk of fallen wall. The twister rumbled like some great giant, through the courtyard. The House of Filius took a direct hit and debris shot through the air, trees were uprooted. Wyman and other knights took shelter behind the wall.

The churiphim and Lilin's battle raged on; already Elspet had downed three of the sisters. While she had deep wounds, a battle with six churiphim was a measure of her power. The demon was a force to reckon with. What powers did Dumitru possess if she was under his command?

The black-haired vampire was hurt, and Elspet intended to shield her. James gripped his Machaira in his right and a Tomahawk on his left, rushing in against the flying debris and whipping winds. He leaped past Elspet and swung down on Andreea. His blade stopped inches from the vampire's neck, her eyes wide and staring into his. A force held his attack back.

James turned and ducked under a swipe from Elspet; she'd leaped from the three remaining churiphim and focused on him.

James swung his sword downward, forcing Elspet to retreat. One of the churiphim plunged her blazing steel through the demon's back. Elspet moaned in protest and faded into a black mass and spun around to face her attacker.

She rammed a palm into the witch's chest, sending her crashing into the other two churiphim.

James pulled a veil of Holy water and poured the liquid into his mouth. When Elspet turned to attack, he lunged in, weapons whirling. They hit their mark, but it was as if hitting air. No damage.

Elspet clutched him by the throat and lifted him off his feet. He swung again. This time, his Machaira made firm contact. She had to take on a solid form to attack. His blade sunk into her chest and her mouth opened wide, hissing. James spat the Holy water into it, sending it down her throat.

She dropped him, recoiling back, clutching her throat. James charged in and noticed Mena behind Elspet, her two Claymores coming down on her as James's Machaira went in. Neither weapon hit.

"Ye will nee have me with tricks, hunter." Elspet glared at James.

A blackish-purple shade glimmered around her, thick, like a liquid sphere. A white flash hurled the hunter away and he slammed on his back. Mena withstood the blast.

Elspet focused on Mena. The witch and the demon faced each other. The purple-black aura wove around Elspet. Mena's glowing orbs spun wildly around her. James felt the air pressure energize around them. His skin tingled. Others felt it too. Hunter and vampire glanced over, momentarily stopping their attacks.

The witch's and the demon's eyes blazed. The earth around them cracked and moaned. The air became warm, making it hard for James to breath.

The glimmering liquid-like aura around Elspet shot forth toward the witch. Before it reached Mena, her voice thundered over the roar of the wind, and released another spell that crackled and let out an ungodly boom that silenced the world and was followed by hot piercing white light.

When James's vision returned, the scene was motionless, the storm clouds were gone, and the sky was rich with hovering stars.

Elspet and the black-haired vampire were gone. The battlefield was littered with both demon and human. The injured churiphim helped each other to their feet, their wounds were already healing.

Only a small scatter of vampires remained with the hunters and knights hacking them down.

Moments later, the battle was over, but the damage was great. Half the foundation of the House of Filius stood.

Mena turned and headed toward the house. "I shall find the Archbishop. Everyone else, survey the area, behead the demon bodies; none must remain."

James walked over to Wyman who was jerking a foot lose from under a thick branch. James extended his hand and helped him up. They both nodded to each other and took measure of their surroundings. The first true battle in the war against Dumitru was barely won.

Elspet laid Andreea on the ground next to the Hudson. "Ye are wounded badly. I'll heal what I can."

Andreea nodded, a groan escaping through her lips. The fire of the churiphim blades lingered in her veins.

Elspet chanted in a low whisper, gliding her hands over the wounds and mollifying the burns.

"Lilin, I come for your head."

Elspet spun to see a churiphim walking toward her, two flaming swords crackling at each hand. Luck was not on their side.

"Aye, ye shall not have that privilege, though ye may try as many hae before." A wry smile etched Elspet's mouth. "Leonette, is it?"

"Remember the name in your last moments." Leonette charged.

Elspet matched her and produced her sword; they clashed, metal ringing.

Andreea barely discerned the movements. Elspet countered each swipe of Leonette's by twirling them away, but the churiphim kept coming at her, landing a hit across Elspet's chest.

Elspet leapt back. "The taste for vengeance has enraged ye. Careful ye daen't loss ye—"

Leonette let out a beastly shout and slammed into Elspet with such speed, it sent her rolling and her sword flying. Elspet barely dodged decapitation this time.

A guttural rumble escaped the vampire and she tumbled to a crouch. "Come, little Tyro. Let's test ye rage."

Leonette lunged in. Elspet ducked under a sword that whooshed above her red hair, the blue flames just licking the tips of her curls. Elspet crunched her knee hard into Leonette's belly, exploding air out of her lungs.

The churiphim kept on and a kick landed hard on Elspet's right cheek. Elspet moved with the force and clutched Leonette's leg, flinging her up and slamming her back hard on the ground.

Leonette's body sparked into flames illuminating the area in a fierce glow.

"Enough of this!" Elspet's face morphed into a shadow, like the silhouette of coal.

Leonette flipped to her feet and moved to swing, but Elspet swooshed behind her, releasing a flurry of swipes the churiphim could not evade. Her flames crackled against the black form of Elspet.

The demon clenched Leonette's wrists and snapped both her forearms. A blood-curdling bellow issued from the churiphim. Elspet silenced it by kicking her chest, dropping her on her back.

The churiphim laid defenseless, coughing, blood trickling at the corners of her lips.

Elspet walked over, picking up her sword, and came to stand over the fallen witch. "Ye could probably learn to harness the churiphim power. Years from now ye could have probably given me a true fight, alas that willnae come to pass." Elspet lifted her sword, the tip pointed at Leonette's heart.

"STOP."

CHAPTER 24

By the time Raven had caught up with Nathaniel and the twins, the storm had dispersed. The group headed north and looped back south to the ships following the Hudson to a ferry dock.

Raven's thirst gnawed at her insides. The long run and the powers she'd exerted had taken their toll. It was fine; she was with her brothers and Nathaniel was there.

Blue light and the clanging of swords came from the direction they headed. They followed the sounds of battle and came upon Elspet standing over Leonette, ready to plunge a sword down on her.

"STOP," Raven shouted.

Elspet glanced back at Raven and her small group. "Ye found ye brothers."

"Do not kill her, please." Raven ran over to Leonette's side.

"The churiphim came upon us, intent on killing." Elspet put away her sword and stepped back. Andreea lay a few feet away with vicious wounds.

"What did you do to her?" Nathaniel rushed to Leonette's side and kneeled down. Leonette kept her gaze glued on Elspet.

The twins stayed back, huddling together.

"Take her if she be ye friend." Elspet lifted Andreea into her arms.

Nathaniel brandished his Machaira and stood. "I'm going to kill you."

"There's been enough blood spilled for one night, daen't ye think boy? Do ye want to add more, in front of them?" Elspet nodded toward the twins.

Raven walked next to Nathaniel and laid a hand over his Machaira. "Nathaniel, she is alive; we will fight another day."

Nathaniel bared his teeth but complied. "I will find you demon. And mark my words. You *will* suffer for this."

Elspet paid him no heed and glided into the air hauling Andreea with her. "Raven, ye precocious child, break out of ye chrysalis and show these people the true gifts bestowed upon ye. Our destiny is entwined. Till next we meet."

The red-haired vampire floated away, fading into the night.

"We have to get to the ferry. Others probably heard the fight," Nathaniel urged.

"We have to take her with us. The other churiphim will kill her if we leave her." Raven crouched down by Leonette. She had passed out. She lifted her, and the group made their way to the ferry. What was done, was done. Now, they had to look forward.

R

Two months passed and Raven had forced her body to survive for days on small quantities of blood taken from Nathaniel by way of a razor, or from people that were sick and allowed Raven to administer bloodletting on them. The hunger and thirst would take over and she would have to seek those who reeked of malevolence.

The days went on as such, and winter came at the heels of fall. Raven would find herself thinking of James. She thought of Elspet and Dumitru. The secret war had been initiated, but who would be the victor? Both sides had struck terror in Raven's heart, both sides had used her, and she wanted to be far away from it all. Yet, she yearned to see James, but it was more than likely she would never talk to him again. She was satisfied with the outcome of a bad situation. She had come away with her brothers and bonded with unlikely friends.

Leonette had opened up to Nathaniel and Raven. She became more human than churiphim as the days passed, though she still talked in dull sentences. It was hard to read her, but Raven began to feel a closeness, an understanding. They were both monsters of sorts. One had been created of darkness, the other to destroy it, and yet, there they were. A churiphim and vampire's bond of friendship.

Raven was glad to have Leonette, glad to have someone to help protect her family. There was a longing in Leonette's eyes. Every day, the churiphim trained, perfecting her skill with the sword and testing the limits of her powers.

Raven would join her occasionally in the night. She wanted to master the art of the blade. Leonette became her teacher. Her training was as challenging as James' had been, but without the harshness.

Nathaniel and Raven had become close, though they wouldn't admit it. For Raven, it was not the life she had envisioned, nor did she lie to herself—she knew it would not last—but for now, she was happy.

Raven and Phillip would play together when the sun set, and they would sit and talk for hours after. He was the same Phillip again. It was all enough in this moment. Yes, she was happy, and she would fight to keep it, fight the thirst that burned for blood at night, master her powers and make the hunger yield to her. This was her birth into darkness.

R

Dumitru stood outside his home, perched next to the terrace railing, and stared out to the soft hue of morning light breaking through the horizon. Elspet joined him. The scars of the churiphim blades were etched into her skin but had almost healed. Andreea, however, was not as fully recovered and slept for days at a time. Elspet had informed Dumitru of the battle, the power of the churiphim. Mena was indeed powerful. Elspet had seen the other rankings, all within the double digits except for an eighth- and ninth-ranked.

"The mission gave us the information needed. The play for control of this new world has begun; we are fully committed."

"Aye, we have no choice in the matter, ye locked us in. More churiphim will come now that they ken of the power ye amass against them. Ye army crumbled to the power of ten of the witches, I hope ye ken weel what ye do."

Dumitru turned and caressed Elspet's face, her beautiful and innocent look. He kissed her brow and entered his home.

In the secret chamber hidden deep underneath, he entered an opened coffin and lay to slumber next to Andreea. She slept soundly in her own coffin; her face was a serene picture of youthful radiance.

Andreea had been in tears, crying out for death the first few days after the battle. The churiphim's blades were like poison to vampires, and it had looked as if she would succumb to it. But Dumitru had stayed with her, holding her and whispering words of comfort. He hadn't eaten through those days. The hunger burned wickedly, but he didn't care. He wanted to feel pain as Andreea felt, though he knew it could never measure to the extremes of her anguish.

In time, the agony subsided, and she had smiled at him. Joy and relief washed over him and took his strength. He closed his eyes, letting himself succumb to the sweet embrace of sleep.

R James and Wyman stood next to Archbishop Archer and four Knights of Templar guards. Mena and her sisters lined up behind them. The House of Filius was already half complete with repairs and added features for any future attacks. The five churiphim they waited for entered the great hall in which they stood. Ranks three through seven entered. Archer, angered by the attack on the House of Filius, had summoned for the strongest ranked. The Core Order agreed. The churiphim came with orders to annihilate Dumitru and his infestation.

The traitor, Leonette, was also to be hunted and executed for her betrayal. She had helped a vampire escape. Nathaniel was to be captured and Raven would be destroyed. The first duty, however, was to find Dumitru. This gave James time.

That night he packed his rations and weapons and took one of the horses. Wyman was waiting for him outside the city walls.

"Archer was expecting you at tonight's meeting," Wyman said.

"Something came up, give him my apologies."

"She's not one of your daughters; she's not human." Wyman stepped in front of the horse and held the animal by the reins.

"I'm going to visit my family." James ushered the horse forward. Wyman released the reins with a scowl.

No, Raven wasn't human, but she was a child. She was special. James had come to understand this. She was special before she had been cursed, and she was special after. He should have let her die that night. He needed to amend his mistake. He would find her and make things right, Raven should have never been an undead. Yes, he would find her and set it right.

CHAPTER 25

Santa Monica, present day

Kylie had been asleep for a couple of hours when the time came to quench my rabid stomach. I left her to the comfort of her dreams and was soon weaving myself through the crowded third street promenade. Musicians, dancers, singers and a medley of other entertainers lined the street to draw in the crowds of people. The voices of singers mingled together with sounds of music that bounced off the walls of restaurants and shops.

When I reached the Santa Monica Pier, the waft of ocean water soaked into my nostrils and the cool breeze washed against my skin. The pier was alive with people enjoying the splendor of colorful night lights and carnival rides.

I wasn't here to enjoy it. Another scent lingered in the air. Malice and ill-content. The vampire I had been tracking lurked somewhere close. The accounts of his victims had flooded onto the internet. Bodies ripped to shreds. He had tortured his victims, slowly draining them and purposely keeping them alive for days. Some were hung by barbed wire and were sexually abused many times over, according to reports. This demon needed to die, and I would make certain of it tonight.

At one a.m., the crowds were gone and only a trickle of people wandered the streets. I hid within the shadows waiting. It wasn't long. The drumming of a heart rang loud above the other noises and sounds of the night. It was a pounding of fear. I focused my hearing; the sharp whimpering of a young woman whispered in the night. The beach was empty, the pier was shrouded in shadows, and it was below the dock the whimpers escaped from. I leapt over the railing that guarded the edge from bumbling humans and landed on the California State Route 1. I shot forth, my feet digging into the loose beach sand. I raced into the black shadows and saw the creature towering over a young girl. She looked to be twenty.

The vampire took notice of me and turned his attention. "She is mine, be gone," he hissed.

"I am not here for her," I replied.

The girl turned to her hands and knees and crawled toward me. She grabbed at her throat, her lips moving but no words escaping it. She mouthed the word: "Help."

The vampire jumped on her, his fangs protruding as he went for the bite. He wouldn't have the satisfaction, not this night. It was a simple thought for me to send him hurtling away. Shock and anger flared in his face. "You bitch. What do you think you're doing?"

I moved over to the girl, she tried to grab me. In the darkness, I could see her large eyes gripped by terror.

Sleep, I commanded. A look of calm and confusion replaced the terror and her eyelids grew heavy. She became limp, and succumbed to my charm.

"I am going to beat you to Hell." The vampire lunged at me, grabbing at air. Surprised, he looked at where I should have been. I had already moved behind him and took an arm first. He ripped out a scream. Blood spewed from his limbless shoulder.

Maddened, he clawed at me. He moved so slowly I could have danced around him twice over before his attack reached. With both my hands, I slapped his forearm and the joint of his elbow, snapping it.

He fell back screeching and biting at the air. I pulled out my Machaira and swiped his neck like a knife through hot butter. His head fell with a pool of blood flowering out into the sand.

I crouched over the girl, turning her and scanning her, making sure she hadn't been bitten. Her purse was thrown a few feet away. I walked over and picked it up. Upon finding the girl's cell phone, I dialed 911. A voice answered on the other side. "Murder under the pier. A girl is hurt."

I placed the phone over the girl's chest and left.

I lingered on the streets afterward, making my way to Hollywood and up to the trail leading to the famous sign. I sat on top of the "H" overlooking the glimmering lights and dribble of traffic. I took in the sight of LA buildings hovering over the shimmering ocean. It was a beautiful jungle of a city, and for the past three months, I had come to love it. I had found James' descendent, Kylie, and would stay at her side, protecting her till her last days. I had promised James I would be his family's dark guardian.

Of course, there was another reason for me being here. Jonas had set root in this city and it was my best chance at finding him. I would never forgive him for locking me to Hell.

I felt the wash of the wind tickling my skin with its cool breeze. I lingered a while longer before leaving; it was getting close to morning and the sun would soon be up. I raced through the back alleys and crossed the busy streets to Santa Monica. When I returned, Kylie was awake and heading out to start her morning. She would meet up with her friends and wouldn't return until I awoke. I had grown to like her over the past two weeks, and she was easy to talk to, though she was very inquisitive.

After she hugged me, she waved goodbye and I escaped to our room. I felt at ease and succumbed to sleep.

Yes, this would be a good home indeed.

About the Author

William Ramos is a Texan, born in Lamesa and raised in Stanton. He began drawing comics at the tender age of four, becoming an accomplished artist by the time he was in his teens. By his early twenties, he'd written his first fantasy epic spanning well over 500,000 words.

William pursues acting and photography while working on his '*Raven's World*' series, and plans to have more books published that focus on other characters and groups in her world.

His next big project will be 'Solare', a fantasy world based on the role-playing games he enacted as a child. Among them, dragons, wizards, and of course, vampires!

Amazon: amazon.com/author/wparks
FB: https://www.facebook.com/WJRParksAuthor/
Instagram: https://www.instagram.com/wjrparks_author/
Website: http://www.Ravenvampire.com

www.ingramcontent.com/pod-product-compliance
Lightning Source LLC
Chambersburg PA
CBHW051646180726
48284CB00006B/1890